WATT

SAMUEL BECKETT

A Jupiter Book

by arrangement with
the OLYMPIA PRESS

LONDON
JOHN CALDER

FIRST PUBLISHED BY OLYMPIA PRESS, PARIS, 1953
FIRST PUBLISHED IN GREAT BRITAIN AS A CALDER JUPITER BOOK IN 1963
BY JOHN CALDER (PUBLISHERS) LIMITED
17 SACKVILLE STREET, LONDON, W.I

PRINTED IN GREAT BRITAIN BY
LATIMER, TREND AND CO. LTD., PLYMOUTH

I

MR. HACKETT turned the corner and saw, in the failing light, at some little distance, his seat. It seemed to be occupied. This seat, the property very likely of the municipality, or of the public, was of course not his, but he thought of it as his. This was Mr. Hackett's attitude towards things that pleased him. He knew they were not his, but he thought of them as his. He knew were not his, because they pleased him.

Halting, he looked at the seat with greater care. Yes, it was not vacant. Mr. Hackett saw things a little more clearly when he was still. His walk was a very agitated walk.

Mr. Hackett did not know whether he should go on, or whether he should turn back. Space was open on his right hand, and on his left hand, but he knew that he would never take advantage of this. He knew also that he would not long remain motionless, for the state of his health rendered this unfortunately impossible. The dilemma was thus of extreme simplicity: to go on, or to turn, and return, round the corner, the way he had come. Was he, in other words, to go home at once, or was he to remain out a little longer?

Stretching out his left hand, he fastened it round a rail. This permitted him to strike his stick against the pavement. The feel, in his palm, of the thudding rubber appeased him, slightly.

But he had not reached the corner when he turned again and hastened towards the seat, as fast as his legs could carry him. When he was so near the seat, that he could have

5

touched it with his stick, if he had wished, he again halted and examined its occupants. He had the right, he supposed, to stand and wait for the tram. They too were perhaps waiting for the tram, for a tram, for many trams stopped here, when requested, from without or within, to do so.

Mr. Hackett decided, after some moments, that if they were waiting for a tram they had been doing so for some time. For the lady held the gentleman by the ears, and the gentleman's hand was on the lady's thigh, and the lady's tongue was in the gentleman's mouth. Tired of waiting for the tram, said[1] Mr. Hackett, they strike up an acquaintance. The lady now removing her tongue from the gentleman's mouth, he put his into hers. Fair do, said Mr. Hackett. Taking a pace forward, to satisfy himself that the gentleman's other hand was not going to waste, Mr. Hackett was shocked to find it limply dangling over the back of the seat, with between its fingers the spent three-quarters of a cigarette.

I see no indecency, said the policeman.

We arrive too late, said Mr. Hackett. What a shame.

Do you take me for a fool? said the policeman.

Mr. Hackett recoiled a step, forced back his head until he thought his throatskin would burst, and saw at last, afar, bent angrily upon him, the red violent face.

Officer, he cried, as God is my witness, he had his hand upon it.

God is a witness that cannot be sworn.

If I interrupted your beat, said Mr. Hackett, a thousand pardons. I did so with the best intentions, for you, for me, for the community at large.

The policeman replied briefly to this.

---

[1] Much valuable space has been saved, in this work, that would otherwise have been lost, by avoidance of the plethoric reflexive pronoun after *say*.

6

If you imagine that I have not your number, said Mr. Hackett, you are mistaken. I may be infirm, but my sight is excellent. Mr. Hackett sat down on the seat, still warm, from the loving. Good evening, and thank you, said Mr. Hackett.

It was an old seat, low and worn. Mr. Hackett's nape rested against the solitary backboard, beneath it unimpeded his hunch protruded, his feet just touched the ground. At the ends of the long outspread arms the hands held the arm-rests, the stick hooked round his neck hung between his knees.

So from the shadows he watched the last trams pass, oh not the last, but almost, and in the sky, and in the still canal, the long greens and yellows of the summer evening.

But now a gentleman passing, with a lady on his arm, espied him.

Oh, my dear, he said, there is Hackett.

Hackett, said the lady. What Hackett? Where?

You know Hackett, said the gentleman. You must have often heard me speak of Hackett. Hunchy Hackett. On the seat.

The lady looked attentively at Mr. Hackett.

So that is Hackett, she said.

Yes, said the gentleman.

Poor fellow, she said.

Oh, said the gentleman, let us now stop, do you mind, and wish him the time of evening. He advanced, exclaiming, My dear fellow, my dear fellow, how are you?

Mr. Hackett raised his eyes, from the dying day.

My wife, cried the gentleman. Meet my wife. My wife. Mr. Hackett.

I have heard so much about you, said the lady, and now I meet you, at last. Mr. Hackett!

I do not rise, not having the force, said Mr. Hackett.

7

Why I should think not indeed, said the lady. She stooped towards him, quivering with solicitude. I should hope not indeed, she said.

Mr. Hackett thought she was going to pat him on the head, or at least stroke his hunch. He called in his arms and they sat down beside him, the lady on the one side, and the gentleman on the other. As a result of this, Mr. Hackett found himself between them. His head reached to the armpits. Their hands met above the hunch, on the backboard. They drooped with tenderness towards him.

You remember Grehan? said Mr. Hackett.

The poisoner, said the gentleman.

The solicitor, said Mr. Hackett.

I knew him slightly, said the gentleman. Six years, was it not.

Seven, said Mr. Hackett. Six are rarely given.

He deserved ten, in my opinion, said the gentleman.

Or twelve, said Mr. Hackett.

What did he do? said the lady.

Slightly overstepped his prerogatives, said the gentleman.

I received a letter from him this morning, said Mr. Hackett.

Oh, said the gentleman, I did not know they might communicate with the outer world.

He is a solicitor, said Mr. Hackett. He added, I am scarcely the outer world.

What rubbish, said the gentleman.

What nonsense, said the lady.

The letter contained an enclosure, said Mr. Hackett, of which, knowing your love of literature, I would favour you with the primeur, if it were not too dark to see.

The primeur, said the lady.

That is what I said, said Mr. Hackett.

I have a petrol-lighter, said the gentleman.

8

Mr. Hackett drew a paper from his pocket and the gentleman lit his petrol-lighter.

Mr. Hackett read:

TO NELLY

To Nelly, said the lady.

To Nelly, said Mr. Hackett.

There was a silence.

Shall I continue? said Mr. Hackett.

My mother's name was Nelly, said the lady.

The name is not uncommon, said Mr. Hackett, even I have known several Nellies.

Read on, my dear fellow, said the gentleman.

Mr. Hackett read:

TO NELLY

To thee, sweet Nell, when shadows fall
Jug-jug! Jug-jug!
I here in thrall
My wanton thoughts do turn.
Walks she out yet with Byrne?
Moves Hyde his hand amid her skirts
As erst? I ask, and Echo answers: Certes.

Tis well! Tis well! Far, far be it
Pu-we! Pu-we!
From me, my tit,
Such innocent joys to chide.
Burn, burn with Byrne, from Hyde
Hide naught—hide naught save what
Is Greh'n's. IT hide from Hyde, with Byrne burn not.

It! Peerless gage of maidenhood!
Cuckoo! Cuckoo!

9

Would that I could
Be certain in my mind
Upon discharge to find
Neath Cupid's flow'r, hey nonny O!
Diana's blushing bud in statu quo.

Then darkly kindle durst my soul
Tuwhit! Tuwhoo!
As on it stole
The murmur to become
Epithalamium,
And Hymen o'er my senses shed
The dewy forejoys of the marriage-bed.

Enough—

Ample, said the lady.

A woman in a shawl passed before them. Her belly could dimly be seen, sticking out, like a balloon.

I was never like that, my dear, said the lady, was I?

Not to my knowledge, my love, said the gentleman.

You remember the night that Larry was born, said the lady.

I do, said the gentleman.

How old is Larry now? said Mr. Hackett.

How old is Larry, my dear? said the gentleman.

How old is Larry, said the lady. Larry will be forty years old next March, D.V.

That is the kind of thing Dee always vees, said Mr. Hackett.

I wouldn't go as far as that, said the gentleman.

Would you care to hear, Mr. Hackett, said the lady, about the night that Larry was born?

Oh do tell him, my dear, said the gentleman.

Well, said the lady, that morning at breakfast Goff turns

to me and he says, Tetty, he says, Tetty, my pet, I should very much like to invite Thompson, Cream and Colquhoun to help us eat the duck, if I felt sure you felt up to it. Why, my dear, says I, I never felt fitter in my life. Those were my words, were they not?

I believe they were, said Goff.

Well, said Tetty, when Thompson comes into the dining-room, followed by Cream and Berry (Coulquhoun I remember had a previous engagement), I was already seated at the table. There was nothing strange in that, seeing I was the only lady present. You did not find that strange, did you, my love?

Certainly not, said Goff, most natural.

The first mouthful of duck had barely passed my lips, said Tetty, when Larry leaped in my wom.

Your what? said Mr. Hackett.

My wom, said Tetty.

You know, said Goff, her woom.

How embarrassing for you, said Mr. Hackett.

I continued to eat, drink and make light conversation, said Tetty, and Larry to leap, like a salmon.

What an experience for you, said Mr. Hackett.

There were moments, I assure you, when I thought he would tumble out on the floor, at my feet.

Merciful heavens, you felt him slipping, said Mr. Hackett.

No trace of this dollar appeared on my face, said Tetty. Did it, my dear?

Not a trace, said Goff.

Nor did my sense of humour desert me. What roly-poly, said Mr. Berry, I remember, turning to me with a smile, what delicious rolypoly, it melts in the mouth. Not only in the mouth, sir, I replied, without an instant's hesitation, not only in the mouth, my dear sir. Not too osy with the sweet, I thought.

Not too what? said Mr. Hackett.

Osy, said Goff. You know, not too osy.

With the coffee and liquors, labour was in full swing, Mr. Hackett, I give you my solemn word, under the groaning board.

Swing is the word, said Goff.

You knew she was pregnant, said Mr. Hackett.

Why er, said Goff, you see er, I er, we er——

Tetty's hand fell heartily on Mr. Hackett's thigh.

He thought I was coy, she cried. Hahahaha. Haha. Ha.

Haha, said Mr. Hackett.

I was greatly worried I admit, said Goff.

Finally they retired, did you not? said Tetty.

We did indeed, said Goff, we retired to the billiard-room, for a game of slosh.

I went up those stairs, Mr. Hackett, said Tetty, on my hands and knees, wringing the carpet-rods as though they were made of raffia.

You were in such anguish, said Mr. Hackett.

Three minutes later I was a mother.

Unassisted, said Goff.

I did everything with my own hands, said Tetty, everything.

She severed the cord with her teeth, said Goff, not having a scissors to her hand. What do you think of that?

I would have snapped it across my knee, if necessary, said Tetty.

That is a thing I often wondered, said Mr. Hackett, what it feels like to have the string cut.

For the mother or the child? said Goff.

For the mother, said Mr. Hackett. I was not found under a cabbage, I believe.

For the mother, said Tetty, the feeling is one of relief, of great relief, as when the guests depart. All my subsequent strings were severed by Professor Cooper, but the feeling was always the same, one of riddance.

Then you dressed and came downstairs, said Mr. Hackett, leading the infant by the hand.

We heard the cries, said Goff.

Judge of their surprise, said Tetty.

Cream's potting had been extraordinary, extraordinary, I remember, said Goff. I never saw anything like it. We were watching breathless, as he set himself for a long thin jenny, with the black of all balls.

What temerity, said Mr. Hackett.

A quite impossible stroke, in my opinion, said Goff. He drew back his queue to strike, when the wail was heard. He permitted himself an expression that I shall not repeat.

Poor little Larry, said Tetty, as though it were his fault.

Tell me no more, said Mr. Hackett, it is useless.

These north-western skies are really extraordinary, said Goff, are they not.

So voluptuous, said Tetty. You think it is all over and then pop! up they flare, with augmented radiance.

Yes, said Mr. Hackett, there are protuberances and pro-tuberances.

Poor Mr. Hackett, said Tetty, poor *dear* Mr. Hackett.

Yes, said Mr. Hackett.

Nothing to the Glencullen Hacketts, I suppose, said Tetty.

It was there I fell off the ladder, said Mr. Hackett.

What age were you then? said Tetty.

One, said Mr. Hackett.

And where was your dear mother? said Tetty.

She was out somewhere, said Mr. Hackett.

And your papa? said Tetty.

Papa was out breaking stones on Prince William's Seat, said Mr. Hackett.

You were all alone, said Tetty.

There was the goat, I am told, said Mr. Hackett.

He turned away from the ladder fallen in the dark yard and his gaze moved down over the fields and the low tottering walls, across the stream and up the farther slope to the bluff already in shadow, and the summer sky. He slipped down with the little sunlit fields, he toiled up with the foothills to the dark bluff, and he heard the distant clink of the hammers.

She left you all alone in the yard, said Tetty, with the goat.

It was a beautiful summer's day, said Mr. Hackett.

And what possessed her to slip off like that? said Goff.

I never asked her, said Mr. Hackett. The pub, or the chapel, or both.

Poor woman, God forgive her, said Tetty.

Faith I wouldn't put it past him, said Mr. Hackett.

Night is now falling fast, said Goff, soon it will be quite dark.

Then we shall all go home, said Mr. Hackett.

On the far side of the street, opposite to where they sat, a tram stopped. It remained stationary for some little time, and they heard the voice of the conductor, raised in anger. Then it moved on, disclosing, on the pavement, motionless, a solitary figure, lit less and less by the receding lights, until it was scarcely to be distinguished from the dim wall behind it. Tetty was not sure whether it was a man or a woman. Mr. Hackett was not sure that it was not a parcel, a carpet for example, or a roll of tarpaulin, wrapped up in dark paper and tied about the middle with a cord. Goff rose, without a word, and rapidly crossed the street. Tetty and Mr. Hackett could see his eager gestures, for his coat was light in colour, and hear his voice, raised in remonstrance. But Watt moved no more, as far as they could see, than if

14

he had been of stone, and if he spoke he spoke so low that they did not hear him.

Mr. Hackett did not know when he had been more intrigued, nay, he did not know when he had been so intrigued. He did not know either what it was that so intrigued him. What is it that so intrigues me, he said, whom even the extraordinary, even the supernatural, intrigue so seldom, and so little. Here there is nothing in the least unusual, that I can see, and yet I burn with curiosity, and with wonder. The sensation is not disagreeable, I must say, and yet I do not think I could bear it for more than twenty minutes, or half an hour.

The lady also was an interested spectator.

Goff rejoined them, very cross. I recognized him at once, he said. He made use, with reference to Watt, of an expression that we shall not record.

For the past seven years, he said, he owes me five shillings, that is to say, six and ninepence.

He does not move, said Tetty.

He refuses to pay, said Mr. Hackett.

He does not refuse to pay, said Goff. He offers me four shillings and fourpence. It is all the money he has in the world.

Then he would owe you only two and threepence, said Mr. Hackett.

I cannot leave him without a penny in his pocket, said Goff.

Why not? said Mr. Hackett.

He is setting out on a journey, said Goff. If I accepted his offer he would be obliged to turn back.

That might be the best thing for him, said Mr. Hackett. Perhaps some day, when we are all dead, looking back he will say, If only Mr. Nesbit had accepted——

Nixon, my name is, said Goff. Nixon.

If only Mr. Nixon had accepted my four and fourpence that night, and I had turned back, instead of going on.

All lies, I suppose, in any case, said Mrs. Nixon.

No no, said Mr. Nixon, he is a most truthful man, really incapable, I believe, of telling an untruth.

You might at least have accepted a shilling, said Mr. Hackett, or one and six.

There he is now, on the bridge, said Mrs. Nixon.

He stood with his back towards them, from the waist up faintly outlined against the last wisps of day.

You haven't told us his name, said Mr. Hackett.

Watt, said Mr. Nixon.

I never heard you mention him, said Mrs. Nixon.

Strange, said Mr. Nixon.

Known him long? said Mr. Hackett.

I cannot really say I know him, said Mr. Nixon.

Like a sewer-pipe, said Mrs. Nixon. Where are his arms?

Since when can't you really say you know him? said Mr. Hackett.

My dear fellow, said Mr. Nixon, why this sudden interest?

Do not answer if you prefer not to, said Mr. Hackett.

It is difficult to answer, said Mr. Nixon. I seem to have known him all my life, but there must have been a period when I did not.

How is that? said Mr. Hackett.

He is considerably younger than I, said Mr. Nixon.

And you never mention him, said Mr. Hackett.

Why, said Mr. Nixon, I may very well have mentioned him, there is really no reason why I should not. It is true. . . . He paused. He does not invite mention, he said, there are people like that.

Not like me, said Mr. Hackett.

He is gone, said Mrs. Nixon.

Is that so, said Mr. Nixon. The curious thing is, my dear

16

fellow, I tell you quite frankly, that when I see him, or think of him, I think of you, and that when I see you, or think of you, I think of him. I have no idea why this is so.

Well well, said Mr. Hackett.

He is on his way now to the station, said Mr. Nixon. Why I wonder did he get down here.

It is the end of the penny fare, said Mrs. Nixon.

That depends where he got on, said Mr. Nixon.

He can scarcely have got on at a point remoter than the terminus, said Mr. Hackett.

But does the penny fare end here, said Mr. Nixon, at a merely facultative stop? Surely it ends rather at the station.

I think you are right, said Mr. Hackett.

Then why did he get off here? said Mr. Nixon.

Perhaps he felt like a little fresh air, said Mr. Hackett, before being pent up in the train.

Weighed down as he is, said Mr. Nixon. Come come.

Perhaps he mistook the stop, said Mrs. Nixon.

But this is not a stop, said Mr. Nixon, in the ordinary sense of the word. Here the tram stops only by request. And since nobody else got off, and since nobody got on, the request must have come from Watt.

A silence followed these words. Then Mrs. Nixon said:

I do not follow you, Goff. Why should he not have requested the tram to stop, if he wished to do so?

There is no reason, my dear, said Mr. Nixon, no earthly reason, why he should not have requested the tram to stop, as he undoubtedly did. But the fact of his having requested the tram to stop proves that he did not mistake the stop, as you suggest. For if he had mistaken the stop, and thought himself already at the railway station, he would not have requested the tram to stop. For the tram always stops at the station.

Perhaps he is off his head, said Mr. Hackett.

He is a little strange at times, said Mr. Nixon, but he is an experienced traveller.

Perhaps, said Mr. Hackett, finding that he had a little time on his hands, he decided to while it away through the sweet cool evening air, rather than in the nasty railway station.

But he will miss his train, said Mr. Nixon, he will miss the last train out, if he does not run.

Perhaps he wished to annoy the conductor, said Mrs. Nixon, or the driver.

But a milder, more inoffensive creature does not exist, said Mr. Nixon. He would literally turn the other cheek, I honestly believe, if he had the energy.

Perhaps, said Mr. Hackett, he suddenly made up his mind not to leave town after all. Between the terminus and here he had time to reconsider the matter. Then, having made up his mind that it is better after all not to leave town just now, he stops the tram and gets down, for it is useless to go on.

But he went on, said Mr. Nixon, he did not go back the way he came, but went on, towards the station.

Perhaps he is going home by a roundabout way, said Mrs. Nixon.

Where does he live? said Mr. Hackett.

He has no fixed address that I know of, said Mr. Nixon.

Then his going on towards the station proves nothing, said Mrs. Nixon. He may be fast asleep in Quin's hotel at the present moment.

With four and four in his pocket, said Mr. Hackett.

Or on a bench somewhere, said Mrs. Nixon. Or in the park. Or on the football field. Or on the cricket field. Or on the bowling green.

Or on the tennis courts, said Mr. Nixon.

I think not, said Mr. Hackett. He gets off the tram,

determined not to leave town after all. But a little furt
reflexion shows him the folly of such a course. This would
explain his attitude after the tram had moved on, and left
him.

The folly of what course? said Mr. Nixon.

Of turning back so soon, said Mr. Hackett, before he was
well started on his way.

Did you see his accoutrement? said Mrs. Nixon. What had
he on his head?

His hat, said Mr. Nixon.

The thought of leaving town was most painful to him,
said Mr. Hackett, but the thought of not doing so no less so.
So he sets off for the station, half hoping he may miss his
train.

You may be right, said Mr. Nixon.

Too fearful to assume himself the onus of a decision, said
Mr. Hackett, he refers it to the frigid machinery of a time-
space relation.

Very ingenious, said Mr. Nixon.

And what do you suppose frightens him all of a sudden?
said Mrs. Nixon.

It can hardly be the journey itself, said Mr. Hackett,
since you tell me he is an experienced traveller.

A silence followed these words.

Now that I have made that clear, said Mr. Hackett, you
might describe your friend a little more fully.

I really know nothing, said Mr. Nixon.

But you must know something, said Mr. Hackett. One
does not part with five shillings to a shadow. Nationality,
family, birthplace, confession, occupation, means of
existence, distinctive signs, you cannot be in ignorance of
all this.

Utter ignorance, said Mr. Nixon.

He is not a native of the rocks, said Mr. Hackett.

ou nothing is known, cried Mr. Nixon. Nothing.
ce followed these angry words, by Mr. Hackett
by Mr. Nixon repented.
a huge big red nose, said Mr. Nixon grudgingly.

Mr. Hackett pondered this.

You are not asleep, my dear, said Mr. Nixon.

I grow drowsy, said Mrs. Nixon.

Here is a man you seem to have known all your life, said
Mr. Hackett, who owes you five shillings for the past seven
years, and all you can tell me is that he has a huge big red
nose and no fixed address. He paused. He added, And that
he is an experienced traveller. He paused. He added, And
that he is considerably younger than you, a common condition I must say. He paused. He added, And that he is truthful, gentle and sometimes a little strange. He glared up
angrily at Mr. Nixon's face. But Mr. Nixon did not see this
angry glare, for he was looking at something quite different.

I think it is time for us to be getting along, he said, is it
not, my dear?

In an instant the last flowers will be engulfed, said Mrs.
Nixon.

Mr. Nixon rose.

Here is a man you have known as long as you can remember, said Mr. Hackett, to whom you lent five shillings seven
years ago, whom you immediately recognize, at a considerable distance, in the dark. You say you know nothing of his
antecedents. I am obliged to believe you.

Nothing obliges you, said Mr. Nixon.

I choose to believe you, said Mr. Hackett. And that you
are unable to tell what you do not know I am willing to
believe also. It is a common failing.

Tetty, said Mr. Nixon.

But certain things you must know, said Mr. Hackett.

For example, said Mr. Nixon.

How you met him, said Mr. Hackett. In what circumstances he touched you. Where he is to be seen.

What does it matter who he is? said Mrs. Nixon. She rose.

Take my arm, my dear, said Mr. Nixon.

Or what he does, said Mrs. Nixon. Or how he lives. Or where he comes from. Or where he is going to. Or what he looks like. What can it possibly matter, to us?

I ask myself the same question, said Mr. Hackett.

How I met him, said Mr. Nixon. I really do not remember any more than I remember meeting my father.

Good God, said Mr. Hackett.

In what circumstances he touched me, said Mr. Nixon. I met him one day in the street. One of his feet was bare. I forget which. He drew me to one side and said he was in need of five shillings to buy himself a boot. I could not refuse him.

But one does not buy a boot, exclaimed Mr. Hackett.

Perhaps he knew where he could have it made to measure, said Mrs. Nixon.

I know nothing of that, said Mr. Nixon. As to where he is to be seen, he is to be seen in the streets, walking about. But one does not see him often.

He is a university man, of course, said Mrs. Nixon.

I should think it highly probable, said Mr. Nixon.

Mr. and Mrs. Nixon moved off, arm in arm. But they had not gone far when they returned. Mr. Nixon stooped and murmured in Mr. Hackett's ear, Mr. Nixon who did not like the sun to go down on the least hint of an estrangement.

Drink, said Mr. Hackett.

Oh my goodness no, said Mr. Nixon, he drinks nothing but milk.

Milk, exclaimed Mr. Hackett.

Even water he will not touch, said Mr. Nixon.

Well, said Mr. Hackett wearily, I am obliged to you, I suppose.

Mr. and Mrs. Nixon moved off, arm in arm. But they had not gone far when they heard a cry. They stopped, and listened. It was Mr. Hackett, crying, in the night, Pleased to have met you, Mrs. Nisbet. Mrs. Nixon, tightening her hold on Mr. Nixon's arm, cried back, The pleasure is mine, Mr. Hackett.

What? cried Mr. Hackett.

She says the pleasure is hers, cried Mr. Nixon.

Mr. Hackett resumed his holds on the armrests. Pulling himself forward, and letting himself fall back, several times in rapid succession, he scratched the crest of his hunch against the backboard. He looked towards the horizon that he had come out to see, of which he had seen so little. Now it was quite dark. Yes, now the western sky was as the eastern, which was as the southern, which was as the northern.

Watt bumped into a porter wheeling a milkcan. Watt fell and his hat and bags were scattered. The porter did not fall, but he let go his can, which fell back with a thump on its tilted rim, rocked rattling on its base and finally came to a stand. This was a happy chance, for had it fallen on its side, full as it perhaps was of milk, then who knows the milk might have run out, all over the platform, and even on the rails, beneath the train, and been lost.

Watt picked himself up, little the worse for his fall, as usual.

The devil raise a hump on you, said the porter.

He was a handsome if dirty fellow. It is so difficult for railway porters to keep sweet and clean, with the work they have to do.

Can't you look where you're going? he said.

Watt did not cry out on this extravagant suggestion, let

fall, it is only fair to say, in the heat of anger. He stooped to pick up his hat and bags, but straightened himself up without having done so. He did not feel at liberty to see to this matter until the porter had finished abusing him.

Mute on top of blind, said the porter.

Watt smiled and clasping his hands raised them to his breastbone and held them there.

Watt had watched people smile and thought he understood how it was done. And it was true that Watt's smile, when he smiled, resembled more a smile than a sneer, for example, or a yawn. But there was something wanting to Watt's smile, some little thing was lacking, and people who saw it for the first time, and most people who saw it saw it for the first time, were sometimes in doubt as to what expression exactly was intended. To many it seemed a simple sucking of the teeth.

Watt used this smile sparingly.

Its effect on the porter was to suggest to him words infinitely more disobliging than any he had already employed. But they were never spoken, by him, to Watt, for suddenly the porter seized his can and wheeled it rapidly away. The stationmaster, a Mr. Lowry, was approaching.

This incident was of too common a kind to excite any great interest among those present. But there were connoisseurs on whom the exceptional quality of Watt was not lost, of his entry, his fall, his rise and subsequent attitudes. These were content.

Among these was the newsagent. He had seen all from his warm nest of books and periodicals. But now that the best was past he came out on the platform, with the intention of closing his stall, for the night. He therefore lowered and locked the corrugated apron. He seemed a man of more than usual acerbity, and to suffer from unremitting mental, moral and perhaps even physical pain. One noticed his cap, perhaps because of the snow-white forehead and damp black curly hair on which it sat. The eye came always in the end to the scowling mouth and from there on up to the rest. His moustache, handsome in itself, was for obscure reasons unimportant. But one thought of him as the man who, among other things, never left off his cap, a plain blue cloth cap, with a peak and knob. For he never left off his bicycle-clips either. These were of a kind that caused his trouser-ends to stick out wide, on either side. He was short and limped dreadfully. When he got started he moved rapidly, in a series of aborted genuflexions.

He picked up Watt's hat and brought it to him, saying, Your hat, sir, I think.

Watt looked at the hat. Was it possible that this was his hat?

He put it on his head.

Now at the end of the platform the newsagent came out of a door, wheeling his bicycle. He would carry it down the winding stone stairs and then ride home. There he would play a game of chess, between masters, out of Mr. Staunton's handbook. The next morning he would carry his bicycle up the stairs again. It was heavy, being a very good bicycle. It would have been simpler to leave it below, but he preferred to have it near him. This man's name was Evans.

Watt picked up his bags and got into the train. He did not choose a compartment. It happened to be empty.

On the platform the porter continued to wheel cans, up and down. At one end of the platform there was one group of cans, and at the other end there was another. The porter chose with care a can in one group and wheeled it to the other. Then he chose with care a can in the other and wheeled it to the one. He is sorting the cans, said Watt. Or perhaps it is a punishment for disobedience, or some neglect of duty.

24

Watt sat with his back to the engine, which now, having got up steam, drew the long line of carriages out of the station. Already Watt preferred to have his back to his destination.

But he had not gone far when, conscious of eyes upon him, he looked up and saw a large gentleman sitting in the corner diagonally opposed to his. This gentleman's feet rested on the wooden seat before him, and his hands were in the pockets of his coat. The compartment then was not so empty as Watt had at first supposed.

My name is Spiro, said the gentleman.

Here then was a sensible man at last. He began with the essential and then, working on, would deal with the less important matters, one after the other, in an orderly way.

Watt smiled.

No offence meant, said Mr. Spiro.

Watt's smile was further peculiar in this, that it seldom came singly, but was followed after a short time by another, less pronounced it is true. In this it resembled the fart. And it even sometimes happened that a third, very weak and fleeting, was found necessary, before the face could be at rest again. But this was rare. And it will be a long time now before Watt smiles again, unless something very unexpected turns up, to upset him.

My friends call me Dum, said Mr. Spiro, I am so bright and cheerful. D-U-M. Anagram of mud.

Mr. Spiro had been drinking, but not more than was good for him.

I edit *Crux*, said Mr. Spiro, the popular catholic monthly. We do not pay our contributors, but they benefit in other ways. Our advertisements are extraordinary. We keep our tonsure above water. Our prize competitions are very nice. Times are hard, water in every wine. Of a devout twist, they do more good than harm. For example: *Rearrange the*

*fifteen letters of the Holy Family to form a question and answer.
Winning entry: Has J. Jurms a po? Yes. Or: What do you
know of the adjuration, excommunication, malediction and ful-
minating anathematisation of the eels of Como, the hurebers of
Beaune, the rats of Lyon, the slugs of Mâcon, the worms of Como,
the leeches of Lausanne and the caterpillars of Valence?*

Now the fields flew by, the hedges and the ditches,
ghastly in the train's light, or appeared to do so, for in
reality it was the train that moved, across a land for ever
still.

Though we know what we know, said Mr. Spiro, we are
not partisan. I personally am a neo-John-Thomist, I make
no bones about that. But I do not allow it to stand in the
way of my promiscuities. *Podex non destra sed sinistra*—what
pettiness. Our columns are open to suckers of every persuasion and freethinkers figure in our roll of honour. My
own contribution to the supplementary redemption, *A
Spiritual Syringe for the Costive in Devotion*, is so elastic, and
unrigid, that a Presbyterian could profit by it, without discomfort. But why do I trouble you with this, you, a perfect
stranger. It is because tonight I must speak, to a fellow
wanderer. Where do you get down, sir?

Watt named the place.

I beg your pardon? said Mr. Spiro.

Watt named the place again.

Then there is not a moment to lose, said Mr. Spiro.

He drew a paper from his pocket and read:

Lourdes
Basses-Pyrénées
France
Sir,
   A rat, or other small animal, eats of a consecrated wafer.
   1. *Does he ingest the Real Body, or does he not?*
   2. *If he does not, what has become of it?*

3. *If he does, what is to be done with him?*
Yours faithfully
Martin Ignatius MacKenzie
(*Author of The Chartered Accountant's Saturday Night*)

Mr. Spiro now replied to these questions, that is to say he replied to question one and he replied to question three. He did so at length, quoting from Saint Bonaventura, Peter Lombard, Alexander of Hales, Sanchez, Suarez, Henno, Soto, Diana, Concina and Dens, for he was a man of leisure. But Watt heard nothing of this, because of other voices, singing, crying, stating, murmuring, things unintelligible, in his ear. With these, if he was not familiar, he was not unfamiliar either. So he was not alarmed, unduly. Now these voices, sometimes they sang only, and sometimes they cried only, and sometimes they stated only, and sometimes they murmured only, and sometimes they sang and cried, and sometimes they sang and stated, and sometimes they sang and murmured, and sometimes they cried and stated, and sometimes they cried and murmured, and sometimes they stated and murmured, and sometimes they sang and cried and stated, and sometimes they sang and cried and murmured, and sometimes they cried and stated and murmured, and sometimes they sang and cried and stated and murmured, all together, at the same time, as now, to mention only these four kinds of voices, for there were others. And sometimes Watt understood all, and sometimes he understood much, and sometimes he understood little, and sometimes he understood nothing, as now.

The racecourse now appearing, with its beautiful white railing, in the fleeing lights, warned Watt that he was drawing near, and that when the train stopped next, then he must leave it. He could not see the stands, the grand, the members', the people's, so   ?   when empty with their white and red, for they were too far off.

So he settled his bags under his hands and held himself in readiness to leave the train, the moment it came to a standstill.

For Watt had once been carried past this station, and on to the next, through his not having prepared himself in time, to get down, when the train stopped.

For this was a line so little frequented, especially at this hour, when the driver, the stoker, the guard and the station staffs all along the line, were anhelating towards their wives, after the long hours of continence, that the train would hardly draw up, when it would be off again, like a bouncing ball.

Personally I would pursue him, said Mr. Spiro, if I were sure it was he, with all the rigour of the canon laws. He took his legs off the seat. He put his head out of the window. And pontifical decrees, he cried. A great rush of air drove him back. He was alone, flying through the night.

The moon was now up. It was not far up, but it was up. It was of an unpleasant yellow colour. Long past the full, it was waning, waning.

Watt's way of advancing due east, for example, was to turn his bust as far as possible towards the north and at the same time to fling out his right leg as far as possible towards the south, and then to turn his bust as far as possible towards the south and at the same time to fling out his left leg as far as possible towards the north, and then again to turn his bust as far as possible towards the north and to fling out his right leg as far as possible towards the south, and then again to turn his bust as far as possible towards the south and to fling out his left leg as far as possible towards the north, and so on, over and over again, many many times, until he reached his destination, and could sit down. So, standing first on one leg, and then on the other, he moved forward, a headlong tardigrade, in a straight line. The knees, on these occasions, did not bend. They could have, but they did not. No knees could better bend than Watt's, when they chose, there was nothing the matter with Watt's knees, as may appear. But when out walking they did not bend, for some obscure reason. Notwithstanding this, the feet fell, heel and sole together, flat upon the ground, and left it, for the air's uncharted ways, with manifest repugnancy. The arms were content to dangle, in perfect equipendency.

Lady McCann, coming up behind, thought she had never, on the public road, seen motions so extraordinary, and few women had a more extensive experience of the public road than Lady McCann. That they were not due to alcohol appeared from their regularity, and dogged air. Watt's was a funambulistic stagger.

More than the legs the head impressed Lady McCann. For the movements of the legs could be accounted for, in a number of ways. And as she reflected on some of the ways, in which the movements of the legs could be accounted for, she recalled the old story of her girlhood days, the old story of the medical students and the gentleman walking before them with stiff and open stride. Excuse me, sir, said one of the students, raising his cap, when they drew abreast, my friend here says it is piles, and I say it is merely the clap. We have all three then been deceived, replied the gentleman, for I thought it was wind myself.

It was therefore less the legs that puzzled Lady McCann, than the head, turning stiffly at every stride, on its stiff neck, under its hard hat, through a quarter of a circle at least. Where had she read that even so, from side to side, bears turn their heads, when baited? In Mr. Walpole, perhaps.

Though not a rapid walker, because of old habit, perhaps, and of her feet, which were old and sore, Lady

McCann saw all this in greater and in greater detail, with every step she took. For they were moving in the same direction, Lady McCann and Watt.

Though not a timorous woman, as a rule, thanks to her traditions, catholic and military, Lady McCann preferred to halt and wait, leaning on her parasol, for the distance between them to increase. So, now halting, now advancing, she followed the high stamping mass, at a judicious remove, until she came to her gate. Here, faithful to the spirit of her cavalier ascendants, she picked up a stone and threw it, with all her might, which, when she was roused, was not negligible, at Watt. And it is to be supposed that God, always favourable to the McCanns of   ?   , guided her hand, for the stone fell on Watt's hat and struck it from his head, to the ground. This was indeed a providential escape, for had the stone fallen on an ear, or on the back of the neck, as it might so easily have done, as it so nearly did, why then a wound had perhaps been opened, never again to close, never, never again to close, for Watt had a poor healing skin, and perhaps his blood was deficient in   ?   . And he still carried, after five or six years, and though he dressed it in a mirror night and morning, on his right ischium a running sore of traumatic origin.

Beyond stopping, and laying down his bags, and picking up his hat, and setting it on his head, and picking up his bags, and setting himself, after one or two false starts, again in motion, Watt, faithful to his rule, took no more notice of this aggression than if it had been an accident. This he found was the wisest attitude, to staunch, if necessary, inconspicuously, with the little red sudarium that he always carried in his pocket, the flow of blood, to pick up what had fallen, and to continue, as soon as possible, on his way, or in his station, like a victim of mere mischance. But he deserved no credit for this. For it was an attitude be-

30

come, with frequent repetition, so part of his being, that there was no more room in his mind for resentment at a spit in the eye, to take a simple example, than if his braces had burst, or a bomb fallen on his bum.

But he had not continued very far when, feeling weak, he left the crown of the road and sat down on the path, which was high, and edged with thick neglected grass. He knew, as he did so, that it would not be easy to get up again, as he must, and move on again, as he must. But the feeling of weakness, which he had been expecting for some time, was such, that he yielded to it, and settled himself on the edge of the path, with his hat pushed back, and his bags beside him, and his knees drawn up, and his arms on his knees, and his head on his arms. The parts of the body are really very friendly at such times, towards one another. But this was a position that could not content him long, in the fresh night air, and soon he stretched himself out, so that one half of him was in the road, and the other on the path. Under the neck and under the distant palms he felt the cool damp grasses of the ditch's edge. And so he rested for a little time, listening to the little nightsounds in the hedge behind him, in the hedge outside him, hearing them with pleasure, and other distant nightsounds too, such as dogs make, on bright nights, at the ends of their chains, and bats, with their little wings, and the heavy daybirds changing to a more comfortable position, and the leaves that are never still, until they lie rotting in a wintry heap, and the breath that is never quiet. But this was a position that Watt, after a short time, found himself unable to sustain, and one of the reasons for that was perhaps this, that he felt the moon pouring its now whitening rays upon him, as though he were not there. For if there were two things that Watt disliked, one was the moon, and the other was the sun. So, settling his hat firmly on his head, and reaching forward for

31

his bags, he rolled himself over into the ditch, and lay there, on his face, half buried in the wild long grass, the foxgloves, the hyssop, the pretty nettles, the high pounting hemlock, and other ditch weeds and flowers. And it was to him lying thus that there came, with great distinctness, from afar, from without, yes, really it seemed from without, the voices, indifferent in quality, of a mixed choir.[1]

SOP. Fifty two point two eight five seven one four
ALT. Fifty two two two fifty two point
TEN. Fiffee fiffee fiffee two tootee tootee tootee tootee
BAS. Hem! fi _____ f

SOP. two eight five seven one four two greatgran
ALT. two eight five seven one four two
TEN. two tootee tootee tootee pointee two eight
BAS. Christ! fi _____ f phew! ty

SOP. ma Ma grew how do you
ALT. five seven one four two gran ma Ma
TEN. fivee sevenee onee fouree two eight fivee sevenee onee fouree
BAS. two point two eight five seven one four

SOP. do blooming thanks and you drooping
ALT. grew how do you do you do blooming
TEN. two ma ma Ma grew how
BAS. two eight five seven one four two Miss oh

[1] What, it may be enquired, was the music of this threne? What at least, it may be demanded, did the soprano sing?

SOP. thanks and	you withered	thanks and	you for
ALT. thanks and	you drooping	thanks and	you withered
TEN. doeedoee doeedoee	do blooming	thanks and	you drooping
BAS. Miss Ma	grew how	do you	do blooming

SOP. gotten thanks and	you thanks for	gotten	too greatgran
ALT. thanks and	you thanks	withered	too granma
TEN. thanks and	you thanks	drooping	too mamamama
BAS. thanks and	you thanks	blooming	too Miss oh

SOP. ma Ma	grew		
ALT. ma Ma	grew		and the
TEN. mamamama Mama	grew	and the	sa
BAS. Miss Ma	grew and the	sa ----	

SOP. and the	same	to you	
ALT. sa ------	me	to you	
TEN. ------	me	to you	
BAS. ------	me Jesus!	to you	

This verse was followed by a second:

> *Fifty-one point one*
> *four two eight five seven one*
> *four two eight five seven one*
> *oh a bun a big fat bun*
> *a big fat yellow bun*
> *for Mr Man and a bun*
> *for Mrs Man and a bun*
> *for Master Man and a bun*
> *for Miss Man and a bun*
> *a big fat bun*
> *for everyone*

> *four two eight five seven one*
> *four two eight five seven one*
> *till all the buns are done*
> *and everyone is gone*
> *home to oblivion.*

The singing then ended.

Of these two verses Watt thought he preferred the former. Bun is such a sad word, is it not? And man is not much better, is it?

But by this time Watt was tired of the ditch, which he had been thinking of leaving, when the voices detained him. And one of the reasons why he was tired of the ditch was perhaps this, that the earth, whose contours and peculiar smell the vegetation at first had masked, now he felt it, and smelt it, the bare hard dark stinking earth. And if there were two things that Watt loathed, one was the earth, and the other was the sky. So he crawled out of the ditch, not forgetting his bags, and resumed his journey, with less difficulty than he had feared, at the point where it had been interrupted, by the feeling of weakness. This feeling of weakness Watt had left, together with his evening meal of goat's milk and insufficiently cooked cod, in the ditch, and it was with confidence that he now advanced, in the middle of the road, with confidence and with awe also, for the chimneys of Mr. Knott's house were visible at last, in the light, of the moon.

The house was in darkness.

Finding the front door locked, Watt went to the back door. He could not very well ring, or knock, for the house was in darkness.

Finding the back door locked also, Watt returned to the front door.

Finding the front door locked still, Watt returned to the back door.

Finding the back door now open, oh not open wide, but on the latch, as the saying is, Watt was able to enter the house.

Watt was surprised to find the back door, so lately locked, now open. Two explanations of this occurred to him. The first was this, that his science of the locked door, so seldom at fault, had been so on this occasion, and that the back door, when he had found it locked, had not been locked, but open. And the second was this, that the back door, when he had found it locked, had in effect been locked, but had subsequently been opened, from within, or without, by some person, while he Watt had been employed in going, to and fro, from the back door to the front door, and from the front door to the back door.

Of these two explanations Watt thought he preferred the latter, as being the more beautiful. For if someone had opened the back door, from within, or without, would not he Watt have seen a light, or heard a sound? Or had the door been unlocked, from within, in the dark, by some person perfectly familiar with the premises, and wearing carpet slippers, or in his stockinged feet? Or, from without, by some person so skilful on his legs, that his footfalls made no sound? Or had a sound been made, a light shown, and Watt not heard the one nor seen the other?

The result of this was that Watt never knew how he got into Mr. Knott's house. He knew that he got in by the back door, but he was never to know, never, never to know, how the back door came to be opened. And if the back door had never opened, but remained shut, then who knows Watt had never got into Mr. Knott's house at all, but turned away, and returned to the station, and caught the first train back to town. Unless he had got in through a window.

No sooner had Watt crossed Mr. Knott's threshold than he saw that the house was not in such darkness as he had at first supposed, for a light was burning in the kitchen.

When Watt reached this light he sat down beside it, on a chair. He set down his bags beside him, on the beautiful red floor, and he took off his hat, for he had reached his destination, discovering his scant red hair, and laid it on the table beside him. And a pretty picture they made, Watt's scalp and red-grey tufts, and the floor burning up, from below.

Watt saw, in the grate, of the range, the ashes grey. But they turned pale red, when he covered the lamp, with his hat. The range was almost out, but not quite. A handful of dry chips and the flames would spring, merry in appearance, up the chimney, with an organ note. So Watt busied himself a little while, covering the lamp, less and less, more and more, with his hat, watching the ashes greyen, redden, greyen, redden, in the grate, of the range.

Watt was so busy doing this, moving his hat to and fro behind him, that he neither saw, nor heard, the door open and a gentleman come in. So his surprise was extreme, when he looked up from his little game. For it was no more than that, an innocent little game, to while away the time.

Here then was something again that Watt would never know, for want of paying due attention to what was going on about him. Not that it was a knowledge that could be of any help to Watt, or any hurt, or cause him any pleasure, or cause him any pain, for it was not. But he found it strange to think, of these little changes, of scene, the little gains, the little losses, the thing brought, the thing removed, the light given, the light taken, and all the vain offerings to the hour, strange to think of all these little things that cluster round the comings, and the stayings, and the goings, that he would know nothing of them, nothing of what they had been, as long as he lived, nothing of when they came, of how they came, and how it was then, compared with

36

before, nothing of how long they stayed, of how they stayed, and what difference that made, nothing of when they went, of how they went, and how it was then, compared with before, before they came, before they went.

The gentleman wore a fine full apron of green baize. Watt thought he had never seen a finer apron. In front there was a great pocket, or pouch, and in this the gentleman's hands were buried. Watt saw the little movements of the stuff, the little bulgings and crumplings, and the sudden indrawings, where it was nipped, between forefinger and thumb probably, for those are the nippers.

The gentleman gazed long at Watt, and then went away, without a word of explanation. Then Watt, for want of something to do, went back to his little game, with the colours. But he soon gave over. And the reason for that was perhaps this, that the ashes would not redden any more, but remained grey, even in the dimmest light.

Finding himself now alone, with nothing in particular to do, Watt put his forefinger in his nose, first in one nostril, and then in the other. But there were no crusts in Watt's nose, tonight.

But in a short time the gentleman reappeared, to Watt. He was dressed for the road, and carried a stick. But no hat was on his head, nor any bag in his hand.

Before leaving he made the following short statement.

Haw! how it all comes back to me, to be sure. That look! That weary watchful vacancy! The man arrives! The dark ways all behind, all within, the long dark ways, in his head, in his side, in his hands and feet, and he sits in the red gloom, picking his nose, waiting for the dawn to break. The dawn! The sun! The light! Haw! The long blue days for his head, for his side, and the little paths for his feet, and all the brightness to touch and gather. Through the grass the little mosspaths, bony with old roots, and the trees

37

sticking up, and the flowers sticking up, and the fruit hanging down, and the white exhausted butterflies, and the birds never the same darting all day into hiding. And all the sounds, meaning nothing. Then at night rest in the quiet house, there are no roads, no streets any more, you lie down by a window opening on refuge, the little sounds come that demand nothing, ordain nothing, explain nothing, propound nothing, and the short necessary night is soon ended, and the sky blue again over all the secret places where nobody ever comes, the secret places never the same, but always simple and indifferent, always mere places, sites of a stirring beyond coming and going, of a being so light and free that it is as the being of nothing. How I feel it all again, after so long, here, and here, and in my hands, and in my eyes, like a face raised, a face offered, all trust and innocence and candour, all the old soil and fear and weakness offered, to be sponged away and forgiven! Haw! Or did I never feel it till now? Now when there is no warrant? Wouldn't surprise me. All forgiven and healed. For ever. In a moment. Tomorrow. Six, five, four hours still, of the old dark, the old burden, lightening, lightening. For one is come, to stay. Haw! All the old ways led to this, all the old windings, the stairs with never a landing that you screw yourself up, clutching the rail, counting the steps, the fever of shortest ways under the long lids of sky, the wild country roads where your dead walk beside you, on the dark shingle the turning for the last time again to the lights of the little town, the appointments kept and the appointments broken, all the delights of urban and rural change of place, all the exitus and redditus, closed and ended. All led to this, to this gloaming where a middle-aged man sits masturbating his snout, waiting for the first dawn to break. For of course he is not as yet familiar with the premises. Indeed it is a wonder to him, and will remain

38

so, how having found the neighbourhood he found the gate, and how having found the gate he found the door, and how having found the door he passed beyond it. No matter, he is content. No. Let us not exaggerate. He is well pleased. For he knows he is in the right place, at last. And he knows he is the right man, at last. In another place he would be the wrong man still, and for another man, yes, for another man it would be the wrong place again. But he being what he has become, and the place being what it was made, the fit is perfect. And he knows this. No. Let us remain calm. He feels it. The sensations, the premonitions of harmony are irrefragable, of imminent harmony, when all outside him will be he, the flowers the flowers that he is among him, the sky the sky that he is above him, the earth trodden the earth treading, and all sound his echo. When in a word he will be in his midst at last, after so many tedious years spent clinging to the perimeter. These first impressions, so hardly won, are undoubtedly delicious. What a feeling of security! They are transports that few are spared, nature is so exceedingly accommodating, on the one hand, and man, on the other. With what sudden colours past trials and errors glow, seen in their new, their true perspective, mere stepping-stones to this! Haw! All is repaid, amply repaid. For he has arrived. He even ventures to remove his hat, and set down his bags, without misgiving. Think of that! He removes his hat without misgiving, he unbuttons his coat and sits down, proffered all pure and open to the long joys of being himself, like a basin to a vomit. Oh, not in idleness. For there is work to do. That is what is so exquisite. Having oscillated all his life between the torments of a superficial loitering and the horrors of disinterested endeavour, he finds himself at last in a situation where to do nothing exclusively would be an act of the highest value, and significance. And what happens? For the first time, since in anguish and disgust he relieved his mother of her milk, definite tasks of unquestionable utility are assigned to him. Is not that charming? But his regret, his indignation, are of short duration, disappearing as a rule at the end of the third or fourth month. Why is this? It is because of the nature of the work to be performed, because of its exceptional fruitfulness, because he comes to understand that he is working not merely for Mr. Knott in person, and for Mr. Knott's establishment, but also, and indeed chiefly, for himself, that he may abide, as he is, where he is, and that where he is may abide about him, as it is. Unable to resist these intenerating considerations, his regrets, lively at first, melt at last, melt quite away and pass over, softly, into the celebrated conviction that all is well, or at least for the best. His indignation undergoes a similar reduction, and calm and glad at last he goes about his work, calm and glad he peels the potato and empties the nightstool, calm and glad he witnesses and is witnessed. For a time. For the day comes when he says, Am I not a little out of sorts, to-day? Not that he feels out of sorts, on the contrary, he feels if possible even better disposed than usual. Haw! He feels if possible even better disposed than usual and he asks himself if he is not perhaps a little seedy. The fool! He has learnt nothing. Nothing. Pardon my vehemence. But that is a terrible day (to look back on), the day when the horror of what has happened reduces him to the ignoble expedient of inspecting his tongue in a mirror, his tongue never so rosy, in a breath never so sweet. It was a Tuesday afternoon, in the month of October, a beautiful October afternoon. I was sitting on the step, in the yard, looking at the light, on the wall. I was in the sun, and the wall was in the sun. I was the sun, need I add, and the wall, and the step, and the yard, and the time of year, and the time of day, to mention only these. To be sitting, at so pleasant a conjuncture of one's courses, in oneself, by oneself, that I think it will freely be admitted is a way no worse than another, and better than some, of whiling away an instant of leisure. Puffing away at the same time at my tobacco-pipe, which was as flat and broad that afternoon as an apothecary's slice, I felt my breast swell, like a pelican's I think it is. For joy? Well, no, perhaps not exactly for joy. For the change of which I speak had not yet taken place. Hymeneal still it lay, the thing so soon to be changed, between me and all the forgotten horrors of joy. But let us not linger on my breast. Look at it now—bugger these buttons!—as flat and—ow!—as hollow as a tambourine. You saw? You heard? No matter. Where was I? The change. In what did it consist? It is hard to say. Something slipped. There I was, warm and bright, smoking my tobacco-pipe, watching the warm bright wall, when suddenly somewhere some little thing slipped, some little tiny thing. Gliss—iss —iss—STOP! I trust I make myself clear. There is a great alp of sand, one hundred metres high, between the pines and the ocean, and there in the warm moonless night, when no one is looking, no one listening, in tiny packets of two or three millions the grains slip, all together, a little slip of one or two lines maybe, and then stop, all together, not one missing, and that is all, that is all for that night, and perhaps for ever that is all, for in the morning with the sun a little wind from the sea may come, and blow them one from another far apart, or a pedestrian scatter them with his foot, though that is less likely. It was a slip like that I felt, that Tuesday afternoon, millions of little things moving all together out of their old place, into a new one near by, and furtively, as though it were forbidden. And I have little doubt that I was the only person living to discover them. To conclude from this that the incident was internal would, I think, be rash. For my—how shall I say?—my personal system was so distended at the period of which I speak that the distinction between what was inside it and what was outside it was not at all easy to draw. Everything that happened happened inside it, and at the same time everything that happened happened outside it. I trust I make myself plain. I did not, need I add, see the thing happen, nor hear it, but I perceived it with a perception so sensuous that in comparison the impressions of a man buried alive in Lisbon on Lisbon's great day seem a frigid and artificial construction of the understanding. The sun on the wall, since I was looking at the sun on the wall at the time, underwent an instantaneous and I venture to say radical change of appearance. It was the same sun and the same wall, or so little older that the difference may safely be disregarded, but so changed that I felt I had been transported, without my having remarked it, to some quite different yard, and to some quite different season, in an unfamiliar country. At the same time my tobacco-pipe, since I was not eating a banana, ceased so completely from the solace to which I was inured, that I took it out of my mouth to make sure it was not a thermometer, or an epileptic's dental wedge. And my breast, on which I could almost feel the feathers stirring, in the charming way breast feathers have, relapsed into the void and bony concavity which my dear tutor used to say reminded him of Crécy. For my spine and sternum have always been concentric, ever since I was a little nipper. It was then in my distress that I had the baseness to call to my aid recent costiveness and want of stomach. But in what did the change *consist*? What was changed, and how? What was changed, if my information is correct, was the sentiment that a change, other than a change of degree, had taken place. What was changed was existence off the ladder. Do not come down the ladder, Ifor, I haf taken it away. This I am happy to inform you is the reversed metamorphosis.

The Laurel into Daphne. The old thing where it always was, back again. As when a man, having found at last what he sought, a woman, for example, or a friend, loses it, or realizes what it is. And yet it is useless not to seek, not to want, for when you cease to seek you start to find, and when you cease to want, then life begins to ram her fish and chips down your gullet until you puke, and then the puke down your gullet until you puke the puke, and then the puked puke until you begin to like it. The glutton castaway, the drunkard in the desert, the lecher in prison, they are the happy ones. To hunger, thirst, lust, every day afresh and every day in vain, after the old prog, the old booze, the old whores, that's the nearest we'll ever get to felicity, the new porch and the very latest garden. I pass on the tip for what it is worth. But how did this sentiment arise, that a change other than a change of degree had taken place? And to what if to any reality did it correspond? And to what forces is the credit for its removal to be attributed? These are questions from which, with patience, it would be an easy matter to extract the next in order, and so descend, so mount, rung by rung, until the night was over. Unfortunately I have information of a practical nature to impart, that is to say a debt to pay, or a score to settle, before I depart. So I shall merely state, without enquiring how it came, or how it went, that in my opinion it was not an illusion, as long as it lasted, that presence of what did not exist, that presence without, that presence within, that presence between, though I'll be buggered if I can understand how it could have been anything else. But that and the rest, haw! the rest, you will decide for yourself, when your time comes, or rather you will leave undecided, to judge by the look of you. For do not imagine me to suggest that what has happened to me, what is happening to me, will ever happen to you, or that what is happening to you,

43

what will happen to you, has ever happened to me, or rather, if it will, if it has, that there is any great chance of its being admitted. For in truth the same things happen to us all, especially to men in our situation, whatever that is, if only we chose to know it. But I am worse than Mr. Ash, a man I once knew to nod to. One evening I ran into him on Westminster Bridge. It was blowing heavily. It was also snowing heavily. I nodded, heavily. In vain. Securing me with one hand, he removed from the other with his mouth two pairs of leather gauntlets, unwound his heavy woollen muffler, unbuttoned successively and flung aside his great coat, jerkin, coat, two waistcoats, shirt, outer and inner vests, coaxed from a washleather fob hanging in company with a crucifix I imagine from his neck a gunmetal half-hunter, sprang open its case, held it to his eyes (night was falling), recovered in a series of converse operations his original form, said, Seventeen minutes past five exactly, as God is my witness, remember me to your wife (I never had one), let go my arm, raised his hat and hastened away. A moment later Big Ben (is that the name?) struck six. This in my opinion is the type of all information whatsoever, be it voluntary or solicited. If you want a stone, ask a turn-over. If you want a turnover, ask plum-pudding. This Ash was what I believe is still called an Admiralty Clerk of the Second Class and with that a sterling fellow. Such vermin pullulate. He died of premature exhaustion, the following week, oiled and houseled, leaving his half-hunter to his house-plumber. Personally of course I regret everything. Not a word, not a deed, not a thought, not a need, not a grief, not a joy, not a girl, not a boy, not a doubt, not a trust, not a scorn, not a lust, not a hope, not a fear, not a smile, not a tear, not a name, not a face, no time, no place, that I do not regret, exceedingly. An ordure, from beginning to end. And yet, when I sat for Fellowship, but for the boil

44

on my bottom . . . The rest, an ordure. The Tuesday scowls, the Wednesday growls, the Thursday curses, the Friday howls, the Saturday snores, the Sunday yawns, the Monday morns, the Monday morns. The whacks, the moans, the cracks, the groans, the welts, the squeaks, the belts, the shrieks, the pricks, the prayers, the kicks, the tears, the skelps, and the yelps. And the poor old lousy old earth, my earth and my father's and my mother's and my father's father's and my mother's mother's and my father's mother's and my mother's father's and my father's mother's father's and my mother's father's mother's and my father's mother's mother's and my mother's father's father's and my father's father's mother's and my mother's mother's father's and my father's father's father's and my mother's mother's mother's and other people's fathers' and mothers' and fathers' fathers' and mothers' mothers' and fathers' mothers' and mothers' fathers' and fathers' mothers' fathers' and mothers' fathers' mothers' and fathers' mothers' mothers' and mothers' fathers' fathers' and fathers' fathers' mothers' and mothers' mothers' fathers' and fathers' fathers' fathers' and mothers' mothers' mothers'. An excrement. The crocuses and the larch turning green every year a week before the others and the pastures red with uneaten sheep's placentas and the long summer days and the new-mown hay and the wood-pigeon in the morning and the cuckoo in the afternoon and the corncrake in the evening and the wasps in the jam and the smell of the gorse and the look of the gorse and the apples falling and the children walking in the dead leaves and the larch turning brown a week before the others and the chestnuts falling and the howling winds and the sea breaking over the pier and the first fires and the hooves on the road and the consumptive postman whistling *The Roses Are Blooming in Picardy* and the standard oil-lamp and of course the snow and to be sure the sleet and

45

bless your heart the slush and every fourth year the February débâcle and the endless April showers and the crocuses and then the whole bloody business starting all over again. A turd. And if I could begin it all over again, knowing what I know now, the result would be the same. And if I could begin again a third time, knowing what I would know then, the result would be the same. And if I could begin it all over again a hundred times, knowing each time a little more than the time before, the result would always be the same, and the hundredth life as the first, and the hundred lives as one. A cat's flux. But at this rate we shall be here all night.

> We shall be here all night,
> Be here all night shall we,
> All night we shall be here,
> Here all night we shall be.
> One dark, one still, one breath,
> Night here, here we, we night,
> One fleeing, fleeing to rest,
> One resting on the flight.

Haw! You heard that one? A beauty. Haw! Hell! Haw! So. Haw! Haw! Haw! My laugh, Mr. ——? I beg your pardon. Like Tyler? Haw! My laugh, Mr. Watt. Christian name, forgotten. Yes. Of all the laughs that strictly speaking are not laughs, but modes of ululation, only three I think need detain us, I mean the bitter, the hollow and the mirthless. They correspond to successive, how shall I say successive . . . suc . . . successive excoriations of the understanding, and the passage from the one to the other is the passage from the lesser to the greater, from the lower to the higher, from the outer to the inner, from the gross to the fine, from the matter to the form. The laugh that now is mirthless once was hollow, the laugh that once was hollow

46

once was bitter. And the laugh that once was bitter? Eye-water, Mr. Watt, eyewater. But do not let us waste our time with that, do not let us waste *any more time* with that, Mr. Watt. No. Where were we. The bitter, the hollow and —haw! haw!—the mirthless. The bitter laugh laughs at that which is not good, it is the ethical laugh. The hollow laugh laughs at that which is not true, it is the intellectual laugh. Not good! Not true! Well well. But the mirthless laugh is the dianoetic laugh, down the snout—haw!—so. It is the laugh of laughs, the *risus purus*, the laugh laughing at the laugh, the beholding, the saluting of the highest joke, in a word the laugh that laughs—silence please—at that which is unhappy. Personally of course I regret all. All, all, all. Not a word, not a——. But have I not been over that already? I have? Then let me speak rather of my present feeling, which so closely resembles the feeling of sorrow, so closely that I can scarcely distinguish between them. Yes. When I think that this hour is my last on earth on Mr. Knott's premises, where I have spent so many hours, so many happy hours, so many unhappy hours, and— worst of all—so many hours that were neither happy nor unhappy, and that before the cock crows, or at very latest very little later, my weary little legs must be carrying me as best they may away, my trunk that is wearier still and my head that is weariest of all, away far away from this state or place on which my hopes so long were fixed, as fast as they can move in and out the weary little fat bottom and belly away, and the shrunk chest, and the poor little fat bald head feeling as though it were falling off, faster and faster through the grey air and further and further away, in any one no matter which of the three hundred and sixty directions open to a desperate man of average agility, and often I turn, tears blinding my eyes, haw! without however pausing in my career (no easy matter),

perhaps longing to be turned into a stone pillar or a crom-
lech in the middle of a field or on the mountain-side for
succeeding generations to admire and for cows and horses
and sheep and goats to come and scratch themselves against
and for men and dogs to make their water against and for
learned men to speculate regarding and for disappointed
men to inscribe with party slogans and indelicate graffiti
and for lovers to scratch their names on, in a heart, with
the date, and for now and then a lonely man like myself
to sit down with his back against and fall asleep, in the
sun, if the sun happened to be shining. And consequently
I feel a feeling that closely resembles in every particular the
feeling of sorrow, sorrow for what has been, is and is to
come, as far as I personally am concerned, for with the
troubles and difficulties of other people I am in no fit state
for the time being to trouble my head, which begins to
feel as though it were falling off, than which I think it
will be readily allowed that for the intellectual type of chap,
haw! like me few sensations can be more painful, just as
for the luxurious type of fellow it would be the feeling of
his private parts on the point of falling off that would very
likely be the most worrying, and so on for the various
other different types of men. Yes, these moments together
have changed us, your moments and my moments, so that
we are not only no longer the same now as when they
began—ticktick! ticktick!—to elapse, but we know that we
are no longer the same, and not only know that we are no
longer the same, but know in what we are no longer the
same, you wiser but not sadder, and I sadder but not wiser,
for wiser I could hardly become without grave personal
inconvenience, whereas sorrow is a thing you can keep on
adding to all your life long, is it not, like a stamp or egg
collection, without feeling very much the worse for it, is it
not Now when one man takes the place of another man,

48

then it is perhaps of assistance to him who takes the place to know something of him whose place he takes, though to be sure at the same time on the other hand the inverse is not necessarily true, I mean that he whose place is taken can hardly be expected to feel any great curiosity about him who takes his place. This interesting relation is I regret often established by procuration. Consider for example the increeping and outbouncing house- and parlour-maids (I say house- and parlour-maids, but you know what I mean), the latter having bounced out before the former crept in, in such a way as to exclude all possibility of encounter whether on the drive or on the way to and from the tram-stop, bus-stop, railway-station, cab-rank, taxi-stand, bar parlour or canal. Now let the name of the former of these two women be Mary, and that of the latter Ann, or, better still, that of the former Ann and that of the latter Mary, and let there exist a third person, the mistress, or the master, for without some such superior existence the exist-ence of the house and parlour-maid, whether on the way to the house and parlour, or on the way from the house and parlour, or motionless in the house and parlour, is hardly conceivable. Then this third person, on whose existence the existences of Ann and Mary depend, and whose exist-ence also in a sense if you like depends on the existences of Ann and Mary, says to Mary, no, says to Ann, for by this time Mary is afar off, in the tram, the bus, the train, the cab, the taxi, the bar parlour or canal, says to Ann, Jane, in the morning when Mary had finished doing this, if Mary may be said to have ever finished doing anything, then she began to do this, that is to say she settled herself firmly in a comfortable semi-upright posture before the task to be performed and remained there quietly eating onions and peppermints turn and turn about, I mean first an onion, then a peppermint, then another onion, then another peppermint, then another onion, then another peppermint, then another onion, then another peppermint, then another onion, then another peppermint, then another onion, then another peppermint, then another onion, then another peppermint, then another onion, then another peppermint, then another onion, then another peppermint, and so on, while little by little the reason for her presence in that place faded from her mind, as with the dawn the figments of the id, and the duster, whose burden up till now she had so bravely born, fell from her fingers, to the dust, where having at once assumed the colour (grey) of its surroundings it disappeared until the following Spring. An average of anything from twenty-six to twenty-seven splendid woollen dusters per mensem were lost in this way by our Mary during her last year of service in this unfortunate house. Now what, it may well be asked, can the fancies have been that so ravished Mary from a sense of her situation? Dreams of less work and higher wages? Erotic cravings? Recollections of childhood? Menopausal discomfort? Grief for a loved one defunct or departed for an unknown destination? Daltonic visualizations of the morning paper's racing programme? Prayers for a soul? She was not a woman to confide. And indeed I think I am correct in saying that she was opposed to conversation on principle as such. Whole days, and even entire weeks, would glide away without Mary's having opened her gob for any purpose other than the reception of her five fingers fastened firmly on a fragment of food, for to the spoon, the knife, and even the fork, considered as aids to ingestion, she had never been able to accustom herself, in spite of excellent references. Her appetite, on the other hand, was quite exceptional. Not that the food absorbed by Mary, over a given period, was greater in mass, or richer in vitamins, than the normal healthy person's allowance for the same time. No. But her

50

appetite was exceptional in this, that it knew no remission. The ordinary person eats a meal, then rests from eating for a space, then eats again, then rests again, then eats again, then rests again, then eats again, then rests again, then eats again, then rests again, then eats again, then rests again, then eats again, then rests again, and in this way, now eating, and now resting from eating, he deals with the difficult problem of hunger, and indeed I think I may add thirst, to the best of his ability and according to the state of his fortune. Let him be a small eater, a moderate eater, a heavy eater, a vegetarian, a naturist, a cannibal, a coprophile, let him look forward to his eating with pleasure or back on it with regret or both, let him eliminate well or let him eliminate ill, let him eructate, vomit, break wind or in other ways fail or scorn to contain himself as a result of an ill-adapted diet, congenital affliction or faulty training during the impressionable years, let him, Jane, I say, be one or more or all or more than all of these, or let him on the other hand be none of these, but something quite different, as would be the case for example if he were on hunger strike or in a catatonic stupor or obliged for some reason best known to his medical advisers to turn for his sustenance to the clyster, the fact remains, and can hardly be denied, that he proceeds by what we call meals, whether taken voluntarily or involuntarily, with pleasure or pain, successfully or unsuccessfully, through the mouth, the nose, the pores, the feed-tube or in an upward direction with the aid of a piston from behind is not of the slightest importance, and that between these acts of nutrition, without which life as it is generally understood would be hard set to continue, there intervene periods of rest or repose, during which no food is taken, unless it be every now and then from time to time an occasional snack, quick drink or light collation, rendered if not indispensable at least welcome by an unforeseen acceleration of the metabolic exchanges due to circumstances of an imprevisible kind, as for example the backing of a loser, the birth of a child, the payment of a debt, the recovery of a loan, the voice of conscience, or any other shock to the great sympathetic, causing a sudden rush of chyme, or chyle, or both, to the semi-digested slowly surely earthward struggling mass of sherry wine, soup, beer, fish, stout, meat, beer, vegetables, sweet, fruit, cheese, stout, anchovy, beer, coffee and benedictine, for example, swallowed lightheartedly but a few short hours before to the strains as likely as not of a piano and cello. Whereas Mary ate all day long, that is to say from early dawn, or at least from the hour at which she woke, which to judge from the hour at which she rose, or rather at which she first appeared in the bowels of this unhappy home, was in no way premature, to late at night, for she retired to rest with great punctuality every evening at eight o'clock, leaving the dinner things on the table, and fell at once into an exhausted sleep, if her snores, of which as I have often been heard to remark I never heard the like, were not simulated, which I for my part will never believe, seeing as how they continued with undiminished sonority all night long, from which I may add I am inclined to suspect that Mary, like so many women, slept on the flat of her back, a dangerous and detestable practice in my opinion, though I know there are times when it is difficult, not to say impossible, to do otherwise. Ahem! Now when I say that Mary ate all day, from her opening her eyes in the morning to her closing them at night, in sleep, I mean that at no moment during this period was Mary's mouth more than half-empty, or, if you prefer, less than half-full, for to the habit generally received of finishing one mouthful before initiating the next Mary had never, notwithstanding her remarkable papers, been able to adapt herself. Now when

52

I say that at no moment of Mary's waking hours was Mary's mouth more than half-empty, or less than half-full, I do not mean that it was always so, for on close and even on casual inspection it would have been found, nine times out of ten, full to overflowing, which goes far towards explaining Mary's indifference to the pleasures of conversation. Now when speaking of Mary's mouth I make use of the expression full to overflowing, I do not merely mean to say that it was so full, nine-tenths of the time, that it threatened to overflow, but in my thought I go further and I assert, without fear of contradiction, that it was so full, nine-tenths of the time, that it did overflow, all over this ill-fated interior, and traces of this exuberance, in the form of partially masticated morsels of meat, fruit, bread, vegetables, nuts and pastry I have frequently found in places as remote in space, and distinct in purpose, as the coal-hole, the conservatory, the American Bar, the oratory, the cellar, the attic, the dairy and, I say it with shame, the servants' W.C., where a greater part of Mary's time was spent than seemed compatible with a satisfactory, or even tolerable, condition of the digestive apparatus, unless we are to suppose that she retired to that place in search of a little fresh air, rest and quiet, for a woman more attached to rest and quiet I have never, I say it without fear of exaggeration, known or even heard of. But to return to where we left her, I see her still, propped up in a kind of stupor against one of the walls in which this wretched edifice abounds, her long grey greasy hair framing in its cowl of scrofulous mats a face where pallor, languor, hunger, acne, recent dirt, immemorial chagrin and surplus hair seemed to dispute the mastery. Flitters of perforated starch entwine an ear. Under the rusty cotton frock, plentifully embossed with scabs of slobber, two cup-like depressions mark the place of the bosom and a conical protuberance that of the abdomen.

53

Between on the one hand a large pouch or bag, containing the forenoon's supplies, cunningly dissimulated in the tattered skirt, and on the other Mary's mouth, Mary's hands flash to and fro, with a regularity that I do not hesitate to compare with that of piston-rods. At the moment that the one hand presses, with open palm, between the indefatigable jaws, a cold potato, onion, tart or sandwich, the other darts into the pouch and there, unerringly, fastens on a sandwich, onion, tart or cold potato, as Mary wills. And the former, on its way down to be filled, meets the latter on its way up to be emptied, at a point equidistant from their points of departure, or arrival. And save for the flying arms, and champing mouth, and swallowing throat, not a muscle of Mary stirs, and over all the dreaming face, which may strike you, Jane, as strange, but, believe me, Jane, I invent nothing. Now with regard to Mary's limbs, ahem, of which I think I am correct in saying that no mention has yet been made, winter and summer. . . . Winter and summer. And so on. Summer! When I lie dying, Mr. Watt, behind the red screen, you know, perhaps that is the word that will sound, summer, and the words for summer things. Not that I ever much cared for them. But some call for the priest, and others for the long days when the sun was a burden. It was summer when I landed here. And now I shall finish and you will hear my voice no more, unless we meet again elsewhere, which considering the probable state of our health is not likely. For then I shall rise, no, I am not seated, then I shall go, just as I am, in the things I stand up in, if you can call this standing up, with not so much as a toothbrush in my pocket to brush my tooth with, morning and evening, or a penny in my purse to buy me a bun in the heat of noonday, without a hope, a friend, a plan, a prospect or a hat to my head to take off to the kind ladies and gentlemen, and make my way as best I may down the path

54

to the gate, for the last time, in the grey of the morning, and pass out with a nod on the hard road and up on the hard path and so go, putting my better foot foremore to the best of my abilities, and the dusty uncut privet brushing my cheek, and so on, and on, hotter and hotter, weaker and weaker, until someone takes pity on me, or God has mercy on me, or better still both, or failing these I fall unable to rise by the way and am taken into custody black with flies by a passing man in blue, leaving you here in my place, with before you all I have behind me, and all I have before me, haw! all I have before me. It was summer. There were three men in the house: the master, whom as you well know we call Mr. Knott; a senior retainer named Vincent, I believe; and a junior, only in the sense that he was of more recent acquisition, named, if I am not mistaken, Walter. The first is here, in his bed, or at least in his room. But the second, I mean Vincent, is not here any more, and the reason for that is this, that when I came in he went out. But the third, I mean Walter, is not here any more either, and the reason for that is this, that when Erskine came in he went out, just as Vincent went out when I came in. And I, I mean Arsene, am not here any more either, and the reason for that is this, that when you came in I went out, just as when I came in Vincent went out and as Walter went out when Erskine came in. But Erskine, I mean the second last to come and the next to go, Erskine is here still, sleeping and little dreaming what the new day holds in store, I mean promotion and a new face and the end in sight. But another evening shall come and the light die away out of the sky and the colour from the earth and the door open on the wind or the rain or the sleet or the hail or the snow or the slush or the storm or the warm still scents of summer or the still of the ice or the earth awakening or the hush of harvest or the leaves falling

55

through the dark from various altitudes, never two coming
to earth at the same time, then bowling red and brown and
yellow and grey briskly for an instant, yes, through the
dark, for an instant, then running together in heaps, here
a heap, and there a heap, to be paddled in by happy boys
and girls on their way home from school looking forward
to Hallow-e'en and Guy Fawkes and Christmas and the
New Year, haw! yes, happy girls and boys looking forward
to the happy New Year, and then perhaps carted off in old
barrows and used as dung the following spring by the
poor, and a man come, shutting the door behind him, and
Erskine go. And then another night fall and another man
come and Watt go, Watt who is now come, for the coming
is in the shadow of the going and the going is in the shadow
of the coming, that is the annoying part about it. And yet
there is one who neither comes nor goes, I refer I need
hardly say to my late employer, but seems to abide in his
place, for the time being at any rate, like an oak, an elm, a
beech or an ash, to mention only the oak, the elm, the beech
and the ash, and we nest a little while in his branches. Yet
come he did once, otherwise how would he be here, and
go sooner or later I suppose he must, though you wouldn't
think it to look at him. But appearances are often deceptive
as my poor old mother, heaving a sigh, used to say to my
poor old father (for I am not illegitimate) in my hearing
(for they always spoke freely before me), a sentiment to
which I can still hear my poor old father, with a sigh,
assent, saying, Thanks be to God, an opinion in which in
tones that haunt me still my poor old mother would
acquiesce, sighing, saying, Amen. Or is there a coming that
is not a coming to, a going that is not a going from, a
shadow that is not the shadow of purpose, or not? For what
is this shadow of the going in which we come, this shadow
of the coming in which we go, this shadow of the coming

and the going in which we wait, if not the shadow of purpose, of the purpose that budding withers, that withering buds, whose blooming is a budding withering? I speak well, do I not, for a man in my situation? And what is this coming that was not our coming and this being that is not our being and this going that will not be our going but the coming and being and going in purposelessness? And though in purposelessness I may seem now to go, yet I do not, any more than in purposelessness then I came, for I go now with my purpose as with it then I came, the only difference being this, that then it was living and now it is dead, which is what you might call what I think the English call six of one and half a dozen of the other, do they not, might you not? Or do I confuse them with the Irish? But to return to Vincent and Walter, they were very much your height, breadth and width, that is to say big bony shabby seedy haggard knock-kneed men, with rotten teeth and big red noses, the result of too much solitude they used to say, just as I am very much Erskine's and Erskine very much mine, that is to say little fat shabby seedy juicy or oily bandy-legged men, with a little fat bottom sticking out in front and a little fat belly sticking out behind, for what would a little fat bottom sticking out in front be without a little fat belly sticking out behind? For though it is rumoured that Mr. Knott would prefer to have no one at all about him, to look after him, yet since he is obliged to have someone at all about him, to look after him, being quite incapable of looking after himself, then the suggestion is that what he likes best is the minimum number of small fat shabby seedy juicy bandy-legged pot-bellied pot-bottomed men about him, to look after him, or, failing this, the fewest possible big bony seedy shabby haggard knock-kneed rotten-toothed red-nosed men about him, to take care of him, thought at the same time it is freely hinted that in default of either of these he would be perfectly content to have men of quite a different stamp or mould about him, as unlike physically you and Vincent and Walter as Erskine and me, if that is conceivable, to fuss over him, as long as they were seedy and shabby and few in number, for to seediness and shabbiness and fewness in number he is greatly attached, if he can be said to be greatly attached to anything, though I have heard it confidently asserted that if he could not have seediness and shabbiness and fewness in number he would be only too delighted to do without them, about him, to make much of him. But that he has never had any but on the one hand big bony seedy shabby haggard knock-kneed rotten-toothed red-nosed men like you and on the other small fat seedy shabby juicy or oily bandy-legged pot-bellied pot-bottomed men like me, about him, to attend to him, seems certain, unless it be so long ago that all trace of them is lost. For Vincent and Walter were not the first, ho no, but before them were Vincent and another whose name I forget, and before them that other whose name I forget and another whose name I also forget, and before them that other whose name I also forget and another whose name I never knew, and before them that other whose name I never knew and another whose name Walter could not recall, and before them that other whose name Walter could not recall and another whose name Walter could not recall either, and before them that other whose name Walter could not recall either and another whose name Walter never knew, and before them that other whose name Walter never knew and another whose name even Vincent could not call to mind, and before them that other whose name even Vincent could not call to mind and another whose name even Vincent could not call to mind either, and before them that other whose name even Vincent could not call to mind either and another whose name even Vincent never knew, and so on, until all trace is lost, owing to the shortness of human memory, one always ousting the other, though perhaps ousting is not the word, just as you ousted me, and Erskine Walter, and I Vincent, and Walter that other whose name I forget, and Vincent that other whose name I also forget, and that other whose name I forget that other whose name I never knew, and that other whose name I also forget that other whose name Walter could not recall, and that other whose name I never knew that other whose name Walter could not recall either, and that other whose name Walter could not recall that other whose name Walter never knew, and that other whose name Walter could not recall either that other whose name even Vincent could not call to mind, and that other whose name Walter never knew that other whose name even Vincent could not call to mind either, and that other whose name even Vincent could not call to mind that other whose name even Vincent never knew, and so on, until all trace is lost, on account of the vanity of human wishes. But that all those of whom all trace is not lost, even though their names be forgotten, were, if not big, bony, seedy, shabby, haggard, knock-kneed, rotten-toothed and red-nosed, at least small, fat, seedy, shabby, oily, bandy-legged, pot-bellied and pot-bottomed, seems certain, if any reliance is to be placed on oral tradition as handed down by word of mouth from one fleeting generation to the next, or, as is more usual, to the next but one. This, if it does not prove beyond all manner of doubt that of all those of whom all trace is lost not one was a body quite different from us, does tend to support the hypothesis so often emitted that there is something about Mr. Knott that draws towards him, to be about him and take care of him, two types of men, and two only, on the one hand the big bony seedy shabby haggard knock-kneed type, with the decayed teeth and the big red nose, and on the other the small fat seedy shabby oily or juicy bandy-legged type, with the little fat bottom and belly sticking out in opposite directions, or, alternatively, that there is something in these two types of men that draw them to Mr. Knott, to be about him and watch over him, though at the same time it is quite possible that if we were in a position to examine the skeleton of one of those of whom not only the name but all trace is lost, of him for example whose name even that other whose name even Vincent (if that was his name) never knew never knew, we might find him to have been quite a different type of chap, neither big nor small, bony nor fat, seedy nor shabby, haggard nor juicy, rotten-toothed nor pot-bellied, red-nosed nor pot-bottomed, quite quite possible, if not quite quite probable. Now though I knew at the outset that I should not have the time to go into these matters as fully as I should wish, or they deserve, yet I felt, perhaps wrongly, that it was my duty to mention them, if only in order for you clearly to understand that about Mr. Knott, attentive to his wants, if speaking of Mr. Knott one may speak of wants, two men and so far as we know never more and never fewer have always been to be found, and that of these two it is not always necessary, as far as we can judge, that one should be bony and so on, and the other fat and so forth, as is now the case with you and Arsene, forgive me, with you and Erskine, for both may be bony and so on, as was the case with Vincent and Walter, or both may be fat and so forth, as was the case with Erskine and me, but that it is necessary, as far as can be ascertained, that of these two men for ever about Mr. Knott in tireless assiduity turning, the one or the other or both should be either bony and so on or fat and so forth, though if we could go back in pure time as easily as we can in pure space the possibility, if not the probability, is not excluded of our finding two or less than two or even more than two men or women or men and women as little bony and so on as fat and so forth eternally turning about Mr. Knott in tireless love. But to go into this matter as longly and as deeply and as fully as I should like, and it deserves, is unfortunately out of the question. Not that space is wanting, for space is not wanting. Not that time is lacking, for time is not lacking. But I hear a little wind come and go, come and go, in the bushes without, and in the hen-house the cock in his sleep uneasily stirs. And I think I have said enough to light that fire in your mind that shall never be snuffed, or only with the utmost difficulty, just as Vincent did for me, and Walter for Erskine, and as you perhaps will do for another, though that is not certain, to judge by the look of you. Not that I have told you all I know, for I have not, being now a good-natured man, and of good will what is more, and indulgent towards the dreams of middle age, which were my dreams, just as Vincent did not tell me all, nor Walter Erskine, nor the others the others, for here we all seem to end by being good-natured men, and of good will, and indulgent towards the dreams of middle age, which were our dreams, whatever may escape us now and then in the way of bitter and I blush to say even blasphemous words and expressions, and perhaps also because what we know partakes in no small measure of the nature of what has so happily been called the unutterable or ineffable, so that any attempt to utter or eff it is doomed to fail, doomed, doomed to fail. Why even I myself, strolling all alone in some hard earned suspension of labour in this charming garden, have tried and tried to formulate this delicious haw! and I may add quite useless wisdom so dearly won, and with which I am so to speak from the crown of my head to the soles of my feet imbued, so that I neither eat nor drink nor breathe in and out nor do my dooodles but more sagaciously than before, like Theseus kissing Ariadne, or Ariadne Theseus, towards the end, on the seashore, and tried in vain, notwithstanding the beauties of the scene, bower and sward, glade and arbour, sunshine and shadow, and the pleasant dawdling motion carrying me about in the midst of them, hither and thither, with unparalleled sagacity. But what I could say, or at least a part, and I trust not the least diverting, I think I have said, and as far as it lay in my power to take you, under the circumstances, I think I have taken you, all things considered. And now for a little along the way that lies between you and me Erskine will go by your side, to be your guide, and then for the rest you will travel alone, or with only shades to keep you company, and that I think you will find, if your experience at all resembles mine, the best part of the outing or at least the least dull, even though the light falls fast, and far below the stumbling feet. Now for what I have said ill and for what I have said well and for what I have not said, I ask you to forgive me. And for what I have done ill and for what I have done well and for what I have left undone, I ask you also to forgive me. And I ask you to think of me always—bugger these buttons—with forgiveness, as you desire to be thought of with forgiveness, though personally of course it is all the same to me whether I am thought of with forgiveness, or with rancour, or not at all. Good night.

But he had not been long gone when he appeared again, to Watt. He stood sideways in the kitchen doorway, looking at Watt, and Watt saw the house-door open behind him and the dark bushes and above them at a great distance something that he thought was perhaps the day again already. And as Watt fixed his eyes on what he thought was perhaps the day again already, the man standing sideways in the kitchen doorway looking at him became two men standing sideways in two kitchen doorways looking at him.

But Watt, catching up his hat, held it before the lamp, that he might the better decide whether what he saw, through the house-door, was really the day again already, or whether it was not. But even as he looked it was effaced, not abruptly, no, and not gently either, but by a firm unhurried hand, wiped away. Then Watt did not know what to think. So turning towards the lamp he drew it towards him, and turned down the wick, and blew down the chimney, until it was quite extinguished. But even then he was no whit better off than before. For if it was really day again already, in some low distant quarter of the sky, it was not yet day again already in the kitchen. But that would come, Watt knew that would come, with patience it would come, little by little, whether he liked it or not, over the yard wall, and through the window, first the grey, then the brighter colours one by one, until getting on to 9 a.m. all the gold and white and blue would fill the kitchen, all the unsoiled light of the new day, of the new day at last, the day without precedent at last.

Mr. Knott was a good master, in a way.

Watt had no direct dealings with Mr. Knott, at this period. Not that Watt was ever to have any direct dealings with Mr. Knott, for he was not. But he thought, at this period, that the time would come when he would have direct dealings with Mr. Knott, on the first-floor. Yes, he thought that time would come for him, as he thought it had ended for Arsene, and for Erskine just begun.

For the moment all Watt's work was on the ground-floor. Even the first-floor slops that he emptied, it was Erskine who carried them down, every morning, in a pail. The first-floor slops could have been emptied, quite as conveniently, if not more conveniently, and the pail rinsed, on the first-floor, but they never were, for reasons that are not known. It is true that Watt had instructions to empty these slops, not in the way that slops are usually emptied, no, but in the garden, before sunrise, or after sunset, on the violet bed in violet time, and on the pansy bed in pansy time, and on the rose bed in rose time, and on the celery banks in celery time, and on the seakale pits in seakale time, and in the tomato house in tomato time, and so on, always in the garden, in the flower garden, and in the vegetable garden, and in the fruit garden, on some young growing thirsty thing at the moment of its most need, except of course in time of frost, or when the snow was on the ground, or when the water was on the ground. Then his instructions were to empty the slops on the dunghill.

But Watt was not so foolish as to suppose that this was

the real reason why Mr. Knott's slops were not emptied away on the first-floor, as they could so easily have been. This was merely the reason offered to the understanding.

It was remarkable that no such instructions existed touching the second-floor slops, that is to say, Watt's slops and Erskine's slops. These, when they had been carried down, Erskine's by Erskine, and Watt's by Watt, Watt was free to dispose of as he pleased. But he was given nevertheless to understand that their commixture with those of the first-floor, if not formally forbidden, was not encouraged.

So Watt saw little of Mr. Knott. For Mr. Knott was seldom on the ground-floor, unless it was to eat a meal, in the dining-room, or to pass through it, on his way to and from the garden. And Watt was seldom on the first-floor, unless it was when he came down to begin his day, in the morning, and then again at evening, when he went up to begin his night.

Even in the dining-room Watt did not see Mr. Knott, although Watt was responsible for the dining-room, and for the service there of Mr. Knott's meals. The reasons for this may appear when the time comes to treat of that complex and delicate matter, Mr. Knott's food.

This is not to say that Watt never saw Mr. Knott at this period, for he did, to be sure. He saw him from time to time, passing through the ground-floor on his way to the garden from his quarters on the first-floor, and on his way back from the garden to his quarters, and he saw him also in the garden itself. But these rare appearances of Mr. Knott, and the strange impression they made on Watt, will be described please God at greater length, at another time.

Callers were few. Tradesmen called, of course, and beggars, and hawkers. The postman, a charming man, called Severn, a great dancer and lover of greyhounds, seldom called. But he did sometimes, always in the evening, with his light eager step and his dog by his side, to deliver a bill, or a begging letter.

The telephone seldom rang, and when it did it was about some indifferent matter touching the plumbing, or the roof, or the food supplies, that Erskine could deal with, or even Watt, without troubling their master.

Mr. Knott saw nobody, heard from nobody, as far as Watt could see. But Watt was not so foolish as to draw any conclusion from this.

But these fleeting acknowledgements of Mr. Knott's establishment, like little splashes on it from the outer world and without which it would have been hard set to keep going, will it is to be hoped be considered in greater detail, later on, and how some were of moment to Watt, and how some were of none. In particular the appearance of the gardener, a Mr. Graves, at the back door, twice and even three times every day, should be gone into with the utmost care, though there is little likelihood of its shedding any light on Mr. Knott, or on Watt, or on Mr. Graves.

But even there where there was no light for Watt, where there is none for his mouthpiece, there may be light for others. Or was there perhaps some light for Watt, on Mr. Knott, on Watt, in such relations as those with Mr. Graves, or with the fishwoman, that he left unspoken. That is by no means impossible.

Mr. Knott never left the grounds, as far as Watt could judge. Watt thought it unlikely that Mr. Knott could leave the grounds, without its coming to his notice. But he did not reject the possibility of Mr. Knott's leaving the grounds, without his being any the wiser. But the unlikelihood, on the one hand of Mr. Knott's leaving the grounds, and on the other of his doing so without exciting the general comment, seemed very great, to Watt.

On only one occasion, during Watt's period of service on the ground-floor, was the threshold crossed by a stranger, by other feet that is than Mr. Knott's, or Erskine's, or Watt's, for all were strangers to Mr. Knott's establishment, as far as Watt could see, with the exception of Mr. Knott himself, and his personnel at any given moment.

This fugitive penetration took place shortly after Watt's arrival. On his answering the door, as his habit was, when there was a knock at the door, he found standing before it, or so he realized later, arm in arm, an old man and a middle-aged man. The latter said:

We are the Galls, father and son, and we are come, what is more, all the way from town, to choon the piano.

They were two, and they stood, arm in arm, in this way, because the father was blind, like so many members of his profession. For if the father had not been blind, then he would not have needed his son to hold his arm, and guide him on his rounds, no, but he would have set his son free, to go about his own business. So Watt supposed, though there was nothing in the father's face to show that he was blind, nor in his attitude either, except that he leaned on his son in a way expressive of a great need of support. But he might have done this, if he had been halt, or merely tired, on account of his great age. There was no family likeness between the two, as far as Watt could make out, and nevertheless he knew that he was in the presence of a father and son, for had he not just been told so. Or were they not perhaps merely stepfather and stepson. We are the Galls, stepfather and stepson—those were perhaps the words that should have been spoken. But it was natural to prefer the others. Not that they could not very well be a true father and son, without resembling each other in the very least, for they could.

How very fortunate for Mr. Gall, said Watt, that he has

his son at his command, whose manner is all devotion and whose mere presence, when he might obviously be earning an honest penny elsewhere, attests an affliction characteristic of the best tuners, and justifies emoluments rather higher than the usual.

When he had led them to the music-room, and left them there, Watt wondered if he had done right. He felt he had done right, but he was not sure. Should he not perhaps rather have sent them flying about their business? Watt's feeling was that anyone who demanded, with such tranquil assurance, to be admitted to Mr. Knott's house, deserved to be admitted, in the absence of precise instructions to the contrary.

The music-room was a large bare white room. The piano was in the window. The head, and neck, in plaster, very white, of Buxtehude, was on the mantelpiece. A ravanastron hung, on the wall, from a nail, like a plover.

After a short time Watt returned to the music-room, with a tray, of refreshments.

Not Mr. Gall Senior, but Mr. Gall Junior, was tuning the piano, to Watt's great surprise. Mr. Gall Senior was standing in the middle of the room, perhaps listening. Watt did not take this to mean that Mr. Gall Junior was the true piano-tuner, and Mr. Gall Senior simply a poor blind old man, hired for the occasion, no. But he took it rather to mean that Mr. Gall Senior, feeling his end at hand, and anxious that his son should follow in his footsteps, was putting the finishing touches to a hasty instruction, before it was too late.

While Watt looked round, for a place to set down his tray, Mr. Gall Junior brought his work to a close. He re-assembled the piano case, put back his tools in their bag, and stood up.

The mice have returned, he said.

The elder said nothing. Watt wondered if he had heard.

Nine dampers remain, said the younger, and an equal number of hammers.

Not corresponding, I hope, said the elder.

In one case, said the younger.

The elder had nothing to say to this.

The strings are in flitters, said the younger.

The elder had nothing to say to this either.

The piano is doomed, in my opinion, said the younger.

The piano-tuner also, said the elder.

The pianist also, said the younger.

This was perhaps the principal incident of Watt's early days in Mr. Knott's house.

In a sense it resembled all the incidents of note proposed to Watt during his stay in Mr. Knott's house, and of which a certain number will be recorded in this place, without addition, or subtraction, and in a sense not.

It resembled them in the sense that it was not ended, when it was past, but continued to unfold, in Watt's head, from beginning to end, over and over again, the complex connexions of its lights and shadows, the passing from silence to sound and from sound to silence, the stillness before the movement and the stillness after, the quickenings and retardings, the approaches and the separations, all the shifting detail of its march and ordinance, according to the irrevocable caprice of its taking place. It resembled them in the vigour with which it developed a purely plastic content, and gradually lost, in the nice processes of its light, its sound, its impacts and its rhythm, all meaning, even the most literal.

Thus the scene in the music-room, with the two Galls, ceased very soon to signify for Watt a piano tuned, an obscure family and professional relation, an exchange of judgments more or less intelligible, and so on, if indeed it had ever signified such things, and became a mere example of light commenting bodies, and stillness motion, and silence sound, and comment comment.

This fragility of the outer meaning had a bad effect on Watt, for it caused him to seek for another, for some meaning of what had passed, in the image of how it had passed.

The most meagre, the least plausible, would have satisfied Watt, who had not seen a symbol, nor executed an interpretation, since the age of fourteen, or fifteen, and who had lived, miserably it is true, among face values all his adult life, face values at least for him. Some see the flesh before the bones, and some see the bones before the flesh, and some never see the bones at all, and some never see the flesh at all, never never see the flesh at all. But whatever it was Watt saw, with the first look, that was enough for Watt, that had always been enough for Watt, more than enough for Watt. And he had experienced literally nothing, since the age of fourteen, or fifteen, of which in retrospect he was not content to say, That is what happened then. He could recall, not indeed with any satisfaction, but as ordinary occasions, the time when his dead father appeared to him in a wood, with his trousers rolled up over his knees and his shoes and socks in his hand; or the time when in his surprise at hearing a voice urging him, in terms of unusual coarseness, to do away with himself, he narrowly escaped being knocked down, by a dray; or the time when alone in a rowing-boat, far from land, he suddenly smelt flowering currant; or the time when an old lady of delicate upbringing, and advantageous person, for she was amputated well above the knee, whom he had pursued with his assiduities on no fewer than three distinct occasions, unstrapped her wooden leg, and laid aside her crutch. Here no tendency appeared, on the part of his father's trousers, for example, to break up into an arrangement of appear-

70

ances, grey, flaccid and probably fistular, or of his father's legs to vanish in the farce of their properties, no, but his father's legs and trousers, as then seen, in the wood, and subsequently brought to mind, remained legs and trousers, and not only legs and trousers, but his father's legs and trousers, that is to say quite different from any of the legs and trousers that Watt had ever seen, and he had seen a great quantity, both of legs and of trousers, in his time. The incident of the Galls, on the contrary, ceased so rapidly to have even the paltry significance of two men, come to tune a piano, and tuning it, and exchanging a few words, as men will do, and going, that this seemed rather to belong to some story heard long before, an instant in the life of another, ill-told, ill-heard, and more than half forgotten.

So Watt did not know what had happened. He did not care, to do him justice, what had happened. But he felt the need to think that such and such a thing had happened then, the need to be able to say, when the scene began to unroll its sequences, Yes, I remember, that is what happened then.

This need remained with Watt, this need not always satisfied, during the greater part of his stay in Mr. Knott's house. For the incident of the Galls father and son was followed by others of a similar kind, incidents that is to say of great formal brilliance and indeterminable purport.

Watt's stay in Mr. Knott's house was less agreeable, on this account, than it would have been, if such incidents had been unknown, or his attitude towards them less anxious, that is to say, if Mr. Knott's house had been another house, or Watt another man. For outside Mr. Knott's house, and of course grounds, such incidents were unknown, or so Watt supposed. And Watt could not accept them for what they perhaps were, the simple games that time plays with space, now with these toys, and now with those, but was obliged, because of his peculiar character, to enquire into what they meant, oh not into what they really meant, his character was not so peculiar as all that, but into what they might be induced to mean, with the help of a little patience, a little ingenuity.

But what was this pursuit of meaning, in this indifference to meaning? And to what did it tend? These are delicate questions. For when Watt at last spoke of this time, it was a time long past, and of which his recollections were, in a sense, perhaps less clear than he would have wished, though too clear for his liking, in another. Add to this the notorious difficulty of recapturing, at will, modes of feeling peculiar to a certain time, and to a certain place, and perhaps also to a certain state of the health, when the time is past, and the place left, and the body struggling with quite a new situation. Add to this the obscurity of Watt's communications, the rapidity of his utterance and the eccentricities of his syntax, as elsewhere recorded. Add to this the material conditions in which these communications were made. Add to this the scant aptitude to receive of him to whom they were proposed. Add to this the scant aptitude to give of him to whom they were committed. And some idea will perhaps be obtained of the difficulties experienced in formulating, not only such matters as those here in question, but the entire body of Watt's experience, from the moment of his entering Mr. Knott's establishment to the moment of his leaving it.

But before passing from the Galls father and son to matters less litigious, or less tediously litigious, it seems advisable that the little that is known, on this subject, should be said. For the incident of the Galls father and son was the first and type of many. And the little that is known about it has not yet all been said. Much has been said, but not all.

72

Not that many things remain to be said, on the subject of the Galls father and son, for they do not. For only three or four things remain to be said, in this connexion. And three or four things are not really many, in comparison with the number of things that might have been known, and said, on this subject, and now never shall.

What distressed Watt in this incident of the Galls father and son, and in subsequent similar incidents, was not so much that he did not know what had happened, for he did not care what had happened, as that nothing had happened, that a thing that was nothing had happened, with the utmost formal distinctness, and that it continued to happen, in his mind, he supposed, though he did not know exactly what that meant, and though it seemed to be outside him, before him, about him, and so on, inexorably to unroll its phases, beginning with the first (the knock that was not a knock) and ending with the last (the door closing that was not a door closing), and omitting none, uninvoked, at the most unexpected moments, and the most inopportune. Yes, Watt could not accept, as no doubt Erskine could not accept, and as no doubt Arsene and Walter and Vincent and the others had been unable to accept, that nothing had happened, with all the clarity and solidity of something, and that it revisited him in such a way that he was forced to submit to it all over again, to hear the same sounds, see the same lights, touch the same surfaces, and so on, as when they had first involved him in their unintelligible intricacies. If he had been able to accept it, then perhaps it would not have revisited him, and this would have been a great saving of vexation, to put it mildly. But he could not accept it, could not bear it. One wonders sometimes where Watt thought he was. In a culture-park?

But if he could say, when the knock came, the knock become a knock, on the door become a door, in his mind, presumably in his mind, whatever that might mean, Yes, I remember, that is what happened then, if then he could say that, then he thought that then the scene would end, and trouble him no more, as the appearance of his father with his trousers rolled up and his shoes and socks in his hands troubled him no more, because he could say, when it began, Yes, yes, I remember, that was when my father appeared to me, in the wood, dressed for wading. But to elicit something from nothing requires a certain skill and Watt was not always successful, in his efforts to do so. Not that he was always unsuccessful either, for he was not. For if he had been always unsuccessful, how would it have been possible for him to speak of the Galls father and son, and of the piano they had come all the way from town to tune, and of their tuning it, and of their passing the remarks they had passed, the one to the other, in the way he did? No, he could never have spoken at all of these things, if all had continued to mean nothing, as some continued to mean nothing, that is to say, right up to the end. For the only way one can speak of nothing is to speak of it as though it were something, just as the only way one can speak of God is to speak of him as though he were a man, which to be sure he was, in a sense, for a time, and as the only way one can speak of man, even our anthropologists have realized that, is to speak of him as though he were a termite. But if Watt was sometimes unsuccessful, and sometimes successful, as in the affair of the Galls father and son, in foisting a meaning there where no meaning appeared, he was most often neither the one, nor the other. For Watt considered, with reason, that he was successful, in this enterprise, when he could evolve, from the meticulous phantoms that beset him, a hypothesis proper to disperse them, as often as this might be found necessary. There was nothing, in this operation, at variance with Watt's habits of mind. For to explain had always been to exorcize, for Watt. And he considered that he was unsuccessful, when he failed to do so. And he considered that he was neither wholly successful, nor wholly unsuccessful, when the hypothesis evolved lost its virtue, after one or two applications, and had to be replaced by another, which in its turn had to be replaced by another, which in due course ceased to be of the least assistance, and so on. And that is what happened, in the majority of cases. Now to give examples of Watt's failures, and of Watt's successes, and of Watt's partial successes, in this connexion, is so to speak impossible. For when he speaks, for example, of the incident of the Galls father and son, does he speak of it in terms of the unique hypothesis that was required, to deal with it, and render it innocuous, or in terms of the latest, or in terms of some other of the series? For when Watt spoke of an incident of this kind, he did not necessarily do so in terms of the unique hypothesis, or of the latest, though this at first sight seems the only possible alternative, and the reason why he did not, why it is not, is this, that when one of the series of hypotheses, with which Watt laboured to preserve his peace of mind, lost its virtue, and had to be laid aside, and another set up in its place, then it sometimes happened that the hypothesis in question, after a sufficient period of rest, recovered its virtue and could be made to serve again, in the place of another, whose usefulness had come to an end, for the time being at least. To such an extent is this true, that one is sometimes tempted to wonder, with reference to two or even three incidents related by Watt as separate and distinct, if they are not in reality the same incident, variously interpreted. As to giving an example of the second event, namely the failure, that is clearly quite out of the question. For there we have to do with events that resisted all Watt's efforts to saddle them with meaning, and a

75

formula, so that he could neither think of them, nor speak of them, but only suffer them, when they recurred, though it seems probable that they recurred no more, at the period of Watt's revelation, to me, but were as though they had never been.

Finally, to return to the incident of the Galls father and son, as related by Watt, did it have that meaning for Watt at the time of its taking place, and then lose that meaning, and then recover it? Or did it have some quite different meaning for Watt at the time of its taking place, and then lose that meaning, and then receive that, alone or among others, which it exhibited, in Watt's relation? Or did it have no meaning whatever for Watt at the moment of its taking place, were there neither Galls nor piano then, but only an unintelligible succession of changes, from which Watt finally extracted the Galls and the piano, in self-defence? These are most delicate questions. Watt spoke of it as involving, in the original, the Galls and the piano, but he was obliged to do this, even if the original had nothing to do with the Galls and the piano. For even if the Galls and the piano were long posterior to the phenomena destined to become them, Watt was obliged to think, and speak, of the incident, even at the moment of its taking place, as the incident of the Galls and the piano, if he was to think and speak of it at all, and it may be assumed that Watt would never have thought or spoken of such incidents, if he had not been under the absolute necessity of doing so. But generally speaking it seems probable that the meaning attributed to this particular type of incident, by Watt, in his relations, was now the initial meaning that had been lost and then recovered, and now a meaning quite distinct from the initial meaning, and now a meaning evolved, after a delay of varying length, and with greater or less pains, from the initial absence of meaning.

One more word on this subject.

Watt learned towards the end of his stay in Mr. Knott's house to accept that nothing had happened, that a nothing had happened, learned to bear it and even, in a shy way, to like it. But then it was too late.

That then is that in which the incident of the Galls father and son resembled other incidents, of which it was merely the first in time, other incidents of note. But to say, as has been said, that the incident of the Galls father and son had this aspect in common with all the subsequent incidents of note, is perhaps to go a little too far. For not all the subsequent incidents of note, with which Watt was called upon to deal, during his stay in Mr. Knott's house, and of course grounds, presented this aspect, no, but some meant something from the very beginning, and continued to mean it, with all the tenacity of, for example, the flowering currant in the rowing-boat, or the capitulation of the one-legged Mrs. Watson, right up to the end.

As to that in which the incident of the Galls father and son differed from the subsequent incidents of its category, that is no longer clear, and cannot therefore be stated, with profit. But it may be taken that the difference was so nice as with advantage to be neglected, in a synopsis of this kind.

Watt thought sometimes of Arsene. He wondered what Arsene had meant, nay, he wondered what Arsene had said, on the evening of his departure. For his declaration had entered Watt's ears only by fits, and his understanding, like all that enters the ears only by fits, hardly at all. He had realized, to be sure, that Arsene was speaking, and in a sense to him, but something had prevented him, perhaps his fatigue, from paying attention to what was being said and from enquiring into what was being meant. Watt was now inclined to regret this, for from Erskine no information was to be obtained. Not that Watt desired information, for he did not. But he desired words to be applied to his situation, to Mr. Knott, to the house, to the grounds, to his duties, to the stairs, to his bedroom, to the kitchen, and in a general way to the conditions of being in which he found himself. For Watt now found himself in the midst of things which, if they consented to be named, did so as it were with reluctance. And the state in which Watt found himself resisted formulation in a way no state had ever done, in which Watt had ever found himself, and Watt had found himself in a great many states, in his day. Looking at a pot, for example, or thinking of a pot, at one of Mr. Knott's pots, of one of Mr. Knott's pots, it was in vain that Watt said, Pot, pot. Well, perhaps not quite in vain, but very nearly. For it was not a pot, the more he looked, the more he reflected, the more he felt sure of that, that it was not a pot at all. It resembled a pot, it was almost a pot, but it was not a pot of which one could say, Pot, pot, and be comforted. It was in vain that it answered, with unexceptionable adequacy, all the purposes, and performed all the offices, of a pot, it was not a pot. And it was just this hairbreadth departure from the nature of a true pot that so excruciated Watt. For if the approximation had been less close, then Watt would have been less anguished. For then he would not have said, This is a pot, and yet not a pot, no, but then he would have said, This is something of which I do not know the name. And Watt preferred on the whole having to do with things of which he did not know the name, though this too was painful to Watt, to having to do with things of which the known name, the proven name, was not the name, any more, for him. For he could always hope, of a thing of which he had never known the name, that he would learn the name, some day, and so be tranquillized. But he could not look forward to this in the case of a thing of which the true name had ceased, suddenly,

78

or gradually, to be the true name for Watt. For the pot remained a pot, Watt felt sure of that, for everyone but Watt. For Watt alone it was not a pot, any more.

Then, when he turned for reassurance to himself, who was not Mr. Knott's, in the sense that the pot was, who had come from without and whom the without would take again,[1] he made the distressing discovery that of himself too he could no longer affirm anything that did not seem as false as if he had affirmed it of a stone. Not that Watt was in the habit of affirming things of himself, for he was not, but he found it a help, from time to time, to be able to say, with some appearance of reason, Watt is a man, all the same, Watt is a man, or, Watt is in the street, with thousands of fellow-creatures within call. And Watt was greatly troubled by this tiny little thing, more troubled perhaps than he had ever been by anything, and Watt had been frequently and exceedingly troubled, in his time, by this imperceptible, no, hardly imperceptible, since he per-ceived it, by this indefinable thing that prevented him from saying, with conviction, and to his relief, of the object that was so like a pot, that it was a pot, and of the creature that still in spite of everything presented a large number of exclusively human characteristics, that it was a man. And Watt's need of semantic succour was at times so great

[1] Watt, unlike Arsene, had never supposed that Mr. Knott's house would be his last refuge. Was it his first? In a sense it was, but it was not the kind of first refuge that promised to be the last. It occurred to him, of course, towards the end of his stay, that it might have been, that he might have made it, this transitory refuge, the last, if he had been more adroit, or less in need of rest. But Watt was very subject to fancies, towards the end of his stay under Mr. Knott's roof. And it was also under the pressure of a similar eleventh hour vision, of what might have been, that Arsene expressed himself on this subject, in the way he did, on the night of his departure. For it is scarcely credible that a man of Arsene's experience could have supposed, in advance, of any given halt, that it was to be the last halt.

that he would set to trying names on things, and on himself, almost as a woman hats. Thus of the pseudo-pot he would say, after reflexion, It is a shield, or, growing bolder, It is a raven, and so on. But the pot proved as little a shield, or a raven, or any other of the things that Watt called it, as a pot. As for himself, though he could no longer call it a man, as he had used to do, with the intuition that he was perhaps not talking nonsense, yet he could not imagine what else to call it, if not a man. But Watt's imagination had never been a lively one. So he continued to think of himself as a man, as his mother had taught him, when she said, There's a good little man, or, There's a bonny little man, or, There's a clever little man. But for all the relief that this afforded him, he might just as well have thought of himself as a box, or an urn.

It was principally for these reasons that Watt would have been glad to hear Erskine's voice, wrapping up safe in words the kitchen space, the extraordinary newel-lamp, the stairs that were never the same and of which even the number of steps seemed to vary, from day to day, and from night to morning, and many other things in the house, and the bushes without and other garden growths, that so often prevented Watt from taking the air, even on the finest day, so that he grew pale, and constipated, and even the light as it came and went and the clouds that climbed the sky, now slow, now rapid, and generally from west to east, or sank down towards the earth on the other side, for the clouds seen from Mr. Knott's premises were not quite the clouds that Watt was used to, and Watt had a great experience of clouds, and could distinguish the various sorts, the cirrhus, the stratus, the tumulus and the various other sorts, at a glance. Not that the fact of Erskine's naming the pot, or of his saying to Watt, My dear fellow, or, My good man, or, God damn you, would have changed the pot into

80

a pot, or Watt into a man, for Watt, for it would not. But it would have shown that at least for Erskine the pot was a pot, and Watt a man. Not that the fact of the pot's being a pot, or Watt's being a man, for Erskine, would have caused the pot to be a pot, or Watt to be a man, for Watt, for it would not. But it would perhaps have lent a little colour to the hope, sometimes entertained by Watt, that he was in poor health, owing to the efforts of his body to adjust itself to an unfamiliar milieu, and that these would be successful, in the end, and his health restored, and things appear, and himself appear, in their ancient guise, and consent to be named, with the time-honoured names, and forgotten. Not that Watt longed at all times for this restoration, of things, of himself, to their comparative innocuousness, for he did not. For there were times when he felt a feeling closely resembling the feeling of satisfaction, at his being so abandoned, by the last rats. For after these there would be no more rats, not a rat left, and there were times when Watt almost welcomed this prospect, of being rid of his last rats, at last. It would be lonely, to be sure, at first, and silent, after the gnawing, the scurrying, the little cries. Things and himself, they had gone with him now for so long, in the foul weather, and in the less foul. Things in the ordinary sense, and then the emptinesses between them, and the light high up before it reached them, and then the other thing, the high heavy hollow jointed unstable thing, that trampled down the grasses, and scattered the sand, in its pursuits. But if there were times when Watt envisaged this dereliction with something like satisfaction, these were rare, particularly in the early stages of Watt's stay in Mr. Knott's house. And most often he found himself longing for a voice, for Erskine's, since he was alone with Erskine, to speak of the little world of Mr. Knott's establishment, with the old words, the old credentials. There was of course the gardener, to speak of the garden. But could the gardener speak of the garden, the gardener who went home every evening, before nightfall, and did not return next morning until the sun was well up, in the sky? No, the gardener's remarks were not evidence, in Watt's opinion. Only Erskine could speak of the garden, as only Erskine could speak of the house, usefully, to Watt. And Erskine never spoke, either of the one, or of the other. Indeed Erskine never opened his mouth, in Watt's presence, except to eat, or belch, or cough, or keck, or muse, or sigh, or sing, or sneeze. It is true that during the first week hardly a day passed that Erskine did not address himself to Watt, on the subject of Watt's duties. But in the first week Watt's words had not yet begun to fail him, or Watt's world to become unspeakable. It is true also that from time to time Erskine would come running to Watt, all in a fluster, with some quite ridiculous question, such as, Did you see Mr. Knott?, or, Has Kate come? But this was much later. Perhaps some day, said Watt, he will ask, Where is the pot?, or, Where did you put that pot? These questions, absurd as they were, constituted nevertheless an acknowledgement of Watt that Watt was not slow to appreciate. But he would have appreciated it more if it had come earlier, before he had grown used to his loss of species.

The song that Erskine sang, or rather intoned, was always the same. It was:

?

Perhaps if Watt had spoken to Erskine, Erskine would have spoken to Watt, in reply. But Watt was not so far gone as all that.

Watt's attention was extreme, in the beginning, to all that went on about him. Not a sound was made, within earshot, that he did not capture and, when necessary, interrogate, and he opened wide his eyes to all that passed, near and at a distance, to all that came and went and paused and stirred, and to all that brightened and darkened and grew and dwindled, and he grasped, in many cases, the nature of the object affected, and even the immediate cause of its being so. To the thousand smells also, which time leaves behind, Watt paid the closest attention. And he provided himself with a portable spittoon.

This constant tension of some of his most noble faculties tired Watt greatly. And the results, on the whole, were meagre. But he had no choice, at first.

One of the first things that Watt learned by these means was that Mr. Knott sometimes rose late and retired early, and sometimes rose very late and retired very early, and sometimes did not rise at all, nor at all retire, for who can retire who does not rise? What interested Watt here was this, that the earlier Mr. Knott rose the later he retired, and that the later he rose the earlier he retired. But between the hour of his rising and the hour of his retiring there seemed no fixed correlation, or one so abstruse that it did not exist, for Watt. For a long time this was a source of great wonder, to Watt, for he said, Here is one who seems on the one hand reluctant to change his state, and on the other impatient to do so. For on Monday, Tuesday and Friday he rose at eleven and retired at seven, and on Wednesday and Saturday he rose at nine and retired at eight, and on Sunday he did not rise at all, nor at all retire. Until Watt realized that between Mr. Knott risen and Mr. Knott retired there was so to speak nothing to choose. For his rising was not a rising from sleep to vigil, nor his setting a setting from vigil to sleep, no, but they were a rising and a setting from and to and to and from a state that was neither sleep nor vigil, nor vigil nor sleep. Even Mr. Knott could hardly be expected to remain day and night in the same position.

Mr. Knott's meals gave very little trouble.

On Saturday night a sufficient quantity of food was prepared and cooked to carry Mr. Knott through the week.

This dish contained foods of various kinds, such as soup of various kinds, fish, eggs, game, poultry, meat, cheese, fruit, all of various kinds, and of course bread and butter, and it contained also the more usual beverages, such as absinthe, mineral water, tea, coffee, milk, stout, beer, whiskey, brandy, wine and water, and it contained also many things to take for the good of the health, such as insulin, digitalin, calomel, iodine, laudanum, mercury, coal, iron, camomile and worm-powder, and of course salt and mustard, pepper and sugar, and of course a little salicylic acid, to delay fermentation.

All these things, and many others too numerous to mention, were well mixed together in the famous pot and boiled for four hours, until the consistence of a mess, or poss, was obtained, and all the good things to eat, and all the good things to drink, and all the good things to take for the good of the health were inextricably mingled and transformed into a single good thing that was neither food, nor drink, nor physic, but quite a new good thing, and of which the tiniest spoonful at once opened the appetite and closed it, excited and stilled the thirst, compromised and stimulated the body's vital functions, and went pleasantly to the head.

It fell to Watt to weigh, to measure and to count, with the utmost exactness, the ingredients that composed this dish, and to dress for the pot those that required dressing, and to mix them thoroughly together without loss, so that not one could be distinguished from another, and to put them on to boil, and when boiling to keep them on the boil, and when boiled to take them off the boil and put out to cool, in a cool place. This was a task that taxed Watt's powers, both of mind and of body, to the utmost, it was so delicate, and rude. And in warm weather it sometimes happened, as he mixed, stripped to the waist, and plying with both hands the great iron rod, that tears would fall, tears of mental fatigue, from his face, into the pot, and from his chest, and out from under his arms, beads of moisture, provoked by his exertions, into the pot also. His moral reserves also were severely tried, so great was his sense of responsibility. For he knew, as though he had been told, that the receipt of this dish had never varied, since its establishment, long long before, and that the choice, the dosage and the quantities of the elements employed had been calculated, with the most minute exactness, to afford Mr. Knott, in a course of fourteen full meals, that is to say, seven full luncheons, and seven full dinners, the maximum of pleasure compatible with the protraction of his health.

This dish was served to Mr. Knott, cold, in a bowl, at twelve o'clock noon sharp and at seven p.m. exactly, all the year round.

That is to say that Watt carried in the bowl, full, to the dining-room at those hours, and left it on the table. An hour later he went back and took it away, in whatever state Mr. Knott had left it. If the bowl still contained food, then Watt transferred this food to the dog's dish. But if it was empty, then Watt washed it up, in readiness for the next meal.

So Watt never saw Mr. Knott at mealtime. For Mr. Knott was never punctual, at his meals. But he was seldom later than twenty minutes, or half an hour. And whether he emptied the bowl, or did not, it never took him more than five minutes to do so, or seven minutes at the outside. So that Mr. Knott was never in the dining-room when Watt brought in the bowl, and he was never there either when

Watt went back, to take the bowl away. So Watt never saw Mr. Knott, never never saw Mr. Knott, at mealtime.

Mr. Knott ate this dish with a little plated trowel, such as confectioners and grocers use, and tea-merchants.

This arrangement represented a great saving of labour. Coal also was economized.

To whom, Watt wondered, was this arrangement due? To Mr. Knott himself? Or to some other person, to a past domestic perhaps of genius for example, or a professional dietician? And if not to Mr. Knott himself, but to some other person (or of course persons), did Mr. Knott know that such an arrangement existed, or did he not?

Mr. Knott was never heard to complain of his food, though he did not always eat it. Sometimes he emptied the bowl, scraping its sides, and bottom, with the trowel, until they shone, and sometimes he left the half of it, or some other fraction, and sometimes he left the whole of it.

Twelve possibilities occurred to Watt, in this connexion:

1. Mr. Knott was responsible for the arrangement, and knew that he was responsible for the arrangement, and knew that such an arrangement existed, and was content.

2. Mr. Knott was not responsible for the arrangement, but knew who was responsible for the arrangement, and knew that such an arrangement existed, and was content.

3. Mr. Knott was responsible for the arrangement, and knew that he was responsible for the arrangement, but did not know that any such arrangement existed, and was content.

4. Mr. Knott was not responsible for the arrangement, but knew who was responsible for the arrangement, but did not know that any such arrangement existed, and was content.

5. Mr. Knott was responsible for the arrangement, but did not know who was responsible for the arrangement, nor that any such arrangement existed, and was content.

6. Mr. Knott was not responsible for the arrangement, nor knew who was responsible for the arrangement, nor that any such arrangement existed, and was content.

7. Mr. Knott was responsible for the arrangement, but did not know who was responsible for the arrangement, and knew that such an arrangement existed, and was content.

8. Mr. Knott was not responsible for the arrangement, nor knew who was responsible for the arrangement, and knew that such an arrangement existed, and was content.

9. Mr. Knott was responsible for the arrangement, but knew who was responsible for the arrangement, and knew that such an arrangement existed, and was content.

10. Mr. Knott was not responsible for the arrangement, but knew that he was responsible for the arrangement, and knew that such an arrangement existed, and was content.

11. Mr. Knott was responsible for the arrangement, but knew who was responsible for the arrangement, but did not know that any such arrangement existed, and was content.

12. Mr. Knott was not responsible for the arrangement, but knew that he was responsible for the arrangement, but did not know that any such arrangement existed, and was content.

Other possibilities occurred to Watt, in this connexion, but he put them aside, and quite out of his mind, as unworthy of serious consideration, for the time being. The time would come, perhaps, when they would be worthy of serious consideration, and then, if he could, he would summon them to his mind, and consider them seriously. But for the moment they did not seem worthy of serious consideration, so he put them quite out of his mind, and forgot them.

Watt's instructions were to give what Mr. Knott left of this dish, on the days that he did not eat it all, to the dog.

Now there was no dog in the house, that is to say, no house-dog, to which this food could be given, on the days that Mr. Knott did not require it.

Watt, reflecting on this, heard a little voice say, Mr. Knott, having once known a man who was bitten by a dog, in the leg, and having once known another man who was scratched by a cat, in the nose, and having once known a fine healthy woman who was butted by a goat, in the loins, and having once known another man who was disembowelled by a bull, in the bowels, and having once frequented a canon who was kicked by a horse, in the crotch, is shy of dogs, and other four-footed friends, about the place, and of his inarticulate bipedal brothers and sisters in God hardly less so, for he once knew a missionary who was trampled to death by an ostrich, in the stomach, and he once knew a priest who, on leaving with a sigh of relief the chapel where he had served mass, with his own hands, to more than a hundred persons, was shat on, from above, by a dove, in the eye.

Watt never knew quite what to make of this particular little voice, whether it was joking, or whether it was serious.

So that it was necessary that a dog from outside should call at the house at least once every day, on the off chance of its being given part, or all, of Mr. Knott's lunch, or dinner, or both, to eat.

Now in this matter great difficulties must have been encountered, notwithstanding the large numbers of hungry and even starving dogs with which the neighbourhood abounded, and doubtless had always abounded, for miles around, in every direction. And the reason for that was perhaps this, that the number of times that the dog went full away was small compared with the number of times that it went away half empty, and the number of times that it went away half empty was small compared with the number of times that it went away as empty as it came. For it was more usual for Mr. Knott to eat all his food than to eat only a part, and to eat only a part than to eat none at all, much much more usual. For while it is true that Mr. Knott very often rose very late and retired very early, yet the number of times was very great on which Mr. Knott rose just in time to eat his lunch, and ate his dinner just in time to retire. The days on which he neither rose nor retired, and so left both his lunch and his dinner untouched, were of course wonderful days, for the dog. But they were very rare.

Now will of its own free will the average hungry or starving dog be constant in its attendance, under such conditions? No, the average hungry or starving dog, if left to its own devices, will not, for it would not be worth its while.

Add to this that the dog's attendance was required, not at any odd hour of the day or night that it might fancy to drop in, no, but between certain definite limiting hours, and these were eight o'clock p.m. and ten o'clock p.m. And the reason for that was this, that at ten o'clock the house was shut up for the night, and it was not known, until eight o'clock, if Mr. Knott had left anything, or all, or nothing, of his food for the day. For though as a general rule Mr. Knott ate every atom, both of his lunch and of his dinner, in which case the dog got nothing, yet what was to prevent him from eating every atom of his lunch, but no dinner, or only part of his dinner, in which case the dog got the uneaten dinner, or portion of dinner, or from eating no lunch, or only part of his lunch, and yet every atom of his dinner, in which case the dog got the uneaten lunch, or portion of lunch, or from eating only part of his lunch, and then again only part of his dinner, in which case the dog benefited by the two uneaten portions, or from not touching either his lunch or his dinner, in which case the dog, if it neither delayed nor precipitated its arrival, went away with its belly full at last.

By what means then were the dog and the food to be brought together, on those days on which, Mr. Knott having left all or part of his food for the day, all or part of the food was available for the dog? For Watt's instructions were formal: On those days on which food was left over, the food left over was to be given to the dog, without loss of time.

This was the problem that must have faced Mr. Knott, in the far distant past, at the moment of his setting up house.

This was one of the many problems that must have faced Mr. Knott then.

Or if not Mr. Knott, then another, of whom all trace is lost. Or if not another, then others, of whom no trace remains.

Watt now passed on to the manner in which this problem had been solved, if not by Mr. Knott, then by that other, and if neither by Mr. Knott nor by that other, then by those others, in a word, to the manner in which this problem had been solved, this problem of how to bring the dog and food together, by Mr. Knott, or by him, or by them, whom it had faced, in that far distant past, when Mr. Knott set up his establishment, for that it could have been solved by some person or persons whom it had never faced seemed improbable, highly improbable, to Watt.

But before he passed on to this, he paused to reflect that the solution of this problem of how to bring the dog and food together in the way described had perhaps been arrived at by the same person or persons by whom the solution of the problem of how Mr. Knott's food was to be prepared had been arrived at, so long before.

And when he had paused to reflect on this, he paused a little longer, before passing on to the solution that seemed to have prevailed, to consider some at least of those that did not seem to have prevailed.

But before pausing a little longer to do this, he hastened to remark that those solutions that did not seem to have prevailed might have been considered, and set aside, as unsatisfactory, by the author or authors of the solution that did seem to have prevailed, or might not.

1. An exceptional hungry or starving dog might have been sought out, that for reasons best known to itself would have considered it worth its while to call at the house, in the manner required.

But the chances of such a dog's existing were small.

But the likelihood of finding such a dog, if it did exist, was slight.

2. An ill-nourished local dog might have been selected, to which with the consent of its proprietor all or part of Mr. Knott's food might have been brought by one of Mr. Knott's men, on the days that Mr. Knott left all or part of his food, for the day.

But then one of Mr. Knott's men would have had to put on his coat and hat and turn out, as likely as not in the pitch dark, and in torrents of rain in all probability, and grope his way in the dark in the pours of rain, with the pot of food in his hand, a wretched and ridiculous figure, to where the dog lay.

But was there any guarantee of the dog's being in, when the man arrived? Might not the dog have gone out, for the night?

But was there any guarantee, supposing the dog to be in when the man arrived, of the dog's being hungry enough to eat the pot of food, when the man arrived with the pot of food? Might not the dog have satisfied its hunger, during the day? Or was there any assurance, supposing the dog to be out when the man arrived, of the dog's being hungry enough, when it came in, in the morning, or during the night, to eat the pot of food that the man had brought? Might not the dog have satisfied its hunger, during the night, and indeed left the house with no other purpose?

3. A messenger might have been employed, a man, or a boy, or a woman, or a girl, to call at the house every evening at say eight fifteen o'clock in the evening, and on those evenings on which food was available for the dog to take that food to a dog, to any dog, and to stand over that dog until it had eaten the food, and if it could not or would not finish the food to take what remained of the food to another dog, to any other dog, and to stand over that other dog until it had eaten what remained of the food, and if it could not or would not finish what remained of the food to take what still remained of the food to another dog, to any other dog, and so on, until all the food was eaten, and not an atom remained, and then to bring back the pot empty.

(This person might have been further employed to clean the boots, and the shoes, either before leaving the house with the pot full, though of course it was not full at all, or on returning to the house with the pot empty, or simply on learning that there was no food available for the dog, that day. This would have greatly relieved the gardener, a Mr. Graves, and enabled him to give the garden the time that he gave to the boots, and to the shoes. And is it not strange most strange that one says of a thing that it is full, when it is not full at all, but not of a thing that it is empty, if it is not empty? And perhaps the reason for that is this, that when one fills, one seldom fills quite full, for that would not be convenient, whereas when one empties one empties completely, holding the vessel upside down, and rinsing it out with boiling water if necessary, with a kind of fury.)

But was there any guarantee that the messenger would indeed give the food to a dog, or dogs, in accordance with his instructions? What was to prevent the messenger from eating the food himself, or from selling all or part of the food to some other party, or from giving it away, or from emptying it away into the nearest ditch or hole, to save time, and trouble?

But what would happen if the messenger, through indisposition, or drunkenness, or carelessness, or idleness, failed to call at the house on an evening on which food was available for the dog?

But might not even the most hardy, the most sober, the most conscientious of messengers, knowing all the local dogs, their habits and their homes, their colours and their shapes, have still some food got, in the old pot, when ten o'cluck strock, from the old clock, and then how would he bring back the pot, the trusty messenger, if the pot was not empty in time, for the following morning would be too late, for Mr. Knott's pots and pans were not allowed to stay out, overnight.

But was a dog the same thing as the dog? For in Watt's instructions there was no mention of a dog, but only of the dog, which could only mean that what was required was not any dog, but one particular dog, that is to say, not one dog one day, and the next another, and perhaps the next a third, no, but every day the same, every day the same poor old dog, as long as the dog lived. But a fortiori were several dogs the same thing as the dog?

4. A man possessed of a famished dog might have been sought out, whose business brought him, accompanied by his dog, past Mr. Knott's house every evening of the year, between the hours of eight and ten. Then on those evenings on which food was available for the dog, in Mr. Knott's window, or some other conspicuous window, a red light

would be set, or perhaps better a green, and on all other evenings a violet light, or perhaps better no light at all, and then the man (and no doubt after a little time the dog too) would lift up his eyes to the window as he passed, and seeing a red light, or a green light, would hasten to the house-door and stand over his dog until his dog had eaten all the food that Mr. Knott had left, but seeing a violet light, or no light at all, would not hasten to the door, with his dog, but continue on his way, down the road, with his dog, as though nothing had happened.

But was it likely that such a man existed?

But was it likely, if he did, that he could be found?

But if he did, and he were found, might he not confound, in his mind, as he passed before the house, on his way home, if he were homeward bound, or on his way out, if he were outward bound, for whither can a man be bound, if bound he be, but on the one hand homeward, and on the other outward, might he not confound, in his mind, the red light with the violet, the violet with the green, the green with the none, the none with the red, and when there was no food him for come ratatat knocking at the door, and when there was for him some food onward plod along the road, followed by his faithful emaciated dog?

But might not Erskine, or Watt, or some other Erskine, or some other Watt, set in the window the wrong light, or the no light, by mistake, or the right light, or the no light, when it was too late, out of forgetfulness, or procrastination, and the man and dog come running to the door, when there was nothing, or onward plod, when there was something?

But would not this greatly add to the worries, the responsibilities, and the exertions, already so heavy, of Mr. Knott's servants?

So Watt considered, not only some of those solutions that had not apparently prevailed, but also some of those

94

objections that were perhaps the cause of their not having done so, distributed as follows:

Solution					Number of Objections
1st	..	..	..	..	.. 2
2nd	..	..	..	..	.. 3
3rd	..	..	..	..	.. 4
4th	..	..	..	..	.. 5

Number of Solutions					Number of Objections
4	..	..	..	..	.. 14
3	..	..	..	..	.. 9
2	..	..	..	..	.. 5
1	..	..	..	..	.. 2

Passing on then to the solution that seemed to have prevailed, Watt found it to be roughly this, that a suitable local dog-owner, that is to say a needy man with a famished dog, should be sought out, and on him settled a handsome annuity of fifty pounds payable monthly, in consideration of his calling at Mr. Knott's house every evening between eight and ten, accompanied by his dog in a famished condition, and on those days on which there was food for his dog of his standing over his dog, with a stick, before witnesses, until the dog had eaten all the food until not an atom remained, and of his then taking himself and his dog off the premises without delay; and that a younger famished dog should by this man at Mr. Knott's expense be acquired and held in reserve, against the day when the first famished dog should die, and that then again another famished dog should in the same way be procured and held in readiness, against the inevitable hour when the second famished dog should pay nature's debt, and so on indefinitely, there being thus two famished dogs always available, the one to eat the food left over by Mr. Knott in the manner described until it died, and the other then for as long as it lived to do the same, and so on indefinitely; and further that a similar young local but dogless man should be sought out, against the day when the first local man should die, to take over and exploit, in the same way and on the same terms, the two surviving famished dogs thus left without a master, and without a home; and that then again another young local dogless man should in the same way be secured, against the dread hour of the second local man's dissolution, and so on indefinitely, there being thus two famished dogs and two needy local men for ever available, the first needy local man to own and exploit the two famished dogs in the manner described as long as he lived, and the other then, as long as he drew breath, to do the same, and so on indefinitely; and that lest, as might very well happen, one of the two famished dogs, or both the famished dogs, should fail to survive their master, and follow him at once to the grave, a third, a fourth, a fifth and even a sixth famished dog should be acquired and suitably maintained at Mr. Knott's expense in some convenient place in a famished condition, or that better still there should be at Mr. Knott's expense on some favourable site established a kennel or colony of famished dogs from which at any time a well-bred well-trained famished dog could be withdrawn and set to work, in the manner described; and that on the off chance of the second poor young local man's passing over, into the beyond, at the same time as the first poor local man, or even before, and stranger things are of hourly occurrence, a third, a fourth, a fifth and even a sixth poor young local dogless man or even woman should be sought out and by fair words and occasional gifts of money and old clothes as far as possible secured to Mr. Knott's service eventually in the manner described, or better still that a suitable large needy local family of say the two parents and from ten to fifteen children and grandchildren passionately attached to their birthplace should be sought out, and by a handsome small initial lump sum to be paid down and by a liberal annual pension of fifty pounds to be paid monthly and by occasional seasonable gifts of loose change and tight clothes and by untiring well-timed affectionate words of advice and encouragement and consolation, attached firmly for good and all in block, their children and their children's children, to Mr. Knott's service, in all matters touching this matter of the dog required to eat the food that Mr. Knott left, and exclusively in these, and that to their care the kennel or colony of famished dogs set up by Mr. Knott in order that there should never be wanting a famished dog to eat his food on those days that he did not eat it himself should be once and for all handed over, for the matter of the kennel was one that touched the matter of the dog. And this seemed to Watt roughly the way in which the solution to the problem of how Mr. Knott's food was to be given to the dog had been reached, and though of course for some time it can have been no more than a tissue now dilating now contracting of thoughts in a skull, very likely very soon it was much more than this, for immense impoverished families abounded for miles around in every conceivable direction, and must have always done so, and very likely very soon a real live famished dog as large as life was coming night after night as regular as clockwork to Mr. Knott's back door, led by and probably preceding an unmistakable specimen of local indigent proliferation, for everyone to see, and admire, and the pension being paid, and every now and then when least expected a half-crown bestowed, or a florin, or a shilling, or a sixpence, or a threepence, or a penny, or a halfpenny, and the cast-off clothes, of which Mr. Knott, who was a great caster-off of clothes, had a large store, being handed over, now a coat, now a waistcoat, now a greatcoat, now a raincoat, now a trousers, now a knickerbockers, now a shirt, now a vest, now a pant, now a combination, now a braces, now a belt, now a collar, now a tie, now a scarf, now a muffler, now a hat, now a cap, now a stocking, now a sock, now a boot and now a shoe, and the good words of counsel, of encouragement and comfort spoken, and lavished the little acts of kindness and of love, just when they were most needed, and the kennel of famished dogs handed over and in full swing, for all the world to see, and admire.

The name of this fortunate family was Lynch and at the moment of Watt's entering Mr. Knott's service this family of Lynch was made up as follows.

There was Tom Lynch, widower, aged eighty-five years, confined to his bed with constant undiagnosed pains in the caecum, and his three surviving boys Joe, aged sixty-five years, a rheumatic cripple, and Jim, aged sixty-four years, a hunchbacked inebriate, and Bill, widower, aged sixty-three years, greatly hampered in his movements by the loss of both legs as the result of a slip, followed by a fall, and his only surviving daughter May Sharpe, widow, aged sixty-two years, in full possession of all her faculties with the exception of that of vision. Then there was Joe's wife née Doyly-Byrne, aged sixty-five years, a sufferer from Parkinson's palsy but otherwise very fit and well, and Jim's wife Kate née Sharpe aged sixty-four years, covered all over with running sores of an unidentified nature but otherwise fit and well. Then there was Joe's boy Tom aged forty-one years, unfortunately subject alternately to fits of exaltation, which rendered him incapable of the least exertion, and of depression, during which he could stir neither hand nor foot, and Bill's boy Sam, aged forty years, paralysed by a merciful providence from no higher than the knees down and from no lower than the waist up, and May's spinster daughter Ann, aged thirty-nine years, greatly reduced in health and spirits by a painful congenital disorder of an unmentionable kind, and Jim's lad Jack aged thirty-eight years, who was weak in the head, and the boon twins Art and Con aged thirty-seven years, who measured in height when in their stockinged feet three feet and four inches and who weighed in weight when stripped to the buff seventy-one pounds all bone and sinew and between whom the resemblance was so marked in every way that even those (and they were many) who knew and loved them most would call Art Con when they meant Art, and Con Art when they meant Con, at least as often as, if not more often than, they called Art Art when they meant Art, and Con Con when they meant Con. And then there was young Tom's wife Mag née Sharpe aged forty-one years, greatly handicapped in her house and outdoor activity by sub-epileptic seizures of monthly incidence, during which she rolled foaming on the floor, or on the yard, or on the vegetable patch, or on the river's brim, and seldom failed to damage herself in one way or another, so that she was obliged to go to bed, and remain there, every month, until she was better, and Sam's wife Liz née Sharpe aged thirty-eight years, fortunate in being more dead than alive as a result of having in the course of twenty years given Sam nineteen children, of whom four survived, and again expecting, and poor Jack who it will be remembered was weak in the head his wife Lil née Sharpe aged thirty-eight years, who was weak in the chest. And then to pass on to the next generation there was Tom's boy young Simon aged twenty, whose it is painful to relate

?

and his young cousin wife his uncle Sam's girl Ann, aged

nineteen, whose it will be learnt with regret beauty and utility were greatly diminished by two withered arms and a game leg of unsuspected tubercular origin, and Sam's two surviving boys Bill and Mat aged eighteen and seventeen respectively, who having come into this world respectively blind and maim were known as Blind Bill and Maim Mat respectively, and Sam's other married daughter Kate aged twenty-one years, a fine girl but a bleeder,[1] and her young cousin husband her uncle Jack's son Sean aged twenty-one years, a sterling fellow but a bleeder too, and Frank's daughter Bridie aged fifteen years, a prop and a stay to the family, sleeping as she did by day and at night receiving in the toolshed so as not to disturb the family for twopence, or threepence, or fourpence, or sometimes even fivepence a time, that depended, or a bottle of ale, and Jack's other son Tom aged fourteen years, who some said took after his father because of the weakness of his head and others said took after his mother because of the weakness of his chest and some said took after his paternal grandfather Jim because of his taste for strong spirits and others said took after his paternal grandmother Kate because of a patch he had on the sacrum the size of a plate of weeping eczema and some said took after his paternal great-grandfather Tom because of the cramps he had in the stomach. And then finally to pass on to the rising generation there were Sean's two little girls Rose and Cerise, aged five and four respectively, and these innocent little girlies were bleeders like their papa and mama, and indeed it was very wrong of Sean, knowing what he was and knowing what Kate was, to do what he did to Kate, so that she conceived and brought forth Rose, and indeed it was very wrong of her to let him, and indeed it was very wrong of Sean again,

---

[1] Haemophilia is, like enlargement of the prostate, an exclusively male disorder. But not in this work.

knowing what he was and what Kate was and now what Rose was, to do again what he did again to Kate, so that Kate conceived again and brought forth Cerise, and indeed it was very wrong of her again to let him again, and then there were Simon's two little boys, Pat and Larry, aged four and three respectively, and little Pat was rickety with little arms and legs like sticks and a big head like a balloon and a big belly like another, and so was little Larry, and the only difference between little Pat and little Larry was this, allowing for the slight difference in age, and name, that little Larry's legs were even more like sticks than little Pat's, whereas little Pat's arms were even more like sticks than little Larry's, and that little Larry's belly was a little less like a balloon than little Pat's, whereas little Pat's head was a little less like a balloon than little Larry's.

Five generations, twenty-eight souls, nine hundred and eighty years, such was the proud record of the Lynch family, when Watt entered Mr. Knott's service.[1]

Then a moment passed and all was changed. Not that there was death, for there was not. Nor that there was birth, for there was not either. But puff puff breath again they breathed, in and out, the twenty-eight, and all was changed.

As by the clouding the unclouding of the sun the sea, the lake, the ice, the plain, the marsh, the mountain-side, or any other similar natural expanse, be it liquid or be it solid.

Till changing changing in twenty over twenty-eight equals five over seven times twelve equals sixty over seven equals eight months and a half approximately, if none died, if none were born, a thousand years!

If all were spared, the living spared, the unborn spared.

In eight months and a half, from the date of Watt's entering Mr. Knott's service.

[1] The figures given here are incorrect. The consequent calculations are therefore doubly erroneous.

But all were not spared.

For Watt had not been four months with Mr. Knott when Liz the wife of Sam lay down and expelled a child, her twentieth, with the greatest of ease as may well be imagined, and for some days after this agreeably surprised all those who knew her (and they were many) by the unusual healthiness of her appearance and by a flow of good spirits quite foreign to her nature, for for many years she had passed rightly for more dead than alive, and she suckled the infant with great enjoyment and satisfaction apparently, the flow of milk being remarkably abundant for a woman of her age and habit of body, which was exsanguine, and then after five or six or perhaps even seven days of this kind of thing grew suddenly weak and to the great astonishment of her husband Sam, her sons Blind Bill and Maim Mat, her married daughters Kate and Ann and their husbands Sean and Simon, her niece Bridie and her nephew Tom, her sisters Mag and Lil, her brothers-in-law Tom and Jack, her cousins Ann, Art and Con, her aunts-in-law May and Mag, her aunt Kate, her uncles-in-law Joe and Jim, her father-in-law Bill and her grandfather-in-law Tom, who were not expecting anything of the kind, grew weaker and weaker, until she died.

This loss was a great loss to the family Lynch, this loss of a woman of forty good-looking years.

For not only was a wife, a mother, a mother-in-law, an aunt, a sister, a sister-in-law, a cousin, a niece-in-law, a niece, a niece-in-law, a daughter-in-law, a granddaughter-in-law and of course a grandmother, snatched from her grandfather-in-law, her father-in-law, her uncles-in-law, her aunt, her aunts-in-law, her cousins, her brothers-in-law, her sisters, her niece, her nephew, her sons-in-law, her daughters, her sons, her husband and of course her four little grandchildren (who however exhibited no sign of emotion other than that of curiosity, being too young no doubt to realize the dreadful thing that had happened, for their total age amounted to no more than sixteen years), never to return, but the Lynch millenium was retarded by almost one year and a half, assuming that during that time all were spared, and so could not be expected before roughly two years from the date of Liz's departure, instead of in a mere five months time, as would have been the case if Liz together with the rest of the family had been spared, and even five or six days sooner if the infant had been spared also, as he was to be sure, but at his mother's expense, with the result that the goal towards which the whole family was striving receded to the tune of a good nineteen months, if not more, assuming all the others to be spared, in the meantime.

But all the others were not spared, in the meantime.

For two months had not passed, since the death of Liz, when to the amazement of the entire family Ann retired to the privacy of her room and gave birth, first to a fine bouncing baby boy, and then to an almost equally fine bouncing baby girl, and they did not remain fine very long, nor did they long continue to bounce, but at their birth they were both very fine indeed, and remarkably resilient.

This brought the total number of souls in the Lynch household up to thirty, and the happy day, on which the eyes of all were set, nearer by twenty-four days approximately, assuming that all were spared, in the meantime.

Now the question that began on all hands openly to be asked was this, Who had done, or whom had Ann persuaded to do, this thing to Ann? For Ann was by no means an attractive woman, and the painful disorder under which she laboured was a matter of common knowledge, not only in the Lynch household, but for miles and miles around in every direction. Several names were freely mentioned in this connexion.

Some said it was her cousin Sam, whose amorous disposition was notorious, not only among the members of his immediate family, but throughout the neighbourhood, and who made no secret of his having committed adultery locally on a large scale, moving from place to place in his self-propelling invalid's chair, with widow women, with married women and with single women, of whom some were young and attractive, and others young but not attractive, and others attractive but not young, and others neither young nor attractive, and of whom some as a result of Sam's intervention conceived and brought forth a son or a daughter or two sons or two daughters or a son and a daughter, for Sam had never managed triplets, and this was a sore point with Sam, that he had never managed triplets, and others conceived but did not bring forth, and others did not conceive at all, though this was exceptional, that they did not conceive at all, when Sam intervened. And when reproached with this Sam with ready wit replied that paralysed as he was, from the waist up, and from the knees down, he had no purpose, interest or joy in life other than this, to set out after a good dinner of meat and vegetables in his wheel-chair and stay out committing adultery until it was time to go home to his supper, after which he was at his wife's disposal. But until then, so far as one knew, he had never affronted Liz under her own roof, or, more strictly speaking, with any of the women that it sheltered, though there were not wanting those to insinuate that he was the father of his cousins Art and Con.

Others said it was her cousin Tom who, in a fit of exaltation, or in a fit of depression, had done this thing to Ann. And to those who objected to this that Tom, when in a fit of exaltation, was incapable of the least exertion, and could move neither hand nor foot, when in a fit of depression, it was replied that the exertion and the motion here involved were not the exertion and the motion from which Tom's fits debarred him, but another exertion and another motion, the suggestion being that the inhibition was not a physical inhibition, but a moral, or aesthetic, and that Tom's recurrent inability on the one hand to discharge certain offices requiring on the part of his bodily frame not the slightest expenditure of energy, such as that of keeping an eye on the kettle, or on the saucepan, and on the other to move from where he stood, or sat, or lay, or to reach out with his hand, or foot, for a tool, such as a hammer, or a chisel, or for a kitchen utensil, such as a shovel, or a bucket, was in neither case an absolute inability, but an inability limited by the nature of the office to be discharged, or the act to be performed. And it was further with cynicism urged, in support of this view, that if Tom had been asked to keep an eye, not on the kettle, or on the saucepan, but on his niece Bridie dressing up for the night, he would have done so, however great his depression at the time, and that his exaltation had often been observed to fall, with remarkable abruptness, in the neighbourhood of a corkscrew and a bottle of stout. For Ann, though apparently plain and rotten with disease, had her partisans, both inside and outside the house. And to those who objected that neither Ann's charms, nor her powers of persuasion, could be compared with Bridie's, or with a bottle of stout's, it was replied that if Tom had not done this thing in a fit of depression, or in a fit of exaltation, then he had done it in the interval between a fit of depression and a fit of exaltation, or in the interval between a fit of exaltation and a fit of depression, or in the interval between a fit of depression and another fit of depression, or in the interval between a fit of exaltation and another fit of exaltation, for with Tom depression and exaltation were not of regular alternance, whatever may have been said to the contrary, but often he emerged from one fit of depression only to be seized soon after by another, and frequently he shook off one fit of exaltation only to fall into the next almost at once, and in these brief intervals Tom would sometimes behave most strangely, almost like a man who did not know what he was doing.

Some said it was her uncle Jack, who it will be remembered was weak in the head. And to those who were not of this opinion those who were were good enough to point out that Jack was not only weak in the head, but married to a woman who was weak in the chest, whereas this could not be said of Ann's chest, that it was weak, whatever might be said of other parts of her, for it was well known that Ann had a splendid bosom, white and fat and elastic, and what could be more natural, in the mind of a man like Jack, weak-minded and tied to a weak-chested woman, than that the thought of this splendid part of Ann, so white, so fat and so elastic, should grow and grow, whiter and whiter, fatter and fatter, and more and more elastic, until all thought of those other parts of Ann (and they were numerous), where whiteness did not dwell, nor fatness, nor elasticity, but greyness, and even greenness, and thinness, and bagginess, were driven quite away.

Other names mentioned in this connexion were those of Ann's uncles Joe, Bill and Jim, and of her nephews, Blind Bill and Maim Mat, Sean and Simon.

That none of Ann's kith and kin, but a stranger from without, had brought Ann to this pass, was considered likely by many, and the names of many strangers from without were freely mentioned, in this connexion.

Then some four months later, when winter seemed safely past, and spring in the air by some was even felt, the brothers Joe, Bill and Jim, or a grand total of more

106

than one hundred and ninety-three years, in the short space of one week were carried off, Joe the eldest being carried off on a Monday, and Bill his junior by one year on the following Wednesday, and Jim their junior by two years and one year respectively on the Friday following, leaving old Tom sonless, and M— and Kate husbandless and May Sharpe bro̊t̊ e̊ Tom and Jack and Art and Con and Sam fatherless, and Mag and Lil father-in-lawless, and Ann uncleless, and Simon and Ann and Bridie and Tom and Sean and Kate and Bill and Mat and Sam's infant by the late Liz grandfatherless, and Rose and Cerise and Pat and Larry great-grandfatherless.

This set back the longed-for day, on which the Lynches' eyes still were fixed, though with less confidence than before, by no less than seventeen years approximately, that is to say far beyond the horizon of expectation or even hope. For old Tom, for example, grew daily worse, and was heard to say, Why was me three boys took, and me with me gripes left?, suggesting that it would have been preferable, in his opinion, if his boys, who whatever their suffering did not suffer from unremitting agony in the caecum, had been left, and he, with his gripes, taken, and many other members of the family also grew daily worse and could not be expected to live, very much longer.

Then they were sorry for what they had said who had said it was her Uncle Joe, and who said it was her Uncle Bill, and who had said it was her Uncle Jim, who had done this thing to Ann, for all three had confessed their sins, to the priest, prior to being carried away, and the priest was an old and intimate friend of the family. And from the corpses of the brothers in a cloud the voices rose and hovering sank to rest among the living, here some, there others, here some again, there others again, until hardly one living but had his voice, and not one voice but was at rest. And of those who had been in agreement, many were now in disagreement, and of those who had been in disagreement, many now were in agreement, though some that had agreed agreed still, and some that had disagreed still disagreed. And so new friendships were formed, and new enmities, and old friendships preserved, and old enmities. And all was agreement and disagreement and amity and enmity, as before, only redistributed. And not one voice but was either for or against, no, not one. But all was objection and answer and answer and objection, as before, only in other mouths. Not that many did not go on saying what they had always said, for many did. But still more did not. And the reason for that was perhaps this, that not only were those who had said what they had said of Jim, of Bill and of Joe, now by the deaths of Joe, of Bill and of Jim incapacitated from going on doing so and obliged to find something new to say, because Bill, Joe and Jim, for all their foolishness, were not so foolish as to allow themselves to be carried away without owning up to the priest to what they had done to Ann, if they had done it, but also a great number of those who had never said anything of Jim, of Joe and of Bill, in this connexion, unless it was that they had not done this thing to Ann, and who were therefore in no way by the deaths of Joe, of Jim and of Bill incapacitated from going on saying what they had always said, in this connexion, nevertheless preferred, when they heard some of those who had always spoken against them, and against whom they had always spoken, now speaking with them, to cease saying what they had always said, in this connexion, and to begin saying something quite new, in order that they might continue to hear speaking against them, and themselves to speak against, the greatest possible number of those who, prior to the deaths of Bill, of Joe and of Jim, had always spoken against them, and against whom they had always spoken. For it is a strange thing, but apparently true, that those who speak speak rather for the pleasure of speaking against than for the pleasure of speaking with, and the reason for that is perhaps this, that in agreement the voice can not be raised perhaps quite so high as it can in disagreement.

This little matter of the food and the dog, Watt pieced it together from the remarks let fall, every now and then, in the evening, by the twin dwarfs Art and Con. For it was they who led the famished dog, every evening, to the door. They had done this since the age of twelve, that is to say for the past quarter of a century, and they continued to do so all the time that Watt remained in Mr. Knott's house, or rather all the time that he remained on the ground-floor, for when Watt was moved to the first-floor, then Watt lost touch with the ground-floor, and saw no more the dog, nor them who brought it. But surely it was still Art and Con who led the dog, every evening, at nine o'clock, to Mr. Knott's back door, even when Watt was no longer there to witness it, for they were sturdy little fellows, and wrapped up in their work.

The dog in service when Watt entered Mr. Knott's service was the sixth dog that Art and Con had employed, in this manner, in twenty-five years.

The dogs employed to eat Mr. Knott's occasional remains were not long-lived, as a rule. This was very natural. For besides what the dog got to eat, every now and then, on Mr. Knott's back doorstep, it got so to speak nothing to eat. For if it had been given food other than the food that Mr. Knott gave it, from time to time, then its appetite might have been spoilt, for the food that Mr. Knott gave it. For Art and Con could never be certain, in the morning, that there would not be waiting for their dog, in the evening, on Mr. Knott's back doorstep, a pot of food so nourishing, and so copious, that only a thoroughly famished dog could get it down. And this was the eventuality for which it was their duty to be always prepared.

Add to this that Mr. Knott's food was a little on the rich and heating side, for a dog.

Add to this that the dog was seldom off the chain, and so got no exercise worth mentioning. This was inevitable. For if the dog had been set free, to run about, as it pleased, then it would have eaten the horsedung, on the road, and all the other nasty things that abound, on the ground, and so ruined its appetite, perhaps for ever, or worse still would have run away, and never come back.

The name of this dog, when Watt entered Mr. Knott's service, was Kate. Kate was not at all a handsome dog. Even Watt, whom his fondness for rats prejudiced against dogs, had never seen a dog that he less liked the look of than Kate. It was not a large dog, and yet it could not be called a small dog. It was a medium-sized dog, of repulsive aspect. It was called Kate not as might be supposed after Jim's Kate, so soon to be made a widow, but after quite a different Kate, a certain Katie Byrne, who was a kind of cousin of Joe's wife May, so soon to be made a widow too, and this Katie Byrne was a great favourite with Art and Con, to whom she always brought a gift of tobacco twist, when she came on a visit, and Art and Con were great chewers of tobacco twist, and never had enough, never never had enough tobacco twist, for their liking.

Kate died while Watt was still on the ground-floor, and was replaced by a dog called Cis. Watt did not know whom this dog was called after. If he had enquired, if, coming out into the open, he had said, Con, or, Art, Kate I know was called after your relative, Katie Byrne, but after whom is Cis called?, then he might have learnt what he so desired to know. But there were limits to what Watt was prepared to do, in pursuit of information. There were times when he was half tempted to believe, as he observed the effect that this name had on Art and Con, notably when associated with certain injunctions, that it was the name of a friend of theirs, a near and dear friend, and that it was in honour of this near and dear friend that they had given the dog the name of Cis rather than some other name. But this was a mere conjecture, and at other times Watt was more inclined to believe that if the dog was called Cis, it was not on account of some living person's being called Cis, no, but simply because the dog had to be called something, to distinguish it, for itself, and for others, from all the other dogs, and that Cis was as good a name as any other, and indeed prettier than many.

Cis was still alive when Watt left the ground-floor, for the first-floor. What became of her later, and of the dwarfs, he had no idea. For once on the first-floor Watt lost sight of the ground-floor, and interest in the ground-floor. This was indeed a merciful coincidence, was it not, that at the moment of Watt's losing sight of the ground-floor, he lost interest in it also.

It was part of Watt's duties to receive Art and Con, when they called in the evening with the dog, and, when there was food for the dog, to witness the dog's eating the food, until not an atom remained. But after the first few weeks Watt abruptly ceased, on his own responsibility, to discharge this office. From then on, when there was food for the dog, he put it outside the door, on the doorstep, in the dog's dish, and he lit a light in the passage window, so that the doorstep should not be in darkness, even on the darkest night, and he contrived, for the dog's dish, a little lid that could be fastened down, by means of clasps, of clasps that clasped tight the sides, of the dish. And Art and Con grew to know that when the dog's dish was not on the doorstep, waiting for them, then there was no food for Kate, or Cis. They did not need to knock, and enquire, no, the bare doorstep was enough. And they even grew to know that when there was no light in the passage window, then there was no food, for the dog. And they learned also not to advance any further, in the evening, than the place whence they could see the passage window, and then to advance farther only if there was a light, in the window, and always to go away, without advancing any farther, if there was none. This was unfortunately of small practical assistance to Art and Con, for coming as one did, suddenly, round a corner of the bushes, on the back door, one did not see the passage window, which was beside the back door, until one was so close to the back door that one could have touched it with one's stick, if one had wished. But Art and Con gradually learned to tell, from no less a distance than ten or fifteen paces, whether there was a light in the passage window, or not. For the light, though hidden by the corner, shone through the passage window and made a glow, in the air, a glow that could be seen, especially when the night was dark, from no less a distance than ten or fifteen paces. Thus all that Art and Con had to do, when the night was favourable, was to advance a little way along the avenue, until they reached the place whence the light, if it was burning, must be visible, as a glow, a feeble glow, in the air, and thence to go on, towards the back door, or to go back, towards the gate, as the case might be. In the height of summer to be sure, only the doorstep bare, or surmounted by the dog's dish, could tell Art and Con and Kate, or Cis, whether there was food for the dog, or not. For in the height of summer Watt did not set a light, in the passage window, when there was food for the dog, no, for in the height of summer the doorstep was not dark until coming up to ten-thirty, or eleven, at night, but burning with all the raging dying summer light, for it looked west, the back doorstep. And to set a light in the passage window, under these conditions, would have been a mere waste of oil. But for more than three-quarters of the year Art's and Con's task was greatly lightened as a result of Watt's refusal to be present when the dog ate the food, and of the measures he was obliged to take, in consequence. Then Watt, if he had put out the plate, a little after eight, took it in again, a little before ten, and washed it up, in readiness for the morrow, before he locked up for the night and went up to his bed, holding the lamp high above his head, to guide his feet, on the stairs, the stairs that never seemed the same stairs, from one night to another, and now were steep, and now shallow, and now long, and now short, and now broad, and now narrow, and now danger-ous, and now safe, and that he climbed, among the moving shadows, every night, shortly after ten o'clock.

This refusal, by Knott, I beg your pardon, by Watt, to assist at the eating, by the dog, of Mr. Knott's remains, might have been supposed to have the gravest conse-quences, both for Watt and for Mr. Knott's establishment.

Watt expected something of this kind. And yet he could not have done otherwise, than he did. It was in vain that he had no love for dogs, greatly preferring rats, he could not have done otherwise, believe it or not, than he did. As it was, nothing happened, but all went on, as before, apparently. No punishment fell on Watt, no thunderbolt, and Mr. Knott's establishment swam on, through the un-ruffled nights and days, with all its customary serenity. And this was a great source of wonder, to Watt, that he had infringed, with impunity, such a venerable tradition, or institution. But he was not so foolish as to found in this a principle of conduct, or a precedent of rebelliousness, ho no, for Watt was only too willing to do as he was told, and

113

as custom required, at all times. And when he was forced to transgress, as in the matter of witnessing the dog's meal, then he was at pains to transgress in such a way, and to surround his transgression with such precautions, such delicacies, that it was almost as though he had not transgressed at all. And perhaps this was counted to him for grace. And he stilled the wonder the trouble in his mind, by reflecting that if he went unpunished for the moment, he would not perhaps always go unpunished, and that if the hurt to Mr. Knott's establishment did not at once appear, it would perhaps one day appear, a little bruise at first, and then a bigger, and then a bigger still, until, growing, growing, it blackened the entire body.

For reasons that remain obscure Watt was, for a time, greatly interested, and even fascinated, by this matter of the dog, the dog brought into the world, and maintained there, at considerable expense, for the sole purpose of eating Mr. Knott's food, on those days on which Mr. Knott was not pleased to eat it himself, and he attached to this matter an importance, and even a significance, that seem hardly warranted. For otherwise would he have gone into the matter at such length? And would he have gone into the Lynch family at such length if, in thought, he had not been obliged to pass, from the dog, to the Lynches, as to one of the terms of the relation that the dog wove nightly, the other of course being Mr. Knott's remains. But much more than with the Lynches, or with Mr. Knott's remains, Watt's concern, while it lasted, was with the dog. But it did not last long, this concern of Watt's, not very long, as such concerns go. And yet it was a major concern, of that period, while it lasted. But once Watt had grasped, in its complexity, the mechanism of this arrangement, how the food came to be left, and the dog to be available, and the two to be united, then it interested him no more, and he enjoyed a comparative peace of mind, in this connexion. Not that for a moment Watt supposed that he had penetrated the forces at play, in this particular instance, or even perceived the forms that they upheaved, or obtained the least useful information concerning himself, or Mr. Knott, for he did not. But he had turned, little by little, a disturbance into words, he had made a pillow of old words, for his head. Little by little, and not without labour. Kate eating from her dish, for example, with the dwarfs standing by, how he had laboured to know what that was, to know which the doer, and what the doer, and what the doing, and which the sufferer, and what the sufferer, and what the suffering, and what those shapes, that were not rooted to the ground, like the veronica, but melted away, into the dark, after a while.

Erskine was for ever running up the stairs and down them again. Not so Watt, who came down only once a day, when he got up, to begin his day, and only once a day went up, when he lay down, to begin his night. Unless when, in his bedroom, in the morning, or in the kitchen, in the evening, he left something behind, that he could not do without. Then of course he went back, up, or down, to fetch this thing, whatever it was. But this was very rare. For what could Watt leave behind, that he could not do without, for a day, for a night? His handkerchief perhaps. But Watt never used a handkerchief. His slopbag. No, he would not have gone back down all the way expressly for his slopbag. No, there was so to speak nothing that Watt could forget, that he could not do without, for the fourteen or fifteen hours that his day lasted, for the ten or nine hours that his night lasted. And yet every now and then he did forget something, some tiny little thing, so that he was obliged to return and fetch it, for he could not have got on, through his day, through his night, without it. But this was very rare. And otherwise he stayed quietly where he was, on the second-floor in his little bedroom by night, and by day on the ground-floor in the kitchen mostly, or wherever else his duties might take him, or in the pleasure garden up and down, or in a tree, or sitting on the ground against a tree or bush, or on a rustic seat. For to the first-floor his duties never took him, at this period, nor to the second, once he had made his bed, and swept clean his little room, which he did every morning the first thing, before coming down, on an empty stomach. Whereas Erskine never did a tap on the ground-floor, but all his duties were on the first-floor. Now Watt did not know, nor care to ask, in what exactly these duties consisted. But whereas Watt's ground-floor duties kept him quietly on the ground-floor, Erskine's first-floor duties did not keep Erskine quietly on the first-floor, but for ever he was flying up the stairs from the first-floor to the second-floor and down them again from the second-floor to the first-floor and down the stairs from the first-floor to the ground-floor and up them again from the ground-floor to the first-floor, for no reason that Watt could see, though to be sure this was a matter in which Watt could not be expected to see very far, because he did not know, and did not care to ask, in what exactly Erskine's duties on the first-floor consisted. Now this is not to say that Erskine did not spend a great deal of his time quietly on the first-floor, for he did, but only that the number of times in the day that he went flying up and down again and down and up again seemed to Watt extraordinary. And what further seemed to Watt extraordinary was the shortness of time that Erskine spent up, when he flew up, before flying down again, and the shortness of time that he spent down, when he flew down, before flying up again, and of course the rapidity of his flight, as though he were always in a hurry to get back. And if it were asked how Watt, who was never on the second-floor from morning to night, could know how long Erskine spent on the second-floor, when he went there in this way, the answer to that would perhaps be this, that Watt, from where he sat in the bottom of the house, could hear Erskine hasten up the stairs to the top of the house, and then hasten down them again to the middle of the house, almost without pause. And the reason for that was perhaps this, that the sound came down the kitchen chimney.

Watt did not care to enquire in so many words into the meaning of all this, for he said, All this will be revealed to Watt, in due time, meaning of course when Erskine went, and another came. But he was not easy until he had said, in short and isolated phrases, or fragments of phrases, separated by considerable periods of time from one another, Perhaps Mr. Knott sends him now upstairs, and now downstairs, on this errand and on that, saying, But hasten back to me, Erskine, don't delay, but hasten back to me. But what kind of errand? Perhaps to fetch him something that he has forgotten, and that suddenly he feels the need of, such as a nice book, or piece of cotton wool or tissue paper. Or perhaps to look out of a top window, to make sure that nobody is coming, or to have a quick look round below stairs, to make sure that no danger threatens the foundations. But am I not here, below stairs, somewhere about, on the alert? But it may be that Mr. Knott has more confidence in Erskine, who has been here longer than I, than in me, who have not been here so long as Erskine. And yet that does not seem like Mr. Knott, to be ever wanting this or that and sending Erskine flying to see to it. But what do I know of Mr. Knott? Nothing. And what to me may seem most unlike him, and what to me may seem most like him, may in reality be most like him, most unlike him, for all I can tell. Or perhaps Mr. Knott sends Erskine flying up and down in this way, simply in order to be rid of him if only for a few moments. Or perhaps Erskine, finding the first-floor trying, is obliged to run upstairs every now and then for a breath of the second-floor, and then every now and then downstairs for a breath of the ground-floor, or even garden, just as in certain waters certain fish, in order to support the middle depths, are forced to rise and fall, now to the surface of the waves and now to the ocean bed. But do such fish exist? Yes, such fish exist, now. But trying in what way? Perhaps who knows Mr. Knott propagates a kind of waves, of depression, or oppression, or perhaps now these, now those, in a way that it is impossible to grasp. But that does not at all agree with my conception of Mr. Knott. But what conception have I of Mr. Knott? None.

Watt wondered if Arsene, Walter, Vincent and the others had passed through the same phase as that through which Erskine then was passing, and he wondered if he Watt would pass through it too, when his time came. Watt could not easily imagine Arsene ever behaving in such a way, nor himself either for that matter. But there were many things that Watt could not easily imagine.

Sometimes in the night Mr. Knott pressed a bell that sounded in Erskine's room, and then Erskine got up and went down. This Watt knew, for from his bed where he lay not far away he would hear the bell sound ting! and Erskine get up and go down. He would hear the sound of the bell because he was not asleep, or only half asleep, or sleeping only lightly. For it is rare that the sound of a bell not far away is not heard by the only half asleep, the only lightly sleeping. Or he would hear, not the sound of the bell, but the sound of Erskine getting up and going down, which came to the same thing. For would Erskine have got up and gone down if the bell had not sounded? No. He might have got up, without the bell's sounding, to do his number one, or number two, in his great big chamber pot.

But get up and go down, without the bell's sounding, no. At other times, when Watt was sleeping deeply, or plunged in meditation, or otherwise engrossed, then of course the bell might sound and sound and Erskine get up and get up and go down and go down and Watt be not a whit the wiser. But that did not matter. For Watt had heard the bell sound, and Erskine get up and go down, often enough to know that sometimes in the night Mr. Knott pressed a bell and that then Erskine, doubtless in obedience to the summons, got up and went down. For were there other fingers in the house, and other thumbs, than Mr. Knott's and Erskine's and Watt's, that might have pressed the bell? For by what but by a finger, or by a thumb, could the bell have been pressed? By a nose? A toe? A heel? A projecting tooth? A knee? An elbow? Or some other prominent bony or fleshy process? No doubt. But whose, if not Mr. Knott's? Watt had not pressed a bell with any part of him, of that he was morally certain, for there was no bell in his room that he could have pressed. And if he had got up and gone down to where the bell was, and he did not know where the bell was, and pressed it there, could he have got back into his room, and into his bed, and sometimes even fallen into a light sleep, in time to hear, from where he lay, in his bed, the bell sound? The fact was that Watt had never seen a bell, in any part of Mr. Knott's house, or heard one, under any other circumstances than those that so perplexed him. On the ground-floor there was no bell of any kind, he could vouch for that, or so cunningly dissembled that no trace appeared, on the walls, or the doorposts. There was the telephone, to be sure, in a passage. But what sounded in Erskine's room, in the night, was not a telephone, Watt was sure of that, but a bell, a simple bell, a simple little probably white electric bell, of the kind that one presses until it sounds ting! and then lets spring back, to the position of silence. Similarly Erskine, if he had pressed the bell, must have pressed it in his own room, and indeed from where he lay, in his bed, as was manifest from the noise that Erskine made in getting out of bed, immediately the bell rang. But was it likely that there was a bell in Erskine's room, that he could press, from his bed, when there was no bell of any kind in any part of Watt's room? And even if there was a bell in Erskine's room, that he could press without leaving his bed, what interest could Erskine have in pressing it, when he knew that at the sound of the bell he must leave his warm bed and go downstairs, inadequately clothed? If Erskine wished to leave his snug bed and go downstairs, half naked, could he not have done so without pressing a bell beforehand? Or was Erskine out of his mind? And he himself Watt, was he not perhaps slightly deranged? And Mr. Knott himself, was he quite right in his head? Were they not all three perhaps a little off the hooks?

The question of who pressed the bell that sounded in Erskine's room, in the night, was a great source of worry to Watt, for a time, and kept him awake at night, on the *qui vive*. If Erskine had been a snorer, and the sound of the bell coincided with the sound of a snore, then the mystery, it seemed to Watt, would have been dissipated, as the mist, by the sun. But there, Erskine was not a snorer. And yet to look at him, or hear him sing his song, you would have taken him for a snorer, a great snorer. And yet he was not a snorer. So the sound of the bell came always on the stillness. But on further reflexion it seemed to Watt that the bell's coinciding with the snore would not have dissipated the mystery, but left it entire. For might not Erskine simulate a snore, at the very moment that he reached out with his arm and pressed the bell, or might he not simulate a long series of snores culminating in the snore that he simulated as he pressed the bell, in order to deceive Watt and make him think that it was not he Erskine who pressed the bell, but Mr. Knott, in some other part of the house? So the fact finally that Erskine did not snore, and that the sound of the bell came always on the silence, made Watt think, not that the bell might be pressed by Erskine, as at first it had made him think, no, but that the bell must be pressed by Mr. Knott. For if Erskine pressed the bell, and did not wish it known, then he would utter a snore, or in some other way dissemble, as he pressed the bell, in order to make Watt think that it was not he Erskine who pressed the bell, but Mr. Knott. But then it occurred to Watt that Erskine might press the bell not caring whether it were known or not, that it was he who did so, and that in that case he would not trouble to utter a snore, or otherwise dissemble, as he pressed the bell, but let the sound of the bell come on the stillness, for Watt to make of what he would.

Watt decided in the end that an examination of Erskine's room was essential, if his mind was to be pacified, in this connexion. Then he would be able to put the matter from him, and forget it, as one puts from one and forgets the peel of an orange, or of a banana.

Watt might have asked Erskine, he might have said, Tell me, Erskine, is there a bell in your room, or is there not? But this would have put Erskine on his guard, and Watt did not desire that. Or Erskine might have answered, Yes!, when the true answer was, No!, or, No!, when the true answer was, Yes!, or he might have answered truly, Yes!, or, No!, and Watt been unable to believe him. And then Watt would have been no better off than before, but rather worse, for he would have set Erskine on his guard.

Now Erskine's room was always locked, and the key in Erskine's pocket. Or rather, Erskine's room was never unlocked, nor the key out of Erskine's pocket, longer than two or three seconds at a stretch, which was the time that

Erskine took to take the key from his pocket, unlock his door on the outside, glide into his room, lock his door again on the inside and slip the key back into his pocket, or take the key from his pocket, unlock his door on the inside, glide out of his room, lock the door again on the outside and slip the key back into his pocket. For if Erskine's room had been *always* locked, and the key *always* in Erskine's pocket, then Erskine himself, for all his agility, would have been hard set to glide in and out of his room, in the way he did, unless he had glided in and out by the window, or the chimney. But in and out by the window he could not have glided, without breaking his neck, nor in and out by the chimney, without being crushed to death. And this was true also of Watt.

The lock was of a kind that Watt could not pick. Watt could pick simple locks, but he could not pick obscure locks.

The key was of a kind that Watt could not counterfeit. Watt could counterfeit simple keys, in a workshop, in a vice, with a file and solder, filing down and building up another and quite different simple key, until the two simplicities were quite alike. But Watt could not counterfeit obscure keys.

Another reason why Watt could not counterfeit Erskine's key was this, that he could not obtain possession of it, even for a moment.

Then how did Watt know that Erskine's key was not a simple key? Why, for having turned and twisted his little wire in the hole.

Then Watt said, Obscure keys may open simple locks, but simple keys obscure locks never. But Watt had hardly said this when he regretted having done so. But then it was too late, the words were said and could never be forgotten, never undone. But a little later he regretted them less. And a little later he did not regret them at all. And a little later they pleased him again, no less than when they had first sounded, so gentle, so cajoling, in his skull. And then again a little later he regretted them again, most bitterly. And so on. Until there were few degrees of remorse, few of complacency, but more particularly of remorse, with which Watt was not familiar, with reference to these words. And this is perhaps worthy of mention, because it was with Watt a common experience, where words were concerned. And though it sometimes happened that a moment's pensiveness was sufficient to fix his attitude, once and for all, towards words when they sounded, so that he liked them, or disliked them, more or less, with an inalterable like or dislike, yet this did not happen often, no, but thinking now this, now that, he did not in the end know what to think, of the words that had sounded, even when they were plain and modest like the above, of a meaning so evident, and a form so inoffensive, that made no matter, he did not know what to think of them, from one year's end to the next, whether to think poorly of them, or highly of them, or with indifference.

And if Watt had not known this, that Erskine's key was not a simple key, then I should never have known it either, nor the world. For all that I know on the subject of Mr. Knott, and of all that touched Mr. Knott, and on the subject of Watt, and of all that touched Watt, came from Watt, and from Watt alone. And if I do not appear to know very much on the subject of Mr. Knott and of Watt, and on the subject of all that touched them, it is because Watt did not know a great deal on these subjects, or did not care to tell. But he assured me at the time, when he began to spin his yarn, that he would tell all, and then again, some years later, when he had spun his yarn, that he had told all. And as I believed him then and then again, so I continued to believe him, long after the yarn was spun, and Watt gone. Not that there is any proof that Watt did indeed tell all he knew, on these subjects, or that he set out to do so, for how could there be, I knowing nothing on these subjects, except what Watt told me. For Erskine, Arsene, Walter, Vincent and the others had all vanished, long before my time. Not that Erskine, Arsene, Walter, Vincent and the others could have told anything of Watt, except perhaps Arsene a little, and Erskine a little more, for they could not, but they might have told something of Mr. Knott. Then we would have had Erskine's Mr. Knott, and Arsene's Mr. Knott, and Walter's Mr. Knott, and Vincent's Mr. Knott, to compare with Watt's Mr. Knott. That would have been a very interesting exercise. But they all vanished, long before my time.

This does not mean that Watt may not have left out some of the things that happened, or that were, or that he may not have foisted in other things that never happened, or never were. Mention has already been made of the difficulties that Watt encountered in his efforts to distinguish between what happened and what did not happen, between what was and what was not, in Mr. Knott's house. And Watt made no secret of this, in his conversations with me, that many things described as happening, in Mr. Knott's house, and of course grounds, perhaps never happened at all, or quite differently, and that many things described as being, or rather as not being, for these were the more important, perhaps were not, or rather were all the time. But apart from this, it is difficult for a man like Watt to tell a long story like Watt's without leaving out some things, and foisting in others. And this does not mean either that I may not have left out some of the things that Watt told me, or foisted in others that Watt never told me, though I was most careful to note down all at the time, in my little note-book. It is so difficult, with a long story like the story that

Watt told, even when one is most careful to note down all at the time, in one's little notebook, not to leave out some of the things that were told, and not to foist in other things that were never told, never never told at all.

Nor was the key the kind of key of which an impression could be taken, in wax, or plaster, or putty, or butter, and the reason for that was this, that possession of the key could not be obtained, even for a moment.

For the pocket in which Erskine kept this key was not the kind of pocket that Watt could pick. For it was no ordinary pocket, no, but a secret one, sewn on to the front of Erskine's underhose. If the pocket in which Erskine kept this key had been an ordinary pocket, such as a coat pocket, of a trousers pocket, or even a waistcoat pocket, then Watt, by picking the pocket when Erskine was not looking, might have obtained possession of the key for long enough to record its impression in wax, or plaster, or putty, or butter. Then when he had recorded the impression he could have put the key back in the same pocket as the pocket from which he had taken it, having first taken care to wipe it clean, with a damp cloth. But to pick a pocket sewn on to the front of a man's underhose, even when the man was looking the other way, without arousing suspicion, was not, Watt knew, in his power.

Now if Erskine had been a lady . . . But there, Erskine was not a lady.

And if it were asked how it is known that the pocket in which Erskine kept this key was sewn on to the front of his underhose, the answer to that would be this, that one day when Erskine was doing his number one against a bush, Watt, who as Lachesis would have it was doing his number one too against the same bush, but on the other side, caught a glimpse, through the bush, for it was a deciduous bush, of the key, gleaming among the flap buttons.

And so always, when the impossibility of my knowing, of Watt's having known, what I know, what Watt knew, seems absolute, and insurmountable, and undeniable, and uncoercible, it could be shown that I know, because Watt told me, and that Watt knew, because someone told him, or because he found out for himself. For I know nothing, in this connexion, but what Watt told me. And Watt knew nothing, on this subject, but what he was told, or found out for himself, in one way or in another.

Watt might have broken the door down, with an axe, or a crow, or a small charge of explosive, but this might have aroused Erskine's suspicions, and Watt did not want that.

So that what with one thing and another, and with Watt's not wishing this, and with Watt's not wanting that, it seemed that Watt, as he was then, could never get into Erskine's room, never never get into Erskine's room, as it was then, and that for Watt to get into Erskine's room, as they were then, Watt would have to be another man, or Erskine's room another room.

And yet, without Watt's ceasing to be what he was, and without the room's ceasing to be what it was, Watt did get into the room, and there learned what he wished to know.

Ruse a by, he said, and as he said, Ruse a by, he blushed, until his nose seemed a normal colour, and hung his head, and twisted and untwisted his big red bony hands.

There was a bell in Erskine's room, but it was broken.

The only other object of note in Erskine's room was a picture, hanging on the wall, from a nail. A circle, obviously described by a compass, and broken at its lowest point, occupied the middle foreground, of this picture. Was it receding? Watt had that impression. In the eastern background appeared a point, or dot. The circumference was black. The point was blue, but blue! The rest was white.

How the effect of perspective was obtained Watt did not know. But it was obtained. By what means the illusion of movement in space, and it almost seemed in time, was given, Watt could not say. But it was given. Watt wondered how long it would be before the point and circle entered together upon the same plane. Or had they not done so already, or almost? And was it not rather the circle that was in the background, and the point that was in the foreground? Watt wondered if they had sighted each other, or were blindly flying thus, harried by some force of merely mechanical mutual attraction, or the playthings of chance. He wondered if they would eventually pause and converse, and perhaps even mingle, or keep steadfast on their ways, like ships in the night, prior to the invention of wireless telegraphy. Who knows, they might even collide. And he wondered what the artist had intended to represent (Watt knew nothing about painting), a circle and its centre in search of each other, or a circle and its centre in search of a centre and a circle respectively, or a circle and its centre in search of its centre and a circle respectively, or a circle and its centre in search of a centre and its circle respectively, or a circle and a centre not its centre in search of its centre and its circle respectively, or a circle and a centre not its centre in search of a centre and a circle respectively, or a circle and a centre not its centre in search of its centre and a circle respectively, or a circle and a centre not its centre in search of a centre and its circle respectively, in boundless space, in endless time (Watt knew nothing about physics), and at the thought that it was perhaps this, a circle and a centre not its centre in search of a centre and its circle respectively, in boundless space, in endless time, then Watt's eyes filled with tears that he could not stem, and they flowed down his fluted cheeks unchecked, in a steady flow, refreshing him greatly.

Watt wondered how this picture would look upside down, with the point west and the breach north, or on its right side, with the point north and the breach east, or on its left side, with the point south and the breach west.

So he took it from its hook and held it before his eyes, at arm's length, upside down, and on its right side, and on its left side.

But in these positions the picture pleased Watt less than it had when on the wall. And the reason for that was perhaps this, that the breach ceased to be below. And the thought of the point slipping in from below at last, when it came home at last, or to its new home, and the thought of the breach open below perhaps for ever in vain, these thoughts, to please Watt as they did, required the breach to be below, and nowhere else. It is by the nadir that we come, said Watt, and it is by the nadir that we go, whatever that means. And the artist must have felt something of this kind too, for the circle did not turn, as circles will, but sailed steadfast in its white skies, with its patient breach for ever below. So Watt put it back on its hook, in the position in which he had found it.

Watt did not of course wonder all these things at the time, but some he wondered at the time, and the others subsequently. But those that he wondered at the time, he again wondered subsequently, together with those that he did not wonder at the time, over and over again. And many other things in this connexion also, of which some at the time, and the others subsequently, Watt wondered subsequently also, time without number.

One of these had to do with the property. Did the picture belong to Erskine, or had it been brought and left behind by some other servant, or was it part and parcel of Mr. Knott's establishment?

Prolonged and irksome meditations forced Watt to the

conclusion that the picture was part and parcel of Mr. Knott's establishment.

The question to this answer was the following, of great importance in Watt's opinion. Was the picture a fixed and stable member of the edifice, like Mr. Knott's bed, for example, or was it simply a manner of paradigm, here to-day and gone tomorrow, a term in a series, like the series of Mr. Knott's dogs, or the series of Mr. Knott's men, or like the centuries that fall, from the pod of eternity?

A moment's reflexion satisfied Watt that the picture had not been long in the house, and that it would not remain long in the house, and that it was one of a series.

There were times when Watt could reason rapidly, almost as rapidly as Mr. Nackybal. And there were other times when his thought moved with such extreme slowness that it seemed not to move at all, but to be at a standstill. And yet it moved, like Galileo's cradle. Watt was greatly worried by this disparity. And indeed it contained cause for worry.

Watt had more and more the impression, as time passed, that nothing could be added to Mr. Knott's establishment, and from it nothing taken away, but that as it was now, so it had been in the beginning, and so it would remain to the end, in all essential respects, any significant presence, at any time, and here all presence was significant, even though it was impossible to say of what, proving that presence at all times, or an equivalent presence, and only the face chang-ing, but perhaps the face ever changing, even as perhaps even Mr. Knott's face ever slowly changed.

This supposition, as far as the picture was concerned, was to be strikingly confirmed, before long. And of the numberless suppositions elaborated by Watt, during his stay in Mr. Knott's house, this was the only one to be confirmed, or for that matter infirmed, by events (if one may speak here of events), or rather the only passage to be confirmed, the only passage of the long supposition, the long dwindling supposition, that constituted Watt's experience in Mr. Knott's house, and of course grounds, to be confirmed.

Yes, nothing changed, in Mr. Knott's establishment, because nothing remained, and nothing came or went, because all was a coming and a going.

Watt seemed highly pleased with this tenth-rate xenium. Spoken as he spoke it, back to front, it had a certain air, it is true.

But what preoccupied Watt most of all, towards the end of his stay on the ground-floor, was the question as to how long he would remain, on the ground-floor, and in his then bedroom, before being transferred to the first-floor, and to Erskine's bedroom, and then how long he would remain, on the first-floor, and in Erskine's bedroom, before leaving the place for ever.

Watt did not for a moment doubt that the ground-floor went with his bedroom, and the first-floor with Erskine's. Yet what could be more uncertain, than such a correspondence? As there seemed no measure between what Watt could understand, and what he could not, so there seemed none between what he deemed certain, and what he deemed doubtful.

Watt's feeling in this matter was that he would serve Mr. Knott for one year on the ground-floor, and then for another year on the first-floor.

In support of this monstrous assumption he assembled the following considerations.

If the period of service, first on the ground-floor, and then on the first-floor, was not one year, then it was less than one year, or more than one year. But if it was less than one year, then there was want, seasons passing, or a season, or a month, or a week, or a day, wholly or in part, on which the light of Mr. Knott's service had not shone, nor its dark brooded, a page of the discourse of the earth unturned. For in a year all is said, in any given latitude. But if it was more than one year, then there was surfeit, seasons passing, or a season, or a month, or a week, or a day, wholly or in part, twice through the beams the shadows of the service of Mr. Knott, a fragment of rigmarole re-read. For the new year says nothing new, to the man fixed in space. Therefore on the ground-floor one year, and on the first another, for the light of the day of the ground-floor was not as the light of the day of the first-floor (notwithstanding their proximity) nor were the lights of their nights the same lights.

But even Watt could not hide from himself for long the absurdity of these constructions, which assumed the period of service to be the same for every servant, and invariably divided into two phases of equal duration. And he felt that the period and distribution of service must depend on the servant, on his abilities, and on his needs; that there were short-time men and long-time men, ground-floor men and first-floor men; that what one might exhaust, what might exhaust one, in two months, another might not, might not another, in ten years; and that to many on the ground-floor the nearness of Mr. Knott must long be a horror, and long a horror to others on the first his farness. But he had hardly felt the absurdity of those things, on the one hand, and the necessity of those others, on the other (for it is rare that the feeling of absurdity is not followed by the feeling of necessity), when he felt the absurdity of those things of which he had just felt the necessity (for it is rare that the feeling of necessity is not followed by the feeling of absurdity). For the service to be considered was not the service of one servant, but of two servants, and even of three servants, and even of an infinity of servants, of whom the first could not out till the second up, nor the second up till the third in, nor the third in till the first out, nor the first out till the third in, nor the third in till the second up, nor the second up till the first out, every going, every being, every coming consisting with a being and a coming, a coming and a going, a going and a being, nay with all the beings and all the comings, with all the comings and all the goings, with all the goings and all the beings, of all the servants that had ever served Mr. Knott, of all the servants that ever would serve Mr. Knott. And in this long chain of consistence, a chain stretching from the long dead to the far unborn, the notion of the arbitrary could only survive as the notion of a pre-established arbitrary. For take any three or four servants, Tom, Dick, Harry and another, if Tom serves two years on the first-floor, then Dick serves two years on the ground-floor, and then Harry comes, and if Dick serves ten years on the first-floor, then Harry serves ten years on the ground-floor, and then the other comes, and so on for any number of servants, the period of service of any given servant on the ground-floor coinciding always with the period of service on the first-floor of his predecessor, and terminating with the arrival of his successor on the premises. But Tom's two years on the first-floor are not *because of* Dick's two years on the ground-floor, or of Harry's coming then, and Dick's two years on the ground-floor are not *because of* Tom's two years on the first-floor, or of Harry's coming then, and Harry's coming then is not *because of* Tom's two years on the first-floor, or of Dick's two years on the ground-floor, and Dick's ten years on the first-floor are not *because of* Harry's ten years on the ground-floor, or of the other's coming then, and Harry's ten years on the ground-floor are not *because of* Dick's ten years on the first-floor, or of the other's coming then, and the other's coming then is not *because of* (tired of underlining this cursed preposition) Dick's ten years on the first-floor, or of Harry's ten years on the ground-floor, no, that would be too horrible to con-

132

template, but Tom's two years on the first-floor, and Dick's two years on the ground-floor, and Harry's coming then, and Dick's ten years on the first-floor, and Harry's ten years on the ground-floor, and the other's coming then, are because Tom is Tom, and Dick Dick, and Harry Harry, and that other that other, of that the wretched Watt was persuaded. For otherwise in Mr. Knott's house, and at Mr. Knott's door, and on the way to Mr. Knott's door, and on the way from Mr. Knott's door, there would be a languor, and a fever, the languor of the task done but not ended, the fever of the task ended but not done, the languor and the fever of the going of the coming too late, the languor and the fever of the coming of the going too soon. But to Mr. Knott, and with Mr. Knott, and from Mr. Knott, were a coming and a being and a going exempt from languor, exempt from fever, for Mr. Knott was harbour, Mr. Knott was haven, calmly entered, freely ridden, gladly left. Driven, riven, bidden, by the storms without, the storms within? The storms without! The storms within! Men like Vincent and Walter and Arsene and Erskine and Watt! Haw! No. But in the stress, in the threat, in the call of storm, in the need, in the having, in the losing of refuge, calm and freedom and gladness. Not that Watt felt calm and free and glad, for he did not, and had never done so. But he thought that perhaps he felt calm and free and glad, or if not calm and free and glad, at least calm and free, or free and glad, or glad and calm, or if not calm and free, or free and glad, or glad and calm, at least calm, or free, or glad, without knowing it. But why Tom Tom? And Dick Dick? And Harry Harry? Because Dick Dick and Harry Harry? Because Harry Harry and Tom Tom? Because Tom Tom and Dick Dick? Watt saw no objection. But it was a conception of which for the moment he had no need, and conceptions of which for the moment Watt had no need

Watt did not for the moment unfurl, but left standing, as one does not unfurl, but leaves standing, in readiness for a rainy day, one's umbrella in one's umbrella-stand. And the reason why Watt for the moment had no need of this conception was perhaps this, that when one's arms are full of waxen lilies, then one does not stop to pick, or smell, or chuck, or otherwise acknowledge, a daisy, or a primrose, or a cowslip, or a buttercup, or a violet, or a dandelion, or a daisy, or a primrose, or any other flower of the field, or any other weed, but treads them down, and when the weight is past, and past the bowed head buried blinded in the white sweetness, then little by little under the load of petals the bruised stems straighten, those that is that have been fortunate enough to escape rupture. For it was not the Tomness of Tom, the Dickness of Dick, the Harryness of Harry, however remarkable in themselves, that pre-occupied Watt, for the moment, but their Tomness, their Dickness, their Harryness then, their then-Tomness, then-Dickness, then-Harryness; nor the ordaining of a being to come by a being past, of a being past by a being to come (no doubt in itself a fascinating study), as in a musical composition bar a hundred say by say bar ten and bar say ten by bar a hundred say, but the interval between them, the ninety bars, the time taken to have been true, the time taken to be proved true, whatever that is. Or of course false, whatever that means.

So at first, in mind as well as body, Watt laboured at the ancient labour.

And so Watt, having opened this tin with his blowlamp, found it empty.

As it turned out, Watt was never to know how long he spent in Mr. Knott's house, how long on the ground-floor, how long on the first-floor, how long altogether. All he could say was that it seemed a long time.

Thinking then, in search of rest, of the possible relations between such series as these, the series of dogs, the series of men, the series of pictures, to mention only these series, Watt remembered a distant summer night, in a no less distant land, and Watt young and well lying all alone stone sober in the ditch, wondering if it was the time and the place and the loved one already, and the three frogs croaking Krak!, Krek! and Krik!, at one, nine, seventeen, twenty-five, etc., and at one, six, eleven, sixteen, etc., and at one, four, seven, ten, etc., respectively, and how he heard

Krak!	—	—	—	—	—	—	—
Krek!	—	—	—	—	Krek!	—	—
Krik!	—	—	Krik!	—	—	Krik!	—
Krak!	—	—	—	—	—	—	—
—	—	Krek!	—	—	—	—	Krek!
—	Krik!	—	—	Krik!	—	—	Krik!
Krak!	—	—	—	—	—	—	—
—	—	—	—	Krek!	—	—	—
—	—	Krik!	—	—	Krik!	—	—
Krak!	—	—	—	—	—	—	—
—	Krek!	—	—	—	—	Krek!	—
Krik!	—	—	Krik!	—	—	Krik!	—
Krak!	—	—	—	—	—	—	—
—	—	—	Krek!	—	—	—	—
—	Krik!	—	—	Krik!	—	—	Krik!
Krak!	—	—	—	—	—	—	—

Krek! — — — — Krek! — —
— — Krik! — — Krik! — —

Krak! — — — — — —
— — Krek! — — — — Krek!
Krik! — — Krik! — — Krik! —

Krak! — — — — — —
— — — — Krek! — — —
— Krik! — — Krik! — — Krik!

Krak! — — — — — —
— Krek! — — — — Krek! —
— — Krik! — — Krik! — —

Krak! — — — — — —
— — — Krek! — — — —
Krik! — — Krik! — — Krik! —

Krak! — — — — — —
Krek! — — — — Krek! — —
— Krik! — — Krik! — — Krik !

Krak! — — — — — —
— — Krek! — — — — Krek!
— — Krik! — — Krik! — —

Krak! — — — — — —
— — — — Krek! — — —
Krik! — — Krik! — — Krik! —

Krak! — — — — — —
— Krek! — — — — Krek! —
— Krik! — — Krik! — — Krik!

Krak! —   —   —   —   —   —   —

    —   —   —   Krek!   —   —   —   —

    —   —   Krik!   —   —   Krik!   —   —

Krak!
Krek!
Krik!

The fishwoman pleased Watt greatly. Watt was not a woman's man, but the fishwoman pleased him greatly. Other women would perhaps please him more, later. But of all the women who had ever pleased him up till then, not one could hold a candle to this fishwoman, in Watt's opinion. And Watt pleased the fishwoman. This was a merciful coincidence, that they pleased each other. For if the fishwoman had pleased Watt, without Watt's pleasing the fishwoman, or if Watt had pleased the fishwoman, without the fishwoman's pleasing Watt, then what would have become of Watt, or of the fishwoman? Not that the fishwoman was a man's woman, for she was not, being of an advanced age and by nature also denied those properties that attract men to women, unless it was perhaps the remains of a distinguished carriage, acquired from the habit of carrying her basket of fish on her head, over long distances. Not that a man, without possessing any of those properties that attract women to men, may not be a woman's man, nor that a woman, without possessing any of those properties that attract men to women, may not be man's woman, for they may. And Mrs. Gorman had had several admirers, both before and after Mr. Gorman, and even during Mr. Gorman, and Watt at least two well-defined romances, in the course of his celibate. Watt was not a man's man either, possessing as he did none of those properties that attract men to men, though of course he had had male friends (what wretch has not?) on more than one occasion. Not that Watt might not have been a man's man, without possessing any of those properties that attract men to men, for he might. But it happened that he was not. As to whether Mrs. Gorman was a woman's woman, or not, that is one of those things that is not known. On the one hand she may have been, on the other she may not. But it seems probable that she was not. Not that it is by any means impossible for a man to be both a man's man and a woman's man, or for a woman to be both a woman's woman and a man's woman, almost in the same breath. For with men and women, with men's men and women's men, with men's women and women's women, with men's and women's men, with men's and women's women, all is possible, as far as can be ascertained, in this connexion.

Mrs. Gorman called every Thursday, except when she was indisposed. Then she did not call, but stayed at home, in bed, or in a comfortable chair, before the fire, if the weather was cold, and by the open window, if the weather was warm, and, if the weather was neither cold nor warm, by the closed window or before the empty hearth. So Thursday was the day that Watt preferred, to all other days. Some prefer Sunday, others Monday, others Tuesday, others Wednesday, others Friday, others Saturday, But Watt preferred Thursday, because Mrs. Gorman called on Thursday. Then he would have her in the kitchen, and open for her a bottle of stout, and set her on his knee, and wrap his right arm about her waist, and lean his head upon her right breast (the left having unhappily been removed in the heat of a surgical operation), and in this position remain, without stirring, or stirring the least possible, forgetful of his troubles, for as long as ten minutes, or a quarter of an hour. And Mrs. Gorman too, as with her left hand she stirred the grey-pink tufts and with her right at studied intervals raised the bottle to her lips, was in her own small way at peace too, for a time.

From time to time, hoisting his weary head, from waist to neck his weary hold transferring, Watt would kiss, in a despairing manner, Mrs. Gorman on or about the mouth, before crumpling back into his post-crucified position. And these kisses, when their first feverish force began to fail, that is to say very shortly following their application, it was Mrs. Gorman's invariable habit to catch up, as it were, upon her own lips, and return, with tranquil civility, as one picks up a glove, or newspaper, let fall in some public place, and restores it with a smile, if not a bow, to its rightful proprietor. So that each kiss was in reality two kisses, first Watt's kiss, velleitary, anxious, and then Mrs. Gorman's, unctious and urbane.

But Mrs. Gorman did not always sit on Watt, for sometimes Watt sat on Mrs. Gorman. Some days Mrs. Gorman was on Watt all the time, other days Watt was on Mrs. Gorman. Nor were there lacking days when Mrs. Gorman began by sitting on Watt, and ended by having Watt sitting on her, or when Watt began by sitting on Mrs. Gorman, and ended by having Mrs. Gorman sitting on him. For Watt was apt to tire, before the time came for Mrs. Gorman to take her leave, of having Mrs. Gorman sitting on him, or of sitting himself on Mrs. Gorman. Then, if it was Mrs. Gorman on Watt, and not Watt on Mrs. Gorman, then he would urge her gently off his lap, to her feet, on the floor, and he himself rise, until they who but a moment before had both been seated, she on him, he on the chair, now stood, side by side, on their feet, on the floor. And then together they would sink to rest, Watt and Mrs. Gorman, the latter on the chair, the former on the latter. But if it was not Mrs. Gorman on Watt, but Watt on Mrs. Gorman, then he would climb down from off her knees, and raise her gently by the hand to her feet, and take her place (bending his knees) on the chair, and draw her down (spreading his thighs) among his lap. And so little could Watt support, on certain days, on the one hand the pressure of Mrs. Gorman from above, and on the other the thrust of Mrs. Gorman from below, that no fewer than two, or three, or four, or five, or six, or seven, or eight, or nine, or ten, or eleven, or even twelve, or even thirteen, changes of position were found necessary, before the time came for Mrs. Gorman to take her leave. Which, allowing one minute for the inter-version, gives an average session of fifteen seconds, and, on the moderate basis of one kiss, lasting one minute, every minute and a half, a total for the day of one kiss only, one double kiss, begun in the first session and consummated in the last, for during the interversions they could not kiss, they were so busy interverting.

Further than this, it will be learnt with regret, they never went, though more than half inclined to do so on more than one occasion. Why was this? Was it the echo murmuring in their hearts, in Watt's heart, in Mrs. Gorman's, of past passion, ancient error, warning them not to sully not to trail, in the cloaca of clonic gratification, a flower so fair, so rare, so sweet, so frail? It is not necessary to suppose so. For Watt had not the strength, and Mrs. Gorman had not the time, indispensable to even the most perfunctory coalescence. The irony of life! Of life in love! That he who has the time should lack the force, that she who has the force should lack the time! That a trifling and in all probability tractable obstruction of some endocrinal Bandusia, that a mere matter of forty-five or fifty minutes by the clock, should as effectively as death itself, or as the Hellespont, separate lovers. For if Watt had had a little more vigour Mrs. Gorman would have just had the time, and if Mrs. Gorman had had a little more time Watt could very likely have developed, with a careful nursing of his languid tides, a breaker not unworthy of the occasion. Whereas as things stood, with Watt's strength, and Mrs. Gorman's time, limited as they were, it is difficult to see what more they could have done than what they did, than sit on each other, turn about, kissing, resting, kissing again and resting again, until it was time for Mrs. Gorman to resume her circuit.

What was this in Mrs. Gorman, what this in Watt, that so appealed to Watt, so melted Mrs. Gorman? Between what deeps the call, the counter-call? Between Watt not a man's man and Mrs. Gorman not a woman's woman? Between Watt not a woman's man and Mrs. Gorman not a man's woman? Between Watt not a man's man and Mrs. Gorman not a man's woman? Between Watt not a woman's man and Mrs. Gorman not a woman's woman? Between Watt neither a man's nor a woman's man and Mrs. Gorman neither a man's nor a woman's woman? In his own vitals, nucleant, he knew them clasped, the men that were not men's, that were not women's men. And Mrs. Gorman was doubtless the theatre of a similar conglutination. But that meant nothing. And were they not perhaps rather drawn, Mrs. Gorman to Watt, Watt to Mrs. Gorman, she by the bottle of stout, he by the smell of fish? This was the view towards which, in later years, when Mrs. Gorman was no more than a fading memory, than a dying perfume, Watt inclined.

Mr. Graves came to the back door four times a day. In the morning, when he arrived, to fetch the key of his shed, and at midday, to fetch his pot of tea, and in the afternoon, to fetch his bottle of stout and return the teapot, and in the evening, to return the key and the bottle.

Watt conceived for Mr. Graves a feeling little short of liking. In particular Mr. Graves's way of speaking did not displease Watt. Mr. Graves pronounced his *th* charmingly.

Turd and fart, he said, for third and fourth. Watt liked these venerable Saxon words. And when Mr. Graves, drinking on the sunny step his afternoon stout, looked up with a twinkle in his old blue eye, and said, in mock deprecation, Tis only me turd or fart, then Watt felt he was perhaps prostituting himself to some purpose.

Mr. Graves had much to say on the subject of Mr. Knott, and of Erskine, Arsene, Walter, Vincent and others, whose names he had forgotten, or never known. But nothing of interest. He quoted as well from his ancestors' experience as from his own. For his father had worked for Mr. Knott, and his father's father, and so on. Here then was another series. His family, he said, had made the garden what it was. He had nothing but good to say of Mr. Knott and of his young gentlemen. This was the first time that Watt had been assimilated to the class of young gentlemen. But Mr. Graves might just as well have been speaking of tavern companions.

But Mr. Grave's chief subject of conversation was his domestic troubles. He did not, it appeared, get on well with his wife, and had not, for some time past. Indeed he did not get on with his wife at all. Mr. Graves seemed to have reached the age at which the failure to get on with one's wife is more generally a cause of satisfaction than of repining. But it greatly discouraged Mr. Graves. All his married life he had got on with his wife, like a house on fire, but now for some time past he had been quite unable to do so. This was very distressing also to Mrs. Graves, that her husband could not get on with her any more, for there was nothing that Mrs. Graves loved better than to be got on well with.

Watt was not the first to whom Mr. Graves had unbosomed himself, in this connexion. For he had unbosomed himself to Arsene, many years before, when his trouble was green, and Arsene had given advice, which Mr. Graves had followed to the letter. But nothing had ever come of it.

Erskine too had been admitted, by Mr. Graves, to his confidence, and Erskine had been most generous with his advice. It was not the same advice as Arsene's, and Mr. Graves had acted on it, to the best of his ability. But nothing had come of it.

Now to Watt Mr. Graves did not say, in so many words, Tell me wat to do, Mr. Watt, in order tat I may get on wid me wife, as in former times. And it was perhaps as well that he did not, for Watt would have been unable to reply, to such a question. And this silence would perhaps have been misconstrued by Mr. Graves, and made to mean that it was all the same to Watt whether Mr. Graves got on with his wife, or whether he did not.

The question was nevertheless implied, and indeed blatantly. For the first time that Mr. Graves ended the relation of his trouble, he did not go away, but remained where he was, silent and expectant, floccillating his hard hat (Mr. Graves always took off his hard hat, even in the open air, when in speech with his betters), and looking up at Watt, who was standing on the step. And as Watt's face wore its habitual expression, which was that of Judge Jeffreys presiding the Ecclesiastical Commission, Mr. Graves's hopes ran high, of hearing something to his advantage. Unfortunately Watt was thinking of birds at the time, their missile flights, their canorous reloadings. But soon tiring of this he turned back into the house, closing the door behind him.

But it was not long before Watt began to put out the key, overnight, by the step, under a stone, and to put out the pot of tea at midday, under a cosy, and to put out the bottle of stout in the afternoon, with a corkscrew, in the shade. And in the evening, when Mr. Graves had gone home, then

Watt would take in the teapot, and the bottle, and the key, which Mr. Graves had put back, where he had found them. But a little later Watt ceased to take in the key. For why take in the key, at six, when it must be put out, at ten? So the key's nail, in the kitchen, knew the key no more, but only Mr. Graves's pocket, and the stone. But if Watt did not take in the key, in the evening, when Mr. Graves was gone, but only the teapot and the bottle, yet he never failed, when he took in the teapot and the bottle, to look under the stone, and make sure the key was there.

Then one bitter night Watt left his warm bed and went down, and took in the key, and he wrapped it in a snippet of blanket, that he had snipped, from his own blanket. And then he put it out again, under the stone. And when he looked the next evening he found it, as he had left it, in its blanket, under the stone. For Mr. Graves was a very understanding man.

Watt wondered if Mr. Graves had a son, as Mr. Gall had, to step into his shoes, when he was dead. Watt thought it most probable. For does one get on with one's wife, all one's married life, like a house on fire, without having at least one son, to step into one's shoes, when one dies, or retires?

Sometimes in the vestibule Watt would catch a glimpse of Mr. Knott, or in the garden, stock still, or moving slowly about.

One day Watt, coming out from behind a bush, almost ran into Mr. Knott, which for an instant troubled Watt greatly, for he had not quite finished adjusting his dress. But he need not have been troubled. For Mr. Knott's hands were behind his back, and his head bowed down, towards the ground. Then Watt in his turn looking down at first saw nothing but the short green grass, but when he had looked a little longer he saw a little blue flower and close by a fat worm burrowing into the earth. So this was what had attracted Mr. Knott's attention, perhaps. So there for a short time they stood together, the master and the servant, the bowed heads almost touching (which gives Mr. Knott's approximate height, does it not, assuming that the ground was level), until the worm was gone and only the flower remained. One day the flower would be gone and only the worm remain, but on this particular day it was the flower that remained, and the worm that went. And then Watt, looking up, saw that Mr. Knott's eyes were closed, and heard his breathing, soft and shallow, like the breathing of a child asleep.

Watt did not know whether he was glad or sorry that he did not see Mr. Knott more often. In one sense he was sorry, and in another glad. And the sense in which he was sorry was this, that he wished to see Mr. Knott face to face, and the sense in which he was glad was this, that he feared to do so. Yes indeed, in so far as he wished, in so far as he feared, to see Mr. Knott face to face, his wish made him sorry, his fear glad, that he saw him so seldom, and at such a great distance as a rule, and so fugitively, and so often sideways on, and even from behind.

Watt wondered if Erskine was better served, in this matter, than he.

But as time, as time will, drew on, and Watt's period of service on the ground floor approached its term, then this wish and this fear, and so this sorrow and this gladness, like so many other wishes and fears, so many other sorrows and gladnesses, grew duller and duller and gradually ceased to be felt, at all. And the reason for that was perhaps this, that little by little Watt abandoned all hope, all fear, of ever seeing Mr. Knott face to face, or perhaps this, that Watt, while continuing to believe in the possibility of his seeing one day Mr. Knott face to face, came to regard its realization as one to which no importance could be attached, or perhaps this, that as Watt's interest in what has been called the spirit of Mr. Knott increased, his interest in what is commonly known as the body diminished (for it is frequent, when one thing increases in one place, for another in another to diminish), or perhaps some quite different reason, such as mere fatigue, having nothing to do with any of these.

Add to this that the few glimpses caught of Mr. Knott, by Watt, were not clearly caught, but as it were in a glass, not a looking-glass, a plain glass, an eastern window at morning, a western window at evening.

Add to this that the figure of which Watt sometimes caught a glimpse, in the vestibule, in the garden, was seldom the same figure, from one glance to the next, but so various, as far as Watt could make out, in its corpulence, complexion, height and even hair, and of course in its way of moving and of not moving, that Watt would never have supposed it was the same, if he had not known that it was Mr. Knott.

Watt had never heard Mr. Knott either, heard him speak, that is to say, or laugh, or cry. But once he thought he heard him say Tweet! Tweet! to a little bird, and once he heard him make a strange noise, *PLOPF* PLOPF *Plopf* Plopf *plopf* plopf plop plo pl. This was in the flower garden.

Watt wondered if Erskine was any better off in this respect. Did he and his master converse? Watt had never heard them do so, as he surely would have done, if they had done so. In an undertone perhaps. Yes, perhaps they conversed in undertones, the master and the servant, in two undertones, the master's undertone, the servant's undertone.

One day towards the end of Watt's stay on the ground-floor, the telephone rang and a voice asked how Mr. Knott was. Here was a teaser, to be sure. The voice said further,

A friend. It might have been a high male voice, or it might have been a deep female voice.

Watt stated this incident as follows:

A friend, sex uncertain, of Mr. Knott telephoned to know how he was.

Cracks soon appeared in this formulation.

But Watt was too tired to repair it. Watt dared not tire himself further.

How often he had pooh-poohed it, this danger of tiring himself further. Pooh-pooh, he had said, pooh-pooh, and set to, to repair the cracks. But not now.

Watt was now tired of the ground-floor, the ground-floor had tired Watt out.

What had he learnt? Nothing.

What did he know of Mr. Knott? Nothing.

Of his anxiety to improve, of his anxiety to understand, of his anxiety to get well, what remained? Nothing.

But was not that something?

He saw himself then, so little, so poor. And now, littler, poorer. Was not that something?

So sick, so alone.

And now.

Sicker, aloner.

Was not that something?

As the comparative is something. Whether more than its positive or less. Whether less than its superlative or more.

Red, bluer, yellowist, that old dream was ended, half ended, ended. Again.

A little before morning.

But at last he awoke to find, on arising, on descending, Erskine gone, and, on descending a little further, a strange man in the kitchen.

He did not know when this was. It was when the yew was dark green, almost black. It was on a morning white

147

and soft, and the earth seemed dressed for the grave. It was to the sound of bells, of chapel bells, of church bells. It was on a morning that the milkboy came singing to the door, shrilly to the door his tuneless song, and went singing away, having measured out the milk, from his can, to the jug, with all his usual liberality.

The strange man resembled Arsene and Erskine, in build. He gave his name as Arthur. Arthur.

III

It was about this time that Watt was transferred to another pavilion, leaving me behind in the old pavilion. We consequently met, and conversed, less than formerly. Not that at any time we had met, or conversed, very much, for we had not. For we seldom left our mansions, Watt seldom left his mansion and I seldom left mine. And when the kind of weather we liked did induce us to leave our mansions, and go out into the garden, it did not always do so at the same time. For the kind of weather that I liked, while resembling the kind of weather that Watt liked, had certain properties that the kind of weather that Watt liked had not, and lacked certain properties that the kind of weather that Watt liked had. So that when, together tempted from our mansions by what each felt to be the kind of weather he liked, we met in the little garden, and perhaps conversed (for though we could not converse without meeting, we could, and often did, meet without conversing), the disappointment of one of us at least was almost certain, and the regret, the bitter regret, at ever having left his mansion at all, and the vow, the hollow vow, never to leave his mansion again, never never to leave his mansion again, on any account. So we knew resistance too, resistance to the call of the kind of weather we liked, but seldom simultaneously. Not that our resisting simultaneously had any bearing on our meeting, our conversing, for it had not. For when we both resisted we no more met, no more conversed, than when the one resisted, the other yielded. But ah, when we yielded both, then we met, and perhaps conversed, in the little garden.

It is so easy to accept, so easy to refuse, when the call is heard, so easy, so easy. But to us, in our windowlessness, in our bloodheat, in our hush, to us who could not hear the wind, nor see the sun, what call could come, from the kind of weather we liked, but a call so faint as to mock acceptance, mock refusal? And it was of course impossible to have any confidence in the meteorological information of our attendants. So it is not to be wondered at if, through sheer ignorance of what was going on without, we spent indoors, now Watt, now I, now Watt and I, many fleeting hours that might have fled, just as well, if not better, certainly not worse, from us with us as we walked, Watt, or I, or Watt and I, and perhaps even went through some of the forms of conversation, in the little garden. No, but what is to be wondered at is this, that to us both, disposed to yield, each in his separate soundless unlit warmth, the call should come, and coax us out, as often as it did, as sometimes it did, into the little garden. Yes, that we should have ever met, and spoken and listened together, and that my arm should ever have rested on his arm, and his on mine, and our shoulders ever touched, and our legs moved in and out, together over more or less the same ground, parallelly the right legs forward, the left ones back, and then without hesitation the reverse, and that, leaning forward, breast to breast, we should ever have embraced (oh, exceptionally, and of course never on the mouth), that seemed to me, the last time I remembered, strange, strange. For we never left our mansions, never, unless at the call of the kind of weather we liked, Watt never left his for me, I never left mine for him, but leaving them independently at the call of the kind of weather we liked we met, and sometimes conversed, with the utmost friendliness, and even tenderness, in the little garden.

No truck with the other scum, cluttering up the passage-ways, the hallways, grossly loud, blatantly morose, and playing at ball, always playing at ball, but stiffly, delicately, out from our mansions, and through this jocose this sniggering muck, to the kind of weather we liked, and back as we went.

The kind of weather we liked was a high wind and a bright sun mixed.[1] But whereas for Watt the important thing was the wind, the sun was the important thing for Sam. With the result that though the sun though bright were not so bright as it might have been, if the wind were high Watt did not audibly complain, and that I, when illuminated by rays of appropriate splendour, could forgive a wind which, while strong, might with advantage have been stronger. It is thus evident that the occasions were few and far between on which, walking and perhaps talking in the little garden, we walked there and perhaps talked with equal enjoyment. For when on Sam the sun shone bright, then in a vacuum panted Watt, and when Watt like a leaf was tossed, then stumbled Sam in deepest night. But ah, when exceptionally the desired degrees of ventilation and radiance were united, in the little garden, then we were peers in peace, each in his own way, until the wind fell, the sun declined.

Not that the garden was so little, for it was not, being of ten or fifteen acres in extent. But it seemed little to us, after our mansions.

In it great pale aspens grew, and yews ever dark, with tropical luxuriance, and other trees, in lesser numbers.

They rose from the wild pathless grass, so that we walked much in shade, heavy, trembling, fierce, tempestuous.

In winter there were the thin shadows writhing, under our feet, in the wild withered grass.

Of flowers there was no trace, save of the flowers that

[1] Watt liked the sun at this time, or at least supported it. Nothing is known about this volte-face. He seemed pleased that all the shadows should move, not only himself.

plant themselves, or never die, or die only after many seasons, strangled by the rank grass. The chief of these was the pissabed.

Of vegetables there was no sign.

There was a little stream, or brook, never dry, flowing now slow, now with torrential rapidity, for ever in its narrow ditch. Unsteadily a rustic bridge bestrode its dark waters, a rustic hump-backed bridge, in a state of extreme dilapidation.

It was through the crown of this construction that one day Watt, treading more heavily than was his wont, or picking his steps with less than his usual care, drove his foot, and part of his leg. And he would certainly have fallen, and perhaps been carried away by the subfluent flood, had I not been at hand to bear him up. For this trifling service, I remember, I received no thanks. But we set to work at once, Watt from the one bank, I from the other, with stout boughs and withes of willow, to repair the havoc. We lay at full length on our stomachs, I at my full length on my stomach, and Watt at his on his, partly (for security) on our banks, partly on the up slopes of the stages, and worked with diligence with arms outstretched until our task was done, and the place mended, and as good as before, if not better. Then, our eyes meeting, we smiled, a thing we did rarely, when together. And when we had lain a little thus, with this exceptional smile, on our faces, then we began to draw ourselves forward, and upward, and persisted in this course until our heads, our noble bulging brows, met, and touched. Watt's noble brow, and my noble brow. And then we did a thing we seldom did, we embraced. Watt laid his hands on my shoulders, and I laid mine on his (I could hardly do otherwise), and then I touched Watt's left cheek with my lips, and then Watt touched my left cheek with his (he could scarcely do less), the whole coolly, and above us tossed the over-arching boughs.

We were attached, you see, to the little bridge. For without it how should we have passed from one part of the garden to the other, without wetting our feet, and perhaps catching a chill, liable to develop into pneumonia, with very likely fatal results.

Of seats, on which to sit down, and rest, there was not the slightest vestige.

Shrubs and bushes, properly so called, were absent from the scene. But thickets rose at every turn, brakes of impenetrable density, and towering masses of brambles, of a beehive form.

Birds of every kind abounded, and these it was our delight to pursue, with stones and clods of earth. Robins, in particular, thanks to their confidingness, we destroyed in great numbers. And larks' nests, laden with eggs still warm from the mother's breast, we ground into fragments, under our feet, with peculiar satisfaction, at the appropriate season, of the year.

But our particular friends were the rats, that dwelt by the stream. They were long and black. We brought them such titbits from our ordinary as rinds of cheese, and morsels of gristle, and we brought them also birds' eggs, and frogs, and fledgelings. Sensible of these attentions, they would come flocking round us at our approach, with every sign of confidence and affection, and glide up our trouser-legs, and hang upon our breasts. And then we would sit down in the midst of them, and give them to eat, out of our hands, of a nice fat frog, or a baby thrush. Or seizing suddenly a plump young rat, resting in our bosom after its repast, we would feed it to its mother, or its father, or its brother, or its sister, or to some less fortunate relative.

It was on these occasions, we agreed, after an exchange of views, that we came nearest to God.

When Watt spoke, he spoke in a low and rapid voice.

Lower voices, voices more rapid, have been heard, will be heard, than Watt's voice, no doubt. But that there ever issued from the mouth of man, or ever shall again, except in moments of delirium, or during the service of the mass, a voice *at once* so rapid and so low, is hard to believe. Watt spoke also with scant regard for grammar, for syntax, for pronunciation, for enunciation, and very likely, if the truth were known, for spelling too, as these are generally received. Proper names, however, both of places and of persons, such as Knott, Christ, Gomorrha, Cork, he articulated with great deliberation, and from his discourse these emerged, palms, atolls, at long intervals, for he seldom specified, in a most refreshing manner. The labour of composition, the uncertainty as to how to proceed, or whether to proceed at all, inseparable from even our most happy improvisations, and from which neither the songs of birds, nor even the cries of quadrupeds, are exempt, had here no part, apparently. But Watt spoke as one speaking to dictation, or reciting, parrot-like, a text, by long repetition become familiar. Of this impetuous murmur much fell in vain on my imperfect hearing and understanding, and much by the rushing wind was carried away, and lost for ever.

This garden was surrounded by a high barbed wire fence, greatly in need of repair, of new wire, of fresh barbs. Through this fence, where it was not overgrown by briars and giant nettles, similar gardens, similarly enclosed, each with its pavilion, were on all sides distinctly to be seen. Now converging, now diverging, these fences presented a striking irregularity of contour. No fence was party, nor any part of any fence. But their adjacence was such, at certain places, that a broad-shouldered or broad-basined man, threading these narrow straits, would have done so with greater ease, and with less jeopardy to his coat, and perhaps to his trousers, sideways than frontways. For a big-bottomed man, on the contrary, or a big-bellied man, frontal motion would be an absolute necessity, if he did not wish his stomach to be perforated, or his arse, or perhaps both, by a rusty barb, or by rusty barbs. A big-bottomed big-bosomed woman, an obese wet-nurse, for example, would be under a similar necessity. While persons at once broad-shouldered and big-bellied, or broad-basined and big-bottomed, or broad-basined and big-bellied, or broad-shouldered and big-bottomed, or big-bosomed and broad-shouldered, or big-bosomed and broad-basined, would on no account, if they were in their right senses, commit themselves to this treacherous channel, but turn about, and retrace their steps, unless they wished to be impaled, at various points at once, and perhaps bleed to death, or be eaten alive by the rats, or perish from exposure, long before their cries were heard, and still longer before the rescuers appeared, running, with the scissors, the brandy and the iodine. For were their cries not heard, then their chances of rescue were small, so vast were these gardens, and so deserted, in the ordinary way.

Some time passed, after Watt's transfer, before we met again. I walked in my garden as usual, that is to say when I yielded to the call of the kind of weather I liked, and similarly Watt walked in his. But as it was no longer the same garden, we did not meet. When finally we did meet, again, in the way described below, it was clear to us both, to me, to Watt, that we might have met much sooner, if we had wished. But there, the wish to meet was lacking. Watt did not wish to meet me, I did not wish to meet Watt. This is not to say that we were opposed to meeting, to resuming our walks, our talks, as before, for we were not, but only that the wish to do so was not felt, by Watt, by me.

Then one fine day, of unparalleled brightness and turbulence, I found my steps impelled, as though by some external agency, towards the fence; and this impulsion was maintained, until I could go no farther, in that direction, without doing myself a serious, if not fatal, injury; then it left me and I looked about, a thing I never used to do, on any account, in the ordinary way. How hideous is the semi-colon. I say an external agency; for of my own volition, which, if not robust, did nevertheless possess, at that period, a kind of kittenish tenacity, I should never have gone near the fence, under any circumstances; for I was very fond of fences, of wire fences, very fond indeed; not of walls, nor palissades, nor opacious hedges, no; but to all that limited motion, without limiting vision, to the ditch, the dyke, the barred window, the bog, the quicksand, the paling, I was deeply attached, at that time, deeply deeply attached. And (which renders, if possible, what follows even more singular that it would be otherwise), so, I believe, was Watt. For when, before his transfer, we walked together in our garden, on no single occasion did we go near the fence, as we surely must have done, if chance had led us, at least once or twice. Watt did not guide me, nor I him, but of our own accord, as though by mutual tacit consent, we never went nearer to the fence than a hundred yards, or a quarter of a mile. Sometimes we saw it afar, faintly the old sagging strands, the leaning posts, trembling in the wind, at the end of a glade. Or we saw a big black bird perched in the void, perhaps croaking, or preening its feathers.

Being now so near the fence, that I could have touched it with a stick, if I had wished, and so looking about me, like a mad creature, I perceived, beyond all possibility of error, that I was in the presence of one of those channels or straits described above, where the limit of my garden and that of another, followed the same course, at so short a remove, the one from the other, and for so considerable a distance, that it was impossible for doubts not to arise, in a reasonable mind, regarding the sanity of the person responsible for the layout. Continuing my inspection, like one deprived of his sense, I observed, with a distinctness that left no room for doubt, in the adjoining garden whom do you think but Watt, advancing backwards towards me. His progress was slow and devious, on account no doubt of his having no eyes in the back of his head, and painful too, I fancy, for often he struck against the trunks of trees, or in the tangles of underwood caught his foot, and fell to the ground, flat on his back, or into a great clump of brambles, or of briars, or of nettles, or of thistles. But still without murmur he came on, until he lay against the fence, with his hands at arm's length grasping the wires. Then he turned, with the intention very likely of going back the way he had come, and I saw his face, and the rest of his front. His face was bloody, his hand also, and thorns were in his scalp. (His resemblance, at that moment, to the Christ believed by Bosch, then hanging in Trafalgar Square, was so striking, that I remarked it.) And at the same instant suddenly I felt as though I were standing before a great mirror, in which my garden was reflected, and my fence, and I, and the very birds tossing in the wind, so that I looked at my hands, and felt my face, and glossy skull, with an anxiety as real as unfounded. (For if anyone, at that time, could be truly said not to resemble the Christ supposed by Bosch, then hanging in Trafalgar Square, I flatter myself it was I.) Why, Watt, I cried, that is a nice state you have got yourself into, to be sure. Not it is, yes, replied Watt. This short phrase caused me, I believe, more alarm, more pain, than if I had received, unexpectedly, at close quarters, a charge of small shot in the ravine. This impression was reinforced by what followed. Wonder I, said Watt, panky-hanky me lend you could, blood away wipe. Wait, wait, I am coming, I cried. And I believe, that in my anxiety to come at Watt then, I would have launched myself against the barrier, bodily, if necessary. Indeed I went so far, with this purpose in view, as hastily to withdraw to a distance of ten or fifteen paces, and to cast round for a sapling, or a bough, susceptible of conversion, rapidly, and without the help of any cutting instrument, into a pole, or perch. While I was thus half-heartedly employed, I thought I saw, in the fence, on my right, a hole, large and irregular. Judge then of my astonishment when, upon approach, I found I was not mistaken. It was a hole, in the fence, a large irregular hole, caused by numberless winds, number-less rains, or by a boar, or by a bull, flying, pursuing, a wild boar, a wild bull, blind with fear, blind with rage, or who knows perhaps with carnal desire, crashing at this point, through the fence, weakened by numberless winds, numberless rains. Through this hole I passed, without hurt, or damage to my pretty uniform, and found myself looking about me, for I had not yet recovered my aplomb, in the couloir. My senses being now sharpened to ten or fifteen times their normal acuity, it was not long before I saw, in the other fence, another hole, in position opposite, and similar in shape, to that through which, some ten or fifteen minutes before, I had made my way. So that I said that no boar had made these holes, nor any bull, but the stress of weather, particularly violent just here. For where was the boar, where the bull, capable, after bursting a hole in the first fence, of bursting a second, exactly similar, in the second? But would not the bursting of the first hole so reduce the infuriated mass as to render impossible, in the course of the same charge, the bursting of the second? Add to this that a bare yard separated the fences, at this point, so that the snout would be, of necessity, in contact with the second fence, before the hind-quarters were clear of the first, and consequently the space be lacking in which, after the bursting of the first hole, the fresh impetus might be developed necessary to the bursting of the second. Nor was it likely that the bull, or boar, after the bursting of the first hole, had withdrawn to a point from which, proceeding as before, he might acquire the impetus necessary to the bursting of the second hole, via the first hole. For either, after the bursting of the first hole, the animal was still blind with passion, or he was so no longer. If he was so still, then the chances were indeed small of his seeing the first hole with the distinctness necessary to his passing through it with the velocity necessary to the bursting of the second hole. And if he was so no longer, but by the bursting of the first hole calmed, and his eyes opened, why then the probability was remote indeed of his desiring to burst another. Nor was it likely that the second hole, or better still Watt's hole (for there was nothing to show that the so-called second hole was not anterior to the so-called first hole, and the so-called first hole not posterior to the so-called second hole), had been burst, independently, at some quite different time, from Watt's side of the fence. For if the two holes had been independently burst, the one from Watt's side of Watt's fence, and the other from mine of mine, by two quite different infuriated boars, or bulls (for that the one had been burst by an infuriated boar, and the other by an infuriated bull, was unlikely), and at two quite different times, the one from Watt's side of Watt's fence, and the other from mine of mine, then their conjunction, at this point, was incomprehensible, to say the least. Nor was it likely that the two holes, the hole in Watt's fence and the hole in mine, had been burst, on the same occasion, by two infuriated bulls, or by two infuriated boars, or by one infuriated bull and one infuriated cow, or by one infuriated boar and one infuriated sow (for that they had been burst, simultaneously, the one by an infuriated bull and the other by an infuriated sow, or the one by an infuriated boar and the other by an infuriated cow, was hard to believe), charging with hostile or libidinous intent, the one from Watt's side of Watt's fence, the other from mine of mine, and clashing, the holes once burst, at the spot where now I stood, trying to understand. For this implied the bursting of the holes, by the bulls, or by the boars, or by the bull and cow, or by the boar and sow, at exactly the same moment, and not first one, and then an instant later the other. For if first one, and then an instant later the other, then the bull, the cow, the boar, the sow, first through its fence, and thrusting with its head against the other, must have prevented, willy nilly, through this other, at this particular point, the passage of the bull, the cow, the bull, the boar, the sow, the boar, hastening to meet it, with all the fury of hate, the fury of love. Nor could I find, though I went down on my knees, and parted the wild grasses, any trace, whether of combat or of copulation. No bull then had burst these holes, nor any boar, nor any two bulls, nor any two boars, nor any two cows, nor any two sows, nor any bull and cow, nor any boar and sow, no, but the stress of weather, rains and winds without number, and suns, and snows, and frosts, and thaws, particularly severe just here. Or was it not after all just possible, through the two fences thus weakened by exposure, for a single exceptionally powerful infuriated or terrified bull, or cow, or boar, or sow, or even some other wild animal, to have passed, whether from Watt's side of Watt's fence, or from mine of mine, as though the two fences were but one?

Turning now to where I had last had the pleasure of seeing Watt, I saw that he was there no longer, nor indeed in any of the other places, and they were numerous, visible to my eye. But when I called, Watt! Watt!, then he came, awkwardly buttoning his trousers, which he was wearing back to front, out from behind a tree, and then backwards, guided by my cries, slowly, painfully, often falling, but as often picking himself up, and without murmur, towards where I stood, until at last, after so long, I could touch him again, with my hand. Then I reached out with my hand, through the hole, and drew him, through the hole, to my side, and with a cloth that I had in my pocket wiped his face, and his hands, and then taking a little box of ointment that I had in my pocket from my pocket I anointed his face, and his hands, and then taking a little hand comb from my pocket I straightened his tufts, and his whiskers, and then taking a little clothes brush from my pocket I brushed his coat, and his trousers. Then I turned him round, until he faced me. Then I placed his hands, on my shoulders, his left hand on my right shoulder, and his right hand on my left shoulder. Then I placed my hands, on his shoulders, on his left shoulder my right hand, and on his right shoulder my left hand. Then I took a single pace forward, with my left leg, and he a single pace back, with his right leg (he could scarcely do otherwise). Then I took a double pace forward with my right leg, and he of course with his left leg a double pace back. And so we paced together between the fences, I forwards, he backwards, until we came to where the fences diverged again. And then turning, I turning, and he turning, we paced back the way we had come, I forwards, and he of course backwards, with our hands on our shoulders, as before. And so pacing back the way we had come, we passed the holes and paced on, until we came to where the fences diverged again. And then turning, as one man, we paced back the way we had paced back the way we had come, I looking whither we were going, and he looking whence we were coming. And so, up and down, up and down, we paced between the fences, together again after so long, and the sun shone bright upon us, and the wind blew wild about us.

To be together again, after so long, who love the sunny wind, the windy sun, in the sun, in the wind, that is perhaps something, perhaps something.

For us moving so between the fences, before they diverged, there was just room.

In Watt's garden, in my garden, we should have been more at our ease. But it never occurred to me to go back into my garden with Watt, or with him to go forward into his. But it never occurred to Watt to go back with me into his garden, or with me to go forward into mine. For my garden was my garden, and Watt's garden was Watt's garden, we had no common garden any more. So we walked to and fro, neither in his garden, in the way described.

So we began, after so long a time, to walk together again, and to talk, from time to time.

As Watt walked, so now he talked, back to front.

The following is an example of Watt's manner, at this period:

Day of most, night of part, Knott with now. Now till up, little seen so oh, little heard so oh. Night till morning from. Heard I this, saw I this then what. Thing quiet, dim. Ears, eyes, failing now also. Hush in, mist in, moved I so.

From this it will perhaps be suspected:

that the inversion affected, not the order of the sentences, but that of the words only;

that the inversion was imperfect;

that ellipse was frequent;

that euphony was a preoccupation;

that spontaneity was perhaps not absent;

that there was perhaps more than a reversal of discourse;

that the thought was perhaps inverted.

So to every man, soon or late, comes envy of the fly, with all the long joys of summer before it.

The utterance was as rapid, and as muffled, as before.

162

These were sounds that at first, though we walked face to face, were devoid of significance for me.

Nor did Watt follow me. Pardon beg, he said, pardon, pardon beg.

Thus I missed I suppose much I suspect of great interest touching I presume the first or initial stage of the second or closing period of Watt's stay in Mr. Knott's house.

For Watt's sense of chronology was strong, in a way, and his dislike of battology was very strong.

Often my hands left his shoulders, to make a note in their little notebook. But his never left mine, unless I detached them personally.

But soon I grew used to these sounds, and then I understood as well as before, that is to say a great part of what I heard.

So all went well until Watt began to invert, no longer the order of the words in the sentence, but that of the letters in the word.

This further modification Watt carried through with all his usual discretion and sense of what was acceptable to the ear, and aesthetic judgement. Nevertheless to one, such as me, desirous above all of information, the change was not a little disconcerting.

The following is an example of Watt's manner, at this period:

Ot bro, lap rulb, krad klub. Ot murd, wol fup, wol fup. Ot niks, sorg sam, sorg sam. Ot lems, lats lems, lats lems. Ot gnut, trat stews, trat stews.

These were sounds that at first, though we walked breast to breast, made little or no sense to me.

Nor did Watt follow me. Geb nodrap, he said, geb nodrap, nodrap.

Thus I missed I suppose much I presume of great interest touching I suspect the second stage of the second or closing period of Watt's stay in Mr. Knott's house.

But soon I grew used to these sounds, and then I understood as well as before.

So all went well until Watt began to invert, no longer the order of the letters in the word, but that of the sentences in the period.

The following is an example of Watt's manner at this period:

Of nought. To the source. To the teacher. To the temple. To him I brought. This emptied heart. These emptied hands. This mind ignoring. This body homeless. To love him my little reviled. My little rejected to have him. My little to learn him forgot. Abandoned my little to find him.

These were sounds that at first, notwithstanding our proximity, were not perfectly clear to me.

Nor did Watt follow me. Beg pardon, pardon, he said, beg pardon.

Thus I missed I presume much I suppose of great interest touching I presume the third stage of the second or closing period of Watt's stay in Mr. Knott's house.

But soon I grew used to these sounds, and then I understood as well as before.

So all went well until Watt began to invert, no longer the order of the sentences in the period, but that of the words in the sentence together with that of the letters in the word.

The following is an example of Watt's manner at this period:

Deen did taw? Tonk. Tog da taw? Tonk. Luf puk saw? Hap! Deen did tub? Ton sparp. Tog da tub? Ton wonk.

These were sounds that at first, though we walked belly to belly, were so much wind to me.

Nor did Watt follow me. Nodrap geb, he said, nodrap, nodrap geb.

Thus I missed I suspect much I presume of great interest

touching the fourth stage of the second or closing period of Watt's stay in Mr. Knott's house.

But soon I grew used to these sounds.

Then all went well until Watt began to invert, no longer the order of the words in the sentence together with that of the letters in the word, but that of the words in the sentence together with that of the sentences in the period.

The following is an example of Watt's manner at this period:

Say he'd, No, waistcoat the, vest the, trousers the, socks the, shoes the, shirt the, drawers the, coat the, dress to ready things got had when. Say he'd, Dress. Say he'd, No, water the, towel the, sponge the, soap the, salts the, glove the, brush the, basin the, wash to ready things got had when. Say he'd, Wash. Say he'd, No, water the, towel the, sponge the, soap the, razor the, powder the, brush the, bowl the, shave to ready things got had when. Say he'd, Shave.

These were sounds that at first, though we walked pubis to pubis, seemed so much balls to me.

Nor did Watt follow me. Pardon, pardon beg, he said, pardon beg.

Thus I missed I presume much I suspect touching I suppose the fifth stage of the second or closing period of Watt's stay in Mr. Knott's house.

But soon I grew used to these sounds.

Until Watt began to invert, no longer the order of the words in the sentence together with that of the sentences in the period, but that of the letters in the word together with that of the sentences in the period.

The following is an example of this manner:

Lit yad mac, ot og. Ton taw, ton tonk. Ton dob, ton trips. Ton vila, ton deda. Ton kawa, ton pelsa. Ton das, don yag. Os devil, rof mit.

This meant nothing to me.

Geb nodrap, nodrap, said Watt, geb nodrap.

Thus I missed I presume much I suppose of great interest touching I suspect the fifth, no, the sixth stage of the second or closing period of Watt's stay in Mr. Knott's house.

But in the end I understood.

Then Watt began to invert, no longer the order of the letters in the word together with that of the sentences in the period, but that of the letters in the word together with that of the words in the sentence together with that of the sentences in the period.

For example:

Dis yb dis, nem owt. Yad la, tin fo trap. Skin, skin, skin. Od su did ned taw? On. Taw ot klat tonk? On. Tonk ot klat taw? On. Tonk ta kool taw? On. Taw ta kool tonk? Nilb, mun, mud. Tin fo trap, yad la. Nem owt, dis yb dis.

It took me some time to get used to this.

Nodrap, nodrap geb, said Watt, nodrap geb.

Thus I missed I suppose much I suspect of great interest touching I presume the seventh stage of the second or closing period of Watt's stay in Mr. Knott's house.

Then he took it into his head to invert, no longer the order of the words in the sentence, nor that of the letters in the word, nor that of the sentences in the period, nor simultaneously that of the words in the sentence and that of the letters in the word, nor simultaneously that of the words in the sentence and that of the sentences in the period, nor simultaneously that of the letters in the word and that of the sentences in the period, nor simultaneously that of the letters in the word and that of the words in the sentence and that of the sentences in the period, ho no, but, in the brief course of the same period, now that of the words in the sentence, now that of the letters in the word, now that of the sentences in the period, now simultaneously that of the words in the sentence and that of the letters in the word, now simultaneously that of the words in the sentence and that of the sentences in the period, now simultaneously that of the letters in the word and that of the sentences in the period, and now simultaneously that of the letters in the word and that of the words in the sentence and that of the sentences in the period.

I recall no example of this manner.

These were sounds that at first, though we walked glued together, were so much Irish to me.

Nor did Watt follow me. Beg nodrap, he said, nodrap, pardon geb.

Thus I missed I suppose much I presume of great interest touching I suspect the eighth or final stage of the second or closing period of Watt's stay in Mr. Knott's house.

But soon I grew used to these sounds, and then I understood as well as ever, that is to say fully one half of what won its way past my tympan.

For my own hearing now began to fail, though my myopia remained stationary. My purely mental faculties on the other hand, the faculties properly so called of ?

| ? | ? |
| ? | ? |

were if possible more vigorous than ever.

To these conversations we are indebted for the following information.

One day they were all four in the garden, Mr. Knott, Watt, Arthur and Mr. Graves. It was a beautiful summer's day. Mr. Knott was moving slowly about, disappearing now behind a bush, emerging now from behind another. Watt was sitting on a mound. Arthur was standing on the lawn, talking to Mr. Graves. Mr. Graves was leaning on a fork. But the great mass of the empty house was hard by. A bound, and they were all in safety.

Arthur said:

Do not despair, Mr. Graves. Some day the clouds will

roll away, and the sun, so long obnubilated, burst forth, for you, Mr. Graves, at last.

Not a kick in me, Mr. Arter, said Mr. Graves.

Oh, Mr. Graves, said Arthur, do not say that.

When I says a kick, said Mr. Graves, I means a ——. He made a gesture with his fork.

Have you tried Bando, Mr. Graves, said Arthur. A capsule, before and after meals, in a little warm milk, and again at night, before turning in. I had tried everything, and was thoroughly disgusted, when a friend spoke to me of Bando. Her husband was never without it, you understand. Try it, she said, and come back in five or six years. I tried it, Mr. Graves, and it changed my whole outlook on life. From being a moody, listless, constipated man, covered with squames, shunned by my fellows, my breath fetid and my appetite depraved (for years I had eaten nothing but high fat rashers), I became, after four years of Bando, vivacious, restless, a popular nudist, regular in my daily health, almost a father and a lover of boiled potatoes. Bando. Spelt as pronounced.

Mr. Graves said he would give it a trial.

The unfortunate thing about Bando, said Arthur, is that it is no longer to be obtained in this unfortunate country. I understand that inferior products, such as Ostreine and Spanish Flies, may still be wheedled out of some of the humaner chemists, up and down the city, in the ten minutes or a quarter of an hour immediately following their midday meal. But for Bando, even on a Saturday afternoon, you will grovel in vain. For the State, taking as usual the law into its own hands, and duly indifferent to the sufferings of thousands of men, and tens of thousands of women, all over the country, has seen fit to place an embargo on this admirable article, from which joy could stream, at a moderate cost, into homes, and other places of rendezvous, now desolate. It cannot enter our ports, nor cross our northern frontier, if not in the form of a casual, hazardous and surreptitious dribble, I mean piecemeal in ladies' underclothing, for example, or gentlemen's golfbags, or the hollow missal of a broad-minded priest, where on discovery it is immediately seized, and confiscated, by some gross customs official half crazed with seminal intoxication and sold, at ten and even fifteen times its advertised value, to exhausted commercial travellers on their way home after an unprofitable circuit. But I shall better illustrate what I mean if I tell you what happened to my old friend, Mr. Ernest Louit, who in the darkest hours of school and university never abandoned me, though often urged to do so, by his well-wishers and by mine. The title of his dissertation I well remember was *The Mathematical Intuitions of the Visicelts*, a subject on which he professed the strongest views, for he was a close companion of the College Bursar, their association (for it was nothing less) being founded on a community of tastes, and even I fear practices, all too common in academic circles, and of which perhaps the most endearing was brandy on awakening, which they did habitually in each other's society. Louit now solicited, through the College Bursar, and finally obtained, a further sum of fifty pounds, fondly calculated to defray the expenses of a six months' research expedition, in the County Clare. His analysis of this risible estimate was as follows:

	£	s.	d.
Travelling	1	15	0
Boots	0	15	0
Coloured Beads	5	0	0
Gratifications	0	10	0
Sustenance	42	0	0
Total	50	0	0

The food necessary for the maintenance of his dog, a bull-terrier, in the condition of ferocious plethora to which it was accustomed, he generously declared himself willing to pay for out of his own pocket, and he added, with his usual candour, and to the great merriment of the Grants Committee, that he thought he could rely on O'Connor to live on the country. To none of these items was any exception found, though the absence of others, usual in such cases, as for example that corresponding to accommodation for the night, caused no little surprise. Invited, through the College Bursar, to account for this omission, Louit replied, through the College Bursar, that being a person of great bodily fastidiousness it was his intention to pass his nights, as long as he remained in that part of the country, in the sweet-smelling hay, or the sweet-smelling straw, as the case might be, of the local barns. This explanation provoked further great hilarity among the members of the committee. And the frankness was admired by many with which Louit, on his return, confessed to having found, in the course of his excursion, three barns in all, of which two contained empty bottles and the third the skeleton of a goat. But in other quarters this and cognate statements were viewed in another and less friendly light. For Ernest, looking very pale and ill, returned to his rooms three weeks before he was due. Invited, through the College Bursar, to produce the boots for the purchase of which fifteen shillings had been allotted to him from the slender College funds, Louit replied, through the same channel, that in the late afternoon of November the twenty-first, in the vicinity of Handcross, they had unfortunately been sucked off his feet by a bog, which in the fading light, and the confusion of his senses consequent on prolonged inanition, he had mistaken for a field of late onions. To the hope then politely expressed that O'Connor had enjoyed his brief outing, Louit with grateful acknowledgement replied that he had been reluctantly obliged, on the same occasion, to hold O'Connor head downward in the morass, until his faithful heart had ceased to beat, and then roast him, in his skin, which he could not bring himself to remove, over a fire of flags and cotton-blossoms. He took no credit for this, O'Connor in his place would have done the same for him. The bones of his old pet, complete save for the medullas, were now in his rooms, in a sack, and might be inspected any afternoon, Sundays excepted, between the hours of two-forty-five and three-fifteen. The College Bursar now wondered, on behalf of the committee, if it would be convenient to Mr. Louit to give some account of the impetus imparted to his studies by his short stay in the country. Louit replied that he would have done so with great pleasure if he had not had the misfortune to mislay, on the very morning of his departure from the west, between the hours of eleven and midday, in the gentlemen's cloakroom of Ennis railway-station, the one hundred and five loose sheets closely covered on both sides with shorthand notes embracing the entire period in question. This represented, he added, an average of no less than five pages, or ten sides, per day. He was now exerting himself to the utmost, and indeed he feared greatly beyond his strength, with a view to recuperating his MS., which, qua MS., could not be of the smallest value to any person other than himself and, eventually, humanity. But it was his experience of railway-station cloakrooms, and in particular those exploited by the western lines, that anything left there at all resembling paper, with the exception perhaps of visiting-cards, postage stamps, betting-slips and perforated railway-tickets, was invariably swallowed up and lost, for ever. So in his efforts, greatly hampered by lack of strength, and absence of funds, to recover his property, his anticipations were of failure, rather than of success. And such a loss would be irreparable, for of the countless observations made during his tour, and of the meditations arising thence, hastily under the most adverse conditions committed to paper, he had to his great regret little or no remembrance. To the relation of these painful events, that is to say the loss of his boots, his dog, his labour, his money, his health and perhaps even the esteem of his academical superiors, Louit had nothing to add, if not that he looked forward to waiting on the committee, at their mutual convenience, with proof that his mission had not been altogether in vain. The day and hour having been appointed, Louit was seen advancing, leading by the hand an old man dressed in kilt, plaid, brogues and, in spite of the cold, a pair of silk socks made fast to the purple calves by an unpretentious pair of narrow mauve suspenders, and holding a large black felt hat under his arm. Louit said, This, gentlemen, is Mr. Thomas Nackybal, native of Burren. There he has spent all his life, thence he was loath to remove, thither he longs to return, to kill his pig, his solitary perennial companion. Mr. Nackybal is now in his seventy-sixth year, and has never, in all that time, received any instruction other than that treating of such agricultural themes, indispensable to the exercise of his profession, as the rock-potato, the clover-thatch, every man his own fertilizer, turf versus combustion and the fly-catching pig, with the result that he cannot, nor ever could, read or write, or, without the assistance of his fingers, and his toes, add, subtract, multiply or divide the smallest whole number to, from, by or into another. So much for the mental Nackybal. The physical —. Stay, Mr. Louit, said the President, holding up his hand. One moment, Mr.

Louit, if you please. A thousand, sir, if you wish, said Louit. On the dais they were five, Mr. O'Meldon, Mr. Magershon, Mr. Fitzwein, Mr. de Baker and Mr. MacStern, from left to right. They consulted together. Mr. Fitzwein said, Mr. Louit, you would not have us believe that this man's mental existence is exhausted by the bare knowledge, emerging from a complete innocence of the rudiments, of what is necessary for his survival. That, replied Louit, is the bold claim I make for my friend, in whose mind, save for the pale music of the innocence you mention, and, in some corner of the cerebellum, where all agricultural ideation has its seat, dumbly flickering, the knowledge of how to extract, from the ancestral half-acre of moraine, the maximum of nourishment, for himself and his pig, with the minimum of labour, all, I am convinced, is an ecstasy of darkness, and of silence. The committee, whose eyes had not left Louit while he spoke these words, transferred them now to Mr. Nackybal, as though the conversation were of his complexion. They then began to look at one another, and much time passed, before they succeeded in doing so. Not that they looked at one another long, no, they had more sense than that. But when five men look at one another, though in theory only twenty looks are necessary, every man looking four times, yet in practice this number is seldom sufficient, on account of the multitude of looks that go astray. For example, Mr. Fitzwein looks at Mr. Magershon, on his right. But Mr. Magershon is not looking at Mr. Fitzwein, on his left, but at Mr. O'Meldon, on his right. But Mr. O'Meldon is not looking at Mr. Magershon, on his left, but, craning forward, at Mr. MacStern, on his left but three at the far end of the table. But Mr. MacStern is not craning forward looking at Mr. O'Meldon, on his right but three at the far end of the table, but is sitting bolt upright looking at Mr. de Baker, on his right. But Mr. de

Baker is not looking at Mr. MacStern, on his left, but at Mr. Fitzwein, on his right. Then Mr. Fitzwein, tired of looking at the back of Mr. Magershon's head, cranes forward and looks at Mr. O'Meldon, on his right but one at the end of the table. But Mr. O'Meldon, tired of craning forward looking at Mr. MacStern, is now craning backward looking at Mr. de Baker, on his left but two. But Mr. de Baker, tired of looking at the back of Mr. Fitzwein's head, is now craning forward looking at Mr. Magershon, on his right but one. But Mr. Magershon, tired of the sight of Mr. O'Meldon's left ear, is now craning forward looking at Mr. MacStern, on his left but two at the end of the table. But Mr. MacStern, tired of looking at the back of Mr. de Baker's head, is now craning forward looking at Mr. Fitzwein, on his right but one. Then Mr. Fitzwein, tired of craning forward looking at Mr. O'Meldon, cranes forward in the other direction and looks at Mr. MacStern, on his left but one at the end of the table. But Mr. MacStern, tired of craning forward looking at Mr. Fitzwein, is now craning backward looking at Mr. Magershon, on his right but two. But Mr. Magershon, tired of craning backward looking at Mr. MacStern, is now craning forward looking at Mr. de Baker, on his left but one. But Mr. de Baker, tired of craning forward looking at Mr. Magershon, is now craning backward looking at Mr. O'Meldon, on his right but two at the end of the table. But Mr. O'Meldon, tired of craning backward looking at Mr. de Baker, is now craning forward looking at Mr. Fitzwein, on his left but one. Then Mr. Fitzwein, tired of craning forward looking at Mr. Mac-Stern's left ear, sits back and turning towards the only member of the committee whose eye he has not yet tried to catch, that is to say Mr. de Baker, is rewarded by a view of that gentleman's hairless sinciput, for Mr. de Baker, tired of craning backward looking at Mr. Magershon's left ear, and having turned in vain to all the members of the committee with the exception of his left-hand neighbour, has sat forward and is now looking down the dingy corollae of Mr. MacStern's right ear. For Mr. MacStern, sick and tired of Mr. Magershon's left ear, and having no other alternative, is now craning forward contemplating the disgusted, and indeed disgusting, right side of Mr. O'Meldon's face. For sure enough Mr. O'Meldon, having eliminated all his colleagues with the exception of his immediate neighbour, has sat back and is now considering the boils, the pimples and the blackheads of Mr. Magershon's nape. For Mr. Magershon, whom Mr. de Baker's left ear has ceased to interest, has sat back and is now benefiting, not indeed for the first time that afternoon, but with a new distinctness, by Mr. Fitzwein's lunch of kidney-beans. Thus of the five times four or twenty looks taken, no two have met, and all this craning forward and backward and looking to the right and to the left has led to nothing, and for all the progress made by the committee in this matter of looking at itself, its eyes might just as well have been closed, or turned towards heaven. Nor is this all. For now Mr. Fitzwein will very likely say, It is is a long time since I looked at Mr. Magershon, let me look at him again now, perhaps who knows he is looking at me. But Mr. Magershon, who it will be remembered has just been looking at Mr. Fitzwein, will certainly have turned his head round the other way, to look at Mr. O'Meldon, in the hope of finding Mr. O'Meldon looking at him, for it is a long time since Mr. Magershon looked at Mr. O'Meldon. But if it is a long time since Mr. Magershon looked at Mr. O'Meldon, it is not a long time since Mr. O'Meldon looked at Mr. Magershon, for he has just been doing so, has he not. And indeed he might be doing so still, for Treasurers' eyes do not readily fall, nor turn aside, were it not for a strange-smelling, at first not unpleasant, but with the passage of time frankly revolting vapour arising from among the recesses of Mr. Magershon's body-linen and issuing, with great volatility, between his nape and his collar-band, a bold and it must be allowed successful effort on the part of that dignitary's pneumo-gastric to compensate the momentary confusion of its superior connexions. So Mr. Magershon turns to Mr. O'Meldon, to find Mr. O'Meldon looking, not at him, as he had hoped (for if he had not hoped to find Mr. O'Meldon looking at him when he turned to look at Mr. O'Meldon, then he would not have turned to look at Mr. O'Meldon, but would have craned forward, or perhaps backward, to look at Mr. MacStern, or perhaps at Mr. de Baker, but more likely the former, as one less lately looked at than the latter), but at Mr. MacStern, in the hope of finding Mr. MacStern looking at him. And this is very natural, for more time has elapsed since Mr. O'Meldon's looking at Mr. MacStern than since Mr. O'Meldon's looking at any of the others, and Mr. O'Meldon cannot be expected to know that since Mr. MacStern's looking at him less time has elapsed than since Mr. MacStern's looking at any of the others, for Mr. MacStern has only just finished looking at Mr. O'Meldon, has he not. So Mr. O'Meldon finds Mr. MacStern looking, not at him, as he had hoped, but, in the hope of finding Mr. de Baker looking at him, at Mr. de Baker. But Mr. de Baker, for the same reason that Mr. Magershon is looking, not at Mr. Fitzwein, but at Mr. O'Meldon, and that Mr. O'Meldon is looking, not at Mr. Magershon, but at Mr. MacStern, and that Mr. MacStern is looking, not at Mr. O'Meldon, but at Mr. de Baker, is looking, not at Mr. MacStern, as Mr. MacStern had hoped (for if Mr. MacStern had not hoped to find Mr. de Baker looking at him, when he turned to look at Mr. de Baker, then he would not have turned to look at Mr. de Baker, no,

176

but would have craned forward, or perhaps backward, to have a look at Mr. Fitzwein, or perhaps at Mr. Magershon, but more probably the former, as one less lately looked at than the latter), but at Mr. Fitzwein, who is now benefiting by the posterior aspect of Mr. Magershon in very much the same way as but a moment before Mr. Magershon by his, and Mr. Θ'Meldon by Mr. Magershon's. And so on. Until of the five times eight or forty looks taken, not one has been reciprocated, and the committee, for all its twisting and turning, is no further advanced, in this matter of look- ing at itself, than at the now irrevocable moment of its setting out to do so. And this is not all. For many, many looks may still be taken, and much, much time still lost, ere every eye find the eye it seeks, and into every mind the energy flow, the comfort and the reassurance, necessary for a resumption of the business in hand. And all this comes of lack of method, which is all the less excusable in a com- mittee as committees, whether large or small, are more often under the necessity of looking at themselves than any other body of men, with the possible exception of commissions. Now perhaps one of the best methods, whereby a committee may rapidly look at itself, and all the fret and weariness, experienced by committees looking at themselves without method, be averted, is perhaps this, that numbers be given to the members of the committee, one, two, three, four, five, six, seven, and so on, as many numbers as there are members of the committee, so that every member of the committee has his number, and no member of the commit- tee is unnumbered, and that these numbers be carefully committed to memory by the members of the committee, until every member of the committee knows, with certain knowledge, not only his own number, but the numbers of all the other members of the committee, and that these numbers be allotted to the members of the committee at the moment of its formation, and maintained unchanged until the hour of its dissolution, for if at every successive meeting of the committee a new numeration were to be adopted, untold confusion would ensue (from the changed numeration) and unspeakable disorder. Then it will be found that every single member of the committee not only has his number, but is content with the number that he has, and willing to learn it off by heart, and not only it, but all the other numbers too, until every number calls at once into his mind a name, a face, a temperament, a function, and every face a number. Then, when the time comes for the committee to look at itself, let all the members but number one look together at number one, and let number one look at them all in turn, and then close, if he cares to, his eyes, for he has done his duty. Then of all those members but number one who have looked together at number one, and by number one been looked at one by one, let all but number two look at number two, and let number two in his turn look at them all in turn, and then remove, if his eyes are sore, his glasses, if he is in the habit of wearing glasses, and rest his eyes, for they are no longer required, for the moment. Then of all those members but number two, and of course number one, who have looked together at number two, and by number two been looked at one by one, let all with the exception of number three look together at number three, and let number three in his turn look at them all in turn, and then get up and go to the window and look out, if he feels like a little exercise and change of scene, for he is no longer needed, for the time being. Then of all those members of the committee with the exception of number three, and of course of numbers two and one, who have looked together at number three and by number three been looked at one by one, let all save number four look at number four, and let number four in his turn look at them one

178

after another, and then gently massage his eyeballs, if he feels the need to do so, for their immediate role is terminated. And so on, until only two members of the committee remain, whom then let at each other look, and then bathe their eyes, if they have their eyebaths with them, with a little laudanum, or weak boracic solution, or warm weak tea, for they have well deserved it. Then it will be found that the committee has looked at itself in the shortest possible time, and with the minimum number of looks, that is to say x squared minus x looks if there are x members of the committee, and y squared minus y if there are y. But slowly two by two the eyes put forth their curious beams again, first in the direction of Mr. Nackybal, and then in that of Louit, who thus emboldened continued, The physical you have before you, the feet are large and flat, and so continued, working slowly up, until he came to the head, of which, as of the rest, he said many things, some good, some fair, some very good, some poor and some excellent. Then Mr. Fitzwein said, But the man is in t—t—tolerable health? Can direct his steps unaided? Can sit down, sit, stand up, stand, eat, drink, go to bed, sleep, rise and attend to his duties, without assistance? Oh yes, sir, said Louit, and he can deject single-handed too. Well, well, said Mr. Fitzwein. He added, And his sexual life, talking of dejection? That of an impoverished bachelor of repulsive appearance, said Louit, no offence meant. I beg your pardon, said Mr. Mac-Stern. Hence the squint, said Louit. Well, said Mr. Fitzwein, it is always a pleasure for us, for me for one for my part, and for my colleagues for two for theirs, to meet a moron from a different crawl of life from our crawl, from my crawl and from their crawl. And to that extent I suppose we are obliged to you, Mr. Louit. But I do not think we grasp, I do not think that I grasp and I should be greatly surprised to learn that my collaborators grasp, what this

179

gentleman has to do with the object of your recent visit, Mr. Louit, your recent brief and, if you will allow me to say so, prodigal visit to the western seaboard. To this for all reply Louit reached with his right hand out and back for the left hand of Mr. Nackybal, whom he remembered having last seen seated, docilely and decently seated, a little to his right, and to his rear. If I tell you all this in such detail, Mr. Graves, the reason is, believe me, that I cannot, much as I should like, and for reasons that I shall not go into, for they are unknown to me, do otherwise. Details, Mr. Graves, details I detest, details I despise, as much as you, a gardener, do. When you sow your peas, when you sow your beans, when you sow your potatoes, when you sow your carrots, your turnips, your parsnips and other root vegetables, do you do so with punctilio? No, but rapidly you open a trench, a rough and ready line, not quite straight, nor yet quite crooked, or a series of holes, at intervals that do not offend, or offend only for a moment, while the holes are still open, your tired old eye, and let fall the seed, absent in mind, as the priest dust, or ashes, into the grave, and cover it with earth, with the edge of your boot in all proability, knowing that if the seed is to prosper and multiply, ten-fold, fifteen-fold, twenty-fold, twenty-five-fold, thirty-fold, thirty-five-fold, forty-fold, forty five-fold, and even fifty-fold, it will do so, and that if it is not, it will not. As a younger man, Mr. Graves, I have no doubt, you used a line, a measure, a plumb, a level, and placed your peas, your beans, your maize, your lentils, in groups of four, or five, or six, or seven, not four in one hole, and five in another, and six in a third, and seven in a fourth, no, but in every hole four, or five, or six, or seven, and your potatoes with the germs uppermost, and mixed your carrot and your turnip seed, your radish and your parsnip seed, with sand, or dust, or ashes, before committing it to the seedplot. Whereas now! And when did you cease, Mr. Graves, to use a line, a measure, a plumb, a level, and so to place and so to thin your seed, before sowing it? At what age, Mr. Graves, and under what circumstances? And did all go at once, Mr. Graves, by the board, the line, the measure, the plumb, the level, and who knows what other mechanical aids, and the way of placing, and the manner of mixing, or did the line go first, and then some time later the measure, and then some time later the plumb (though I confess I do not see the use of the plumb), and then some time later the level, and then some time later the punctilious placing, and then some time later the meticulous mixing? Or was it by twos and threes at a time, Mr. Graves, until you arrived, little by little, at your present freedom, when all you need is seed, earth, excrement, water and a stick? But neither Mr. Nackybal's left hand, nor his right, was free, for with the former he was supporting the weight of his bulk now acutely inclined, whilst with the latter, invisible beneath the kilt, he was scratching, gently but firmly, learnedly, through the worn but still heating material of his winter drawers, a diffuse ano-scrotal prurit (worms? nerves? piles? or worse?) of sixty-four years standing. The faint rasp could be heard of the heel of the hand coming and going, coming and going, and this, joined to the attitude of the rapt the suffering body, and to the expression, attentive, gloating, shocked, expectant, of the face, entirely misled the committee, so that it exclaimed, What vitality! At his age! The open-air life! The single life! Ego autem![1] (Mr. Mac Stern). But now Mr. Nackybal, having obtained a temporary relief, brought out, as he raised himself up, his right hand from under his skirt, and drew it, palm outwards, several times back and forth beneath his nose, a characteristic gesture. Then he

[1] A Latin expression meaning: I (Ego) also (autem).

resumed the pose, the decent pose, from which the sudden access of his old trouble had startled him, his hands on his knees, his old hairy mottled knotted hands on his bare old bony blue knees, the right old hairy mottled hand on the bony right bare old knee, and the left old knotted mottled hand on the left old blue old bony knee, and looking, as at some scene long familiar, or for some other reason devoid of interest, with listening lack-lustre eyes out of the window, at the sky supported here and there by a cupola, a dome, a roof, a spire, a tower, a tree-top. But now, the moment being come, Louit led Mr. Nackybal to the foot of the and there, looking him affectionately full in the more exactly full in the quarter-face, that is to say affectionately full in the ear, for the more Louit turn face, his full affectionate face, towards Mr. Nackybal, the more Mr. Nackybal turned his, his tired red old hairy face away, said, in slow loud solemn tones, Four hundred and eight thousand one hundred and eighty-four. Mr. Nackybal now, to the general surprise, transferred, from the sky, eyes, docile, stupid, liquid, staring eyes, towards Mr. Fitz-wein, who after a moment exclaimed, to the further general surprise, A gazelle! A sheep! An old sheep! Mr. de Baker, sir, said Louit, will you be so friendly now as to make a faithful note of what I say, and of what my friend here says, from now on? Why of course to be sure, Mr. Louit, said Mr. de Baker. I am greatly obliged to you, Mr. de Baker, said Louit. Tut tut, don't mention it, Mr. Louit, said Mr. de Baker. I may count on you then, Mr. de Baker, said Louit. To be sure you may, Mr. Louit, said Mr. de Baker. You are too kind, Mr. de Baker, said Louit. Foh, not at all, not at all, Mr. Louit, said Mr. de Baker. A goat! An old quinch! cried Mr. Fitzwein. You set my mind at rest, Mr. de Baker, said Louit. Not another word, Mr. Louit, said Mr. de Baker, not a word more. And relieve it at the same time

182

of a great load of anxiety, Mr. de Baker, said Louit. His eyes coil into my very soul, said Mr. Fitzwein. His very what?, said Mr. O'Meldon. His very soul, said Mr. Magershon. Bless me, what was that! exclaimed Mr. MacStern. What do you think it was? The angelus? said Mr. de Baker. Does one remark such things, among men of the world? said Mr. Magershon. At least it was frank, said Mr. O'Meldon. Then I may proceed without misgiving, Mr. de Baker, said Louit. You certainly may indeed as far as I personally am concerned, Mr. Louit, said Mr. de Baker. And wrap it round as with wet bands, said Mr. Fitzwein. God bless you, Mr. Baker, said Louit. And you, Mr. Louit, said Mr. de Ba... No no, you, Mr. de Baker, you, said Louit. Why by all means, Mr. Louit, me, if you insist, but you too, said Mr. de Baker. You mean God bless us both, Mr. de Baker? said Louit. Diable, said Mr. de Baker (the French extraction). His face is familiar, said Mr. Fitzwein. Tom! cried Louit. Mr. Nackybal turned his face towards the call, and saw that it was stamped with anxiety. Bah! said Louit, the decisive moment is at hand. Then, in a loud voice, he said, Three hundred and eighty-nine th—. To me, at all events, said Mr. Fitzwein. Three hundred and eighty-nine thousand, vociferated Louit, and seventeen. Eh? said Mr. Nackybal. Have you got that down, Mr. de Baker, said Louit. I have, Mr. Louit, said Mr. de Baker. Would you be good enough to repeat, Mr. de Baker, said Louit. Certainly, Mr. Louit. I repeat: Mr. Louit: Three hundred and eighty-nine thousand and seventy. Mr. Nack —. Three hundred and eighty-nine thousand and seven*teen*, said Louit, not and seven*ty*, and seven*teen*. Oh, I beg your pardon, Mr. Louit, I heard and seventy, said Mr. de Baker. I said and seven*teen*, Mr. de Baker, said Louit, as I thought distinctly. How extraordinary, I distinctly heard and seven*ty*, said Mr. de Baker. What did you hear, Mr.

MacStern? I heard and seven*teen*, with great distinctness, said Mr. MacStern. Oh you did, did you, said Mr. de Baker. The *n* is still ringing in my ears, said Mr. MacStern. And you, Mr. O'Meldon, said Mr. de Baker. And I what? said Mr. O'Meldon. Heard what, seven*teen* or seven*ty*? said Mr. de Baker. What did you hear, Mr. de Baker? said Mr. O'Meldon. And seven*ty*, said Mr. de Baker. And seven what? said Mr. O'Meldon. And seven*teeeee*, said Mr. de Baker. Naturally, said Mr. O'Meldon. Ha, said Mr. de Baker. I said and seventeen, said Louit. And seven what? said Mr. Magershon. And seven*teen*, said Louit. I thought so, said Mr. Magershon. But were not sure, said Mr. de Baker. Obviously, said Mr. Magershon. And you, Mr. President, said Mr. de Baker. Eh? said Mr. Fitzwein. I say, And you, Mr. President, said Mr. de Baker. I don't follow you, Mr. de Baker, said Mr. Fitzwein. Was it seven*teen* you heard, or seven*ty*? said Mr. de Baker. I heard forty-six, said Mr. Fitzwein. I said and seventeen, said Louit. We believe you, Mr. Louit, we believe you, said Mr. Magershon. Will you emend, Mr. de Baker, said Louit. Why of course with pleasure, Mr. Louit, said Mr. de Baker. Thank you very much, Mr. de Baker, said Louit. Not at all, not at all, Mr. Louit, said Mr. de Baker. How does it read now? said Louit. It reads now, said Mr. de Baker: Mr. Louit: Three hundred and eighty-nine thousand and seventeen. Mr. Nackybal: Eh? Has he your leave to sit down? said Louit. Has who our leave to sit down? said Mr. Magershon. He is tired standing, said Louit. Where have I seen that face before, said Mr. Fitzwein. How long will this go on? said Mr. MacStern. Is that all? said Mr. Magershon. He hears better seated, said Louit. Let him lie down, if he wishes, said Mr. Fitzwein. Louit helped Mr. Nackybal to lie down and knelt down beside him. Tom, can you hear me? he cried. Yes, sir, said Mr. Nackybal. Three hundred and eighty-nine thousand and seventeen, cried Louit. One moment while I get that down, said Mr. de Baker. A moment passed. Proceed, said Mr. de Baker. Reply, cried Louit. Sivinty-thray, said Mr. Nackybal. Sivinty-thray? said Mr. de Baker. Perhaps he means seventy-three, said Mr. O'Meldon. Does he mean seventy-three? said Mr. Fitzwein. He said seventy-three, said Louit. Did he indeed, said Mr. de Baker. My God, said Mr. MacStern. His what? said Mr. O'Meldon. His God, said Mr. Magershon. Would you be good enough to read out what you have got, Mr. de Baker, said Louit. What I have got? said Mr. de Baker. What you have got down in your book, to make sure it is correct, said Louit. Yours is not a trusting nature, Mr. Louit, said Mr. de Baker. So much depends on the accuracy of the record, said Louit. He is right, said Mr. MacStern. Where shall I begin? said Mr. de Baker. Just my words and my friend's, said Louit. The rest doesn't interest you, said Mr. de Baker. No, said Louit. Mr. de Baker said, Looking back over my notes, I find what follows: Mr. Louit: Tom, can you hear me? Mr. Nackybal: Yes, sir. Mr. Louit: Three hundred and eighty-nine thousand and seventy. Mr. Nack—. And seven*teen*, said Louit. Really, Mr. de Baker, said Mr. Fitzwein. How often have you to be told? said Mr. O'Meldon. Think of sweet seventeen, said Mr. Magershon. Ha ha, very good, said Mr. de Baker. Mr. Magershon said, Would it not perhaps be preferable, with such exceptionally large and involved figures—er—at stake, if our Treasurer would consent to take over the record, just for today? I do not intend any disparagement of our Record Secretary, who as we all know is a superb Record Secretary, but perhaps with such unprecedentedly high and complicated figures involved, just for one afternoon—. No no, that would never do, said Mr. Fitzwein. Mr. MacStern said, Perhaps if our Record Secretary would be so good as to transcribe the figures, not in figures, but in words—. Yes yes, how would that be? said Mr. Fitzwein. What difference would that make? said Mr. O'Meldon. Mr. MacStern replied, Why then he would simply write down the words that he hears, instead of their ciphered equivalents, which requires long practice, especially in the case of numbers of five and six letters, I beg your pardon, I mean figures. Perhaps after all that is an excellent idea, said Mr. Magershon. Would you be good enough to do that, Mr. de Baker, do you think? said Mr. Fitzwein. But it is my invariable habit, said Mr. de Baker. No no, I believe you, said Mr. Fitzwein. Then one does not see what is to be done, said Mr. Magershon. The best of us may make a slip, said Louit. Thank you, Mr. Louit, said Mr. de Baker. Pray do not mention it, Mr. de Baker, said Louit. Wonderful most wonderful, exclaimed Mr. O'Meldon. What is wonderful most wonderful? said Mr. MacStern. The two figures are related, said Mr. O'Meldon, as the cute to its roob. The cute to its what? said Mr. Fitzwein. He means the cube to its root, said Mr. MacStern. What did I say? said Mr. O'Meldon. The cute to its roob, ha ha, said Mr. de Baker. What does that mean, the cube to its root? said Mr. Fitzwein. It means nothing, said Mr. MacStern. What do you mean, it means nothing? said Mr. O'Meldon. Mr. MacStern replied, To its which root? A cube may have any number of roots. Like the long Turkey cucumber, said Mr. Fitzwein. Not all cubes, said Mr. O'Meldon. Who spoke of all cubes? said Mr. MacStern. Not this cube, said Mr. O'Meldon. I know nothing of that, said Mr. MacStern. I am completely in the dark, said Mr. Fitzwein. I too, said Mr. Magershon. What is wonderful most wonderful? said Mr. Fitzwein. Mr. O'Meldon replied, That Mr. Ballynack—. Mr. Nackybal, said Louit. Mr. O'Meldon said, That Mr. Nackybal, in his head, in the short space of thirty-five or forty seconds, should have elicited the cube root of a number of six figures. Mr. MacStern said, Forty seconds! At least five minutes have elapsed since the figure was first mentioned. What is wonderful about that? said Mr. Fitzwein. Perhaps our President has forgotten, said Mr. MacStern. Two is the cube root of eight, said Mr. O'Meldon. Indeed, said Mr. Fitzwein. Yes, twice two is four and twice four is eight, said Mr. O'Meldon. So two is the cube root of eight, said Mr. Fitzwein. Yes, and eight is the cube of two, said Mr. O'Meldon. Eight is the cube of two, said Mr. Fitzwein. Yes, said Mr. O'Meldon. What is there so wonderful about that? said Mr. Fitzwein. Mr. O'Meldon replied, That two should be the cube root of eight, and eight the cube of two, has long ceased to be a matter for surprise. What is surprising is this, that Mr. Nallyback, in his head, in so short a time, should have elicited the cube root of a number of six figures. Oh, said Mr. Fitzwein. Is it then so difficult? said Mr. Magershon. Impossible, said Mr. MacStern. Well well, said Mr. Fitzwein. A feat never yet achieved by man, and only once by a horse, said Mr. O'Meldon. A horse! exclaimed Mr. Fitzwein. An episode in the Kulturkampf, said Mr. O'Meldon. Oh, I see, said Mr. Fitzwein. Louit did not conceal his satisfaction. Mr. Nackybal lay on his side, apparently asleep. But Mr. Nackynack is not a horse, said Mr. Fitzwein. Far from it, said Mr. O'Meldon. You are sure of what you advance? said Mr. Magershon. No, said Mr. O'Meldon. There is something fishy here, said Mr. MacStern. Not horsey, fishy, ha ha, very good, said Mr. de Baker. I protest, said Louit. Against what? said Mr. Fitzwein. Against the word fishy, said Louit. Make a note of that, Mr. de Baker, said Mr. Fitzwein. Louit took a sheet of paper from his pocket, and handed it to Mr. O'Meldon. Why, what in the world is this, Mr. Louit? said Mr. O'Meldon. A list of perfect cubes, said Louit, of six figures and under, ninety-nine in all, with their corresponding cubic roots. What do you want me to do with this, Mr. Louit? said Mr. O'Meldon. Examine my friend, said Louit. Oh, said Mr. Fitzwein. In my absence, since you question our good faith, said Louit. Tut tut, Mr. Louit, said Mr. Magershon. Strip him naked, bandage his eyes, send me away, said Louit. You forget telepathy, or the transference of thought, said Mr. MacStern. Louit said, Cover the cubes when you ask for the cubes of the roots, cover the roots when you ask for the roots of the cubes. What difference will that make? said Mr. O'Meldon. You won't know the answers before him, said Louit. Mr. Fitzwein left the room, followed by his assistants. Louit roused Mr. Nackybal and helped him to rise. Mr. O'Meldon came back, Louit's paper in his hand. I may keep this, Mr. Louit, he said. Certainly, said Louit. Thank you, Mr. Louit, said Mr. O'Meldon. Not at all, Mr. O'Meldon, said Louit. Good evening to you both, said Mr. O'Meldon. Louit said, Good evening, Mr. O'Meldon. Say good evening nicely to Mr. O'Meldon, Tom, say, Good evening, Mr. O'Meldon. Ning, said Mr. Nackybal. Charming, charming, said Mr. O'Meldon. Mr. O'Meldon left the room. Louit and Mr. Nackybal, arm in arm, followed soon after. Soon the room, empty now, was grey with shadows of the evening. A porter came, turned on the lights, straightened the chairs, saw that all was well and went away. Then the vast room was dark, for night had fallen, again. Well, Mr. Graves, the next day, believe it or not, at the same hour, in the same place, in the immense and lofty hall flooded now with light, the same persons assembled and Mr. Nackybal was thoroughly examined, both in cubing and extracting, from the table that Louit had provided. The precautions recommended by Louit were adopted, except that Louit was not sent out of the room, but posted with his back to it before the open window, and that Mr. Nackybal was permitted to retain many of his underclothes. From this severe trial Mr. Nackybal emerged with distinction, having in his cubing made only twenty-five slight mistakes out of the forty-six cubes demanded, and in his rooting, out of the fifty-three extractions propounded, committed a mere matter of four trifling errors. The interval between question and response, sometimes brief, sometimes as long as one minute, averaged, according to Mr. O'Meldon, who had come with his stop-watch, anything from thirty-four to thirty-five seconds. Once Mr. Nackybal did not answer at all. This was an occasion of some unpleasantness. Mr. O'Meldon, his eyes on the sheet, announced, Five hundred and nineteen thousand three hundred and thirteen. A minute passed, a minute and a quarter, a minute and a half, a minute and three-quarters, two minutes, two minutes and a quarter, two minutes and a half, two minutes and three-quarters, three minutes, three minutes and a quarter, three minutes and a half, three minutes and three-quarters, and still Mr. Nackybal did not reply! Come come, sir, said Mr. O'Meldon, with acerbity, five hundred and nineteen thousand three hundred and thirteen. Still Mr. Nackybal did not reply! Either he knows or he doesn't, said Mr. Magershon. Here Mr. de Baker laughed till the tears ran down his cheeks. Mr. Fitzwein said, If you don't hear, say you don't hear. If you don't know, say you don't know. Don't keep us waiting here all night. Louit turned round and said, Is the number on the list? Silence, Mr. Louit, said Mr. Fitzwein. Is the number on the list? thundered Louit, taking a stride forward, and white, under his green, with indignation. I accuse the Treasurer, he said, pointing his finger at that gentleman, as though there were two, or three or four, or five, or even six treasurers in the room, instead of only one, of calling out a number that is not on the list and has no more a cube root than my arse. Mr. Louit! cried

Mr. Fitzwein. His what? said Mr. O'Meldon. His arse, said Mr. Magershon. I accuse him, said Louit, of attempting, with deliberate and premeditated malevolence, to bait and bewilder an old man who is doing his best, out of friendship to me, to—to—who is doing his best. Annoyed by this feeble conclusion, Louit added, I call that the act of a —, —, —, —, —, —, —, —, —, —, and here followed a flow of language so gross that a less sweet-tempered man than Mr. O'Meldon would certainly have been offended, it was so gross and fluent. But Mr. O'Meldon's temper was of such sweetness, that when Mr. Fitzwein rose, and with indignant words began to close the session, Mr. O'Meldon rose and calmed Mr. Fitzwein, explaining how it was that he and no other was to blame, who had taken a nought for a one, and not, as he ought, for a nought. But you did not do this on p—p—purpose, with malice prepense, said Mr. Fitzwein. Then there was a silence until Mr. O'Meldon, hanging his head, and swinging it slowly to and fro, and shifting his weight from one foot to the other, replied, Oh, no no no no no, as heaven is my witness, I did not. In that case I must ask Mr. Lingard to make you an apology, said Mr. Fitzwein. Oh no no no no no, no apologies, cried Mr. O'Meldon. Mr. Lingard? said Mr. Magershon. I said Mr. Lingard? said Mr. Fitzwein. Certainly you did, said Mr. Magershon. What can I have been thinking of, said Mr. Fitzwein. My mother was a Miss Lingard, said Mr. MacStern. Ah to be sure, I remember, a charming woman, said Mr. Fitzwein. She died in giving me birth, said Mr. MacStern. I can well believe that, said Mr. de Baker. Charming, charming woman, said Mr. Fitzwein. When the demonstration was over, then it was question-time. Through the western windows of the vast hall shone the low red winter sun, stirring the air, the chambered air, with its angry farewell shining, whilst via the opposite or oriental apertures or lights the murmur rose, appeasing, of the myriad faint clarions of night. It was question-time. Mr. Fitzwein said, And can he square and square-root too? Mr. O'Meldon said, If he can cube he can square, if he can cube-root he can square-root. My question was aimed at Mr. Louit, said Mr. Fitzwein. Cubing and squaring is not the point, said Louit. How is that? said Mr. Fitzwein. Louit replied, A visualizer can cube and square in his head, seeing the figures come and go. You stand by the extirpation of the root? said Mr. Fitzwein. Of the cube root, said Louit. Not of the square root? said Mr. Fitzwein. No, said Louit, How is that? said Mr. Fitzwein. A visualizer can extract the square root in his head, said Louit, as with a paper and a sheet of pencil. But not the cube root? said Mr. Fitzwein. Louit said nothing, for what could he have said? And the fourth root? said Mr. O'Meldon. The square root of the square root, said Louit. And the fifth root? said Mr. Fitzwein. Did he rise on the second day? said Louit. And the sixth root? said Mr. de Baker. The square root of the cube root, or the cube root of the square root, said Louit. And the seventh root? said Mr. MacStern. Dance on the waters? said Louit. And the eighth root? said Mr. O'Meldon. The square root of the square root of the square root, said Louit. It was question-time. Rose and gloom, farewell and hail, mingled, clashed, vanquished, victor, victor, vanquished, in the vast indifferent chamber. And the ninth root? said Mr. Fitzwein. The cube root of the cube root, said Louit. And the tenth root? said Mr. de Baker. Involves the fifth, said Louit. And the eleventh root? said Mr. MacStern. Into whiskey? said Louit. And the twelfth root? said Mr. O'Meldon. The square root of the square root of the cube root, or the cube root of the square root of the square root, or the square root of the cube root of the square root, said Louit. And the thirteenth root? said Mr. Fitzwein. Enough! cried Mr. Magershon.

I beg your pardon? said Mr. Fitzwein. Enough, said Mr. Magershon. Who are you to say enough? said Mr. Fitzwein. Gentlemen, gentlemen, said Mr. MacStern. Mr. Louit, said Mr. O'Meldon. Sir, said Louit. In the two columns of figures before me, this afternoon, said Mr. O'Meldon, the one, or column of roots, has no number of more than two digits, and the other, or column of cubes, none of more than six. Column of cubes! cried Mr. MacStern. What is the matter now? said Mr. Fitzwein. How beautiful, said Mr. MacStern. That is so, Mr. Louit, is it not? said Mr. O'Meldon. I have no ear for music, said Louit. I do not refer to that, said Mr. O'Meldon. To what might you refer? said Mr. Fitzwein. I refer, said Mr. O'Meldon, on the one hand to the absence, in the one column, or column of roots, of any number of more than two digits, and on the other, in the other column, or column of cubes, to the absence of any number of more than six digits. That is so, Mr. Louit, is it not? You have the list before you, said Louit, Column of roots is very pretty too, I think, said Mr. de Baker. Yes, but not so pretty as column of cubes, said Mr. MacStern. Well, perhaps not quite, but very nearly, said Mr. de Baker. Mr. de Baker sang

> *Said the column of cubes to the column of roots,*
> *Oh what will you have to drink?*
> *Said the column of cubes to the column of roots,*
> *Oh what will you have to drink?*
> *Said the column of cubes to the column of roots,*
> *Oh what will you have to drink?*
> *Why, thank you, sir, said the column of roots,*
> *I'll have a bottle of ink.*

Hahahaha, haha, ha, hum, said Mr. de Baker. Any more questions, before I go home to bed, said Mr. Fitzwein. I was raising a point, said Mr. O'Meldon, when I was interrupted. Perhaps he could go on from where he left off, said Mr. Magershon. The point I was raising, said Mr. O'Meldon, when I was interrupted, is this, that of the two columns of figures here before me this afternoon, the one, or—. He has said this twice already, said Mr. MacStern. If not three times, said Mr. de Baker. Go on from where you left off, said Mr. Magershon, not from where you began. Or are you like Darwin's caterpillar? Darwin's what? said Mr. de Baker. Darwin's caterpillar? said Mr. Magershon. What was the matter with him? said Mr. MacStern. The matter with him was this, said Mr. Magershon, that when he was disturbed in the building of his hammock—. Are we here to discuss caterpillars? said Mr. O'Meldon. Raise your point for the love of God, said Mr. Fitzwein, and let me get home to my wife. He added, And children. The point I was in the act of raising, said Mr. O'Meldon, when I was so rudely interrupted, was this, that if in the left-hand column, or column of roots, instead of there being figures of two digits at the most, there were figures of three digits, and even four digits, to go no further, then in the right-hand column, or column of cubes, instead of there being figures of six digits at the most, there would be figures of seven, eight, nine, ten, eleven and even twelve digits. A silence followed these words. Would there not, Mr. Louit, said Mr. O'Meldon. Very likely, said Louit. Then why, said Mr. Meldon, leaning forward and bringing down his fist with a thump on the table, why are there not? Are there not what? said Mr. Fitzwein. What I have just said, said Mr. O'Meldon. What was that? said Mr. Fitzwein. Mr. O'Meldon replied, On the one hand, in the one column—. Or column of roots, said Mr. de Baker. Mr. O'Meldon continued, Figures of three digits and even four—. To go no further, said Mr. MacStern. Mr. O'Meldon continued,

And on the other, in the other—. Or column of cubes, said Mr. Magershon. Mr. O'Meldon continued, Figures of seven—. Of eight, said Mr. de Baker. Of nine, said Mr. MacStern. Of ten, said Mr. Magershon. Of eleven, said Mr. de Baker. And even of twelve, said Mr. MacStern. Digits, said Mr. Magershon. Why should there be? said Mr. Fitzwein. Little by little the bird, said Louit. Am I then to suppose, Mr. Louit, said Mr. O'Meldon, that if I were to ask this fellow for the cube root of say—he bent over his paper—let us say nine hundred and seventy-three million two hundred and fifty-two thousand two hundred and seventy-one, he could not supply it? Not this evening, said Louit. Or, said Mr. O'Meldon, reading again from his paper, nine hundred and ninety-eight billion seven hundred million one hundred and twenty-nine thousand nine hundred and ninety-nine, for example? Not just now, some other time, said Louit. Ha, said Mr. O'Meldon. Is your point now raised, Mr. O'Meldon, said Mr. Fitzwein. It is, said Mr. O'Meldon. I am glad to hear that, said Mr. Fitzwein. You will tell us about it later, said Mr. Magershon. Where have I seen that face before, said Mr. Fitzwein. Just one more thing, said Mr. MacStern. The sun has now sunk, in the west, said Mr. de Baker, turning his head, and extending his arm, in that direction. Then the others turned too, and looked long, at the place where the sun had been, but a moment before. But Mr. de Baker whirled round and pointed in the opposite direction, saying, While in the orient night is falling fast. Then the others to those shimmering windows turned them round, to the sky dark grey below, and lighter grey above. For the night seemed less to fall, than to rise, from below, like another day. But finally as from the filling grave, or with the loved one disappearing conveyance, mark well my words, Mr. Graves, with the loved one disappearing conveyance, slowly their sighing bodies they tore away, and Mr. Fitzwein began briskly to gather up his papers, for in that ending light he had found the place, the ancient place, where he had seen that face before, and so he rose and rapidly left the hall (as though he could have rapidly left the hall without rising), followed more leisurely by his assistants, in this order, first Mr. O'Meldon, and then Mr. MacStern, and then Mr. de Baker, and then Mr. Magershon, as chance would have it, or some other force. And then Mr. O'Meldon, pausing on his way to shake Louit by the hand, and pat Mr. Nackybal on the head, with a quick pat that he wiped off at once discreetly on his trousers, was overtaken and left behind, first by Mr. MacStern, and then by Mr. de Baker, and then by Mr. Magershon. And then Mr. MacStern, halting to formulate that one more thing, was overtaken and left behind, first by Mr. de Baker, and then by Mr. Magershon. And then Mr. de Baker, kneeling to secure his lace, which had come undone, as laces will, was passed by Mr. Magershon, who swept on slowly alone, like something out of Poe, towards the door, and would indeed have reached it, and passed through it, had not a sudden thought stiffened him in his stride, so that he stood, two feet between the foot-following feet, on left sole and right toe, in the uncertain equilibrium of erect consternation. And now the order was reversed in which, following Mr. Fitzwein, now in the eleven tram, they had set out, so that the first was last, and the last first, and the second third, and the third second, and that which had been, in order of march, Mr. O'Meldon, Mr. MacStern, Mr. de Baker and Mr. Magershon, was now, brooding, kneeling, brooding, greeting, Mr. Magershon, Mr. de Baker, Mr. MacStern and Mr. O'Meldon. But hardly had Mr. O'Meldon, ceasing to greet, moved on towards Mr. MacStern, when Mr. MacStern, ceasing to brood, moved on, accompanied by Mr. O'Meldon, towards Mr.

de Baker. But hardly had Mr. O'Meldon and Mr. Mac-
Stern, ceasing, first Mr. O'Meldon, then Mr. MacStern,
the first to greet, the second to brood, moved on together
towards Mr. de Baker, when Mr. de Baker, ceasing to
kneel, moved on, accompanied by Mr. Meldon and Mr.
MacStern, towards Mr. Magershon. But hardly had Mr.
O'Meldon and Mr. MacStern and Mr. de Baker, ceasing,
first Mr. O'Meldon, then Mr. MacStern, then Mr. de
Baker, the first to greet, the second to brood, the third to
kneel, moved on together towards Mr. Magershon, when
Mr Magershon, ceasing to brood, moved on, accompanied
by Mr. O'Meldon and Mr. MacStern and Mr. de Baker
towards the door. And so through the door, after the customary coagulation, the holding back, the thrust resisting,
the sideways stepping, the onward urging, and the little
landing along, and down the noble stairs, and out into the
court now rife with night, one by one they passed, Mr.
MacStern, Mr. O'Meldon, Mr. Magershon, and Mr. de
Baker, in that order, as chance would have it, or some
other agency. So that who was first first and second last
now was second, and who was first second and second third
now was first, and who was first third and second second
now was last, and who was first last and second first now
was third. And soon after Mr. Nackybal put on his outer
clothes and went away. And soon after Louit went away.
And Louit, going down the stairs, met the bitter stout
porter Power coming up. And as they passed the porter
raised his cap and Louit smiled. And they did well. For had
not Louit smiled, then Power had not raised his cap, and
had not Power raised his cap, then Louit had not smiled,
but they had passed, each on his way, Louit down, Power
up, the one unsmiling, and the other covered. Now the next
day—.

But here Arthur seemed to tire, of his story, for he left

196

Mr. Graves, and went back, into the house. Watt was thankful for this, for he too was tired, of Arthur's story, to which he had listened with the closest attention. And he could truly say, as he did, in after times, that of all the things he ever saw or heard, during his stay in Mr. Knott's establishment, he heard none so well, saw none so clear, as Arthur and Mr. Graves that sunny afternoon, on the lawn, and Louit, and Mr. Nackybal, and Mr. O'Meldon, and Mr. Magershon, and Mr. Fitzwein, and Mr. de Baker, and Mr. MacStern, and all the things they did, and the words they said. He understood it all too, very well, though he could not vouch for the accuracy of the figures, which he had not taken the trouble to check, having no head for figures. And if the words were not the exact words employed by Arthur, by Louit, by Mr. Nackybal and the others, they were not far out. He enjoyed this incident too, at the time, more than he had enjoyed anything for a long time, or would enjoy anything again, for a considerable time. But it tired him, in the end, and he was glad when Arthur left off, and went away. Then Watt climbed down, from off his mound, thinking how nice it would be to go back into the cool house gloom, and drink a glass of milk. But he did not care to leave Mr. Knott all alone in the garden, though there was really no reason why he should not. Then he saw the branches of a tree in agitation, and Mr. Knott climbing down among them, from branch it almost seemed to branch, lower and lower, until he reached the ground. Then Mr. Knott turned towards the house, and Watt followed after, very pleased with the afternoon he had spent, on his mound, and looking forward to the nice glass of cold milk that he would drink, in the cool, in the gloom, in a moment. And Mr. Graves remained alone, leaning on his fork, all alone, while the shadows lengthened.

Watt learned later, from Arthur, that the telling of this

story, while it lasted, before Arthur grew tired, had transported Arthur far from Mr. Knott's premises, of which, of the mysteries of which, of the fixity of which, Arthur had sometimes more, than he could bear.

Arthur was a very nice open fellow, not at all like Erskine.

In another place, he said, from another place, he might have told this story to its end, told the true identity of Mr. Nackybal (his real name was Tisler and he lived in a room on the canal), told his method of cube-rooting in his head (he merely knew by heart the cubes of one to nine, and even this was not indispensable, and that one gives one, and two eight, and three seven, and four four, and five five, and six six, and seven three, and eight two, and nine nine, and of course nought nought), and told the delinquencies of Louit, his fall and subsequent ascension, running Bando.

But on Mr. Knott's premises, from Mr. Knott's premises, this was not possible, for Arthur.

For what stopped Arthur, and made him go silent, in the middle of his story, was not really fatigue with his story, for he was not really fatigued, but the desire to return, to leave Louit and return, to Mr. Knott's house, to its mysteries, to its fixity. For he had been absent longer from them, than he could bear.

But perhaps in another place, from another place, Arthur would never have begun this story.

For there was no other place, but only there where Mr. Knott was, whose mysteries, whose fixity, whose fixity of mystery, so thrust forth, with such a thrust.

But if he had begun, in some other place, from some other place, to tell this story, then he would very likely have told it to the end.

For there was no place, but only there where Mr. Knott

was, whose peculiar properties, having first thrust forth, with such a thrust, called back so soon, with such a call.

Watt sympathized with this predicament. Had not he himself, in the beginning, resorted to similar shifts?

Was he finished with them now? Well, almost.

Fixity was not the word he would have chosen.

Watt had little to say on the subject of the second or closing period of his stay in Mr. Knott's house.

In the course of the second or closing period of Watt's stay in Mr. Knott's house, the information acquired by Watt, on that subject, was scant.

Of the nature of Mr. Knott himself Watt remained in particular ignorance.

Of the many excellent reasons for this, two seemed to Watt to merit mention: on the one hand the exiguity of the material propounded to his senses, and on the other the decay of these. What little there was to see, to hear, to smell, to taste, to touch, like a man in a stupor he saw it, heard it, smelt it, tasted it, touched it.

In empty hush, in airless gloom, Mr. Knott abode, in the large room set aside for his exclusive enjoyment, and that of his attendant. And from it this ambience followed him forth, and when he moved, in the house, in the garden, with him moved, dimming all, dulling all, stilling all, numbing all, where he passed.

The clothes that Mr. Knott wore, in his room, about the house, amid his garden, were very various, very very various. Now heavy, now light; now smart, now dowdy; now sober, now gaudy; now decent, now daring (his skirt-less bathing-costume, for example). Often too he wore, by his fireside, or as he mooched about the rooms, the stairs, the passage-ways of his home, a hat, or a cap, or, imprison-ing his rare his wanton hair, a net. And as often his head was bare.

As for his feet, sometimes he wore on each a sock, or on the one a sock and on the other a stocking, or a boot, or a shoe, or a slipper, or a sock and boot, or a sock and shoe, or a sock and slipper, or a stocking and boot, or a stocking and shoe, or a stocking and slipper, or nothing at all. And sometimes he wore on each a stocking, or on the one a stocking and on the other a boot, or a shoe, or a slipper, or a sock and boot, or a sock and shoe, or a sock and slipper, or a stocking and boot, or a stocking and shoe, or a stocking and slipper, or nothing at all. And sometimes he wore on each a boot, or on the one a boot and on the other a shoe, or a slipper, or a sock and boot, or a sock and shoe, or a sock and slipper, or a stocking and boot, or a stocking and shoe, or a stocking and slipper, or nothing at all. And sometimes he wore on each a shoe, or on the one a shoe and on the other a slipper, or a sock and boot, or a sock and shoe, or a sock and slipper, or a stocking and boot, or a stocking and shoe, or a stocking and slipper, or nothing at all. And sometimes he wore on each a slipper, or on the one a slipper and on the other a sock and boot, or a sock and shoe, or a sock and slipper, or a stocking and boot, or a stocking and shoe, or a stocking and slipper, or nothing at all. And sometimes he wore on each a sock and boot, or on the one a sock and boot and on the other a sock and shoe, or a sock and slipper, or a stocking and boot, or a stocking and shoe, or a stocking and slipper, or nothing at all. And sometimes he wore on each a sock and shoe, or on the one a sock and shoe and on the other a sock and slipper, or a stocking and boot, or a stocking and shoe, or a stocking and slipper, or nothing at all. And sometimes he wore on each a sock and slipper, or on the one a sock and slipper and on the other a stocking and boot, or a stocking and shoe, or a stocking and slipper, or nothing at all. And sometimes he wore on each a stocking and boot, or on the one a stocking and boot and on the other a stocking and shoe, or a stocking and slipper, or nothing at all. And sometimes he wore on each a stocking and shoe, or on the one a stocking and shoe and on the other a stocking and slipper, or nothing at all. And sometimes he wore on each a stocking and slipper, or on the one a stocking and slipper and on the other nothing at all. And sometimes he went barefoot.

To think, when one is no longer young, when one is not yet old, that one is no longer young, that one is not yet old, that is perhaps something. To pause, towards the close of one's three-hour day, and consider: the darkening ease, the brightening trouble; the pleasure pleasure because it was, the pain pain because it shall be; the glad acts grown proud, the proud acts growing stubborn; the panting the trembling towards a being gone, a being to come; and the true true no longer, and the false true not yet. And to decide not to smile after all, sitting in the shade, hearing the cicadas, wishing it were night, wishing it were morning, saying, No, it is not the heart, no, it is not the liver, no, it is not the prostate, no it is not the ovaries, no, it is muscular, it is nervous. Then the gnashing ends, or it goes on, and one is in the pit, in the hollow, the longing for longing gone, the horror of horror, and one is in the hollow, at the foot of all the hills at last, the ways down, the ways up, and free, free at last, for an instant free at last, nothing at last.

But whatever he put on, in the beginning, for by midnight he was always in his nightshirt, whatever he put on then, on his head, on his body, on his feet, he did not touch again, but kept on all the day, in his room, in his house, in his grounds, until the time came to put on his nightshirt, once again. Yes, not one button would he touch, to button or unbutton it, except those that nature obliged him to, and these he habitually left unbuttoned, from the moment of his putting on his clothes, and adjusting them to his satisfaction, to the moment of his taking them off, once more. So that he was not seldom to be seen, in his room, in his house, in his grounds, in strange and unseasonable costume, as though he were unaware of the weather, or of the time of year. And to see him sometimes thus, barefoot and for boating dressed, in the snow, in the slush, in the icy winter wind, or, when summer came again, by his fire, charged with furs, was to wonder, Does he seek to know again, what is cold, what is heat? But this was an anthropomorphic insolence of short duration.

For except, one, not to need, and, two, a witness to his not needing, Knott needed nothing, as far as Watt could see.

If he ate, and he ate well; if he drank, and he drank heartily; if he slept, and he slept sound; if he did other things, and he did other things regularly, it was not from need of food, or drink, or sleep, or other things, no, but from the need never to need, never never to need, food, and drink, and sleep, and other things.

This was Watt's first surmise of any interest on the subject of Mr. Knott.

And Mr. Knott, needing nothing if not, one, not to need, and, two, a witness to his not needing, of himself knew nothing. And so he needed to be witnessed. Not that he might know, no, but that he might not cease.

This, on the subject of Mr. Knott, was Watt's second, and closing, conjecture not entirely gratuitous.

Halting, faint with dubiety, from Watt's lips they fell.

His habitual tone was one of assurance.

But what kind of witness was Watt, weak now of eye, hard of hearing, and with even the more intimate senses greatly below par?

A needy witness, an imperfect witness.

The better to witness, the worse to witness.

That with his need he might witness its absence.

That imperfect he might witness it ill.

That Mr. Knott might never cease, but ever almost cease.

Such appeared to be the arrangement.

When Mr. Knott moved about the house he did so as one unfamiliar with the premises, fumbling at doors immemorially locked, kneeling rapt on window-seats, stumbling in the dark, seeking high and low the water-closet, pausing irresolute at the foot of the stairs, pausing irresolute at the head of the stairs.

When Mr. Knott moved in the midst of his garden, he did so as one unacquainted with its beauties, looking at the trees, looking at the flowers, looking at the bushes, looking at the vegetables, as though they, or he, had been created in the course of the night.

But it was in his room, though he sometimes offered to leave it by the hanging-cupboard, that Mr. Knott seemed least a stranger, and appeared to best advantage.

Here he stood. Here he sat. Here he knelt. Here he lay. Here he moved, to and fro, from the door to the window, from the window to the door; from the window to the door, from the door to the window; from the fire to the bed, from the bed to the fire; from the bed to the fire, from the fire to the bed; from the door to the fire, from the fire to the door; from the fire to the door, from the door to the fire; from the window to the bed, from the bed to the window; from the bed to the window, from the window to the bed; from the fire to the window, from the window to the fire; from the window to the fire, from the fire to the window; from the bed to the door, from the door to the bed; from the door to the bed, from the bed to the door; from the door to the window, from the window to the fire; from the fire to the window, from the window to the door; from the window to the door, from the door to the bed; from the bed to the door, from the door to the window; from the fire to the bed, from the bed to the window; from the window to the bed, from the bed to the fire; from the bed to the fire, from the fire to the door; from the door to the fire, from the fire to the bed; from the door to the window, from the window to the bed; from the bed to the window, from the window to the door; from the window to the door, from the door to the fire; from the fire to the door, from the door to the window; from the fire to the bed, from the bed to the door; from the door to the bed, from the bed to the fire; from the bed to the fire, from the fire to the window; from the window to the fire, from the fire to the bed; from the door to the fire, from the fire to the window; from the window to the fire, from the fire to the door; from the window to the bed, from the bed to the door; from the door to the bed, from the bed to the window; from the fire to the window, from the window to the bed; from the bed to the window, from the window to the fire; from the bed to the door, from the door to the fire; from the fire to the door, from the door to the bed.

This room was furnished solidly and with taste.

This solid and tasteful furniture was subjected by Mr. Knott to frequent changes of position, both absolute and relative. Thus it was not rare to find, on the Sunday, the tallboy on its feet by the fire, and the dressing-table on its head by the bed, and the night-stool on its face by the door, and the wash-hand-stand on its back by the window; and, on the Monday, the tallboy on its back by the bed, and the dressing-table on its face by the door, and the night-stool on its back by the window, and the wash-hand-stand on its feet by the fire; and, on the Tuesday, the tallboy on its face by the door, and the dressing-table on its back by the window, and the night-stool on its feet by the fire, and the wash-hand-stand on its head by the bed; and, on the

Wednesday, the tallboy on its back by the window, and the dressing-table on its feet by the fire, and the night-stool on its head by the bed, and the wash-hand-stand on its face by the door; and, on the Thursday, the tallboy on its side by the fire, and the dressing-table on its feet by the bed, and the night-stool on its head by the door, and the wash-hand-stand on its face by the window; and, on the Friday, the tallboy on its feet by the bed, and the dressing-table on its head by the door, and the night-stool on its face by the window, and the wash-hand-stand on its side by the fire; and, on the Saturday, the tallboy on its head by the door, and the dressing-table on its face by the window, and the night-stool on its side by the fire, and the wash-hand-stand on its feet by the bed; and, on the Sunday week, the tallboy on its face by the window, and the dressing-table on its side by the fire, and the night-stool on its feet by the bed, and the wash-hand-stand on its head by the door; and, on the Monday week, the tallboy on its back by the fire, and the dressing-table on its side by the bed, and the night-stool on its feet by the door, and the wash-hand-stand on its head by the window; and, on the Tuesday week, the tallboy on its side by the bed, and the dressing-table on its feet by the door, and the night-stool on its head by the window, and the wash-hand-stand on its back by the fire; and, on the Wednesday week, the tallboy on its feet by the door, and the dressing-table on its head by the window, and the night-stool on its back by the fire, and the wash-hand-stand on its side by the bed; and, on the Thursday week, the tallboy on its head by the window, and the dressing-table on its back by the fire, and the night-stool on its side by the bed, and the wash-hand-stand on its feet by the door; and, on the Friday week, the tallboy on its face by the fire, and the dressing-table on its back by the bed, and the nightstool on its side by the door, and the wash-hand-stand on its feet by the window; and, on the Saturday week, the tallboy on its back by the bed, and the dressing-table on its side by the door, and the night-stool on its feet by the window, and the wash-hand-stand on its face by the fire; and, on the Sunday fortnight, the tallboy on its side by the door, and the dressing-table on its feet by the window, and the night-stool on its face by the fire, and the wash-hand-stand on its back by the bed; and, on the Monday fortnight, the tallboy on its feet by the window, and the dressing-table on its face by the fire, and the night-stool on its back by the bed, and the wash-hand-stand on its side by the door; and, on the Tuesday fortnight, the tallboy on its head by the fire, and the dressing-table on its face by the bed, and the night-stool on its back by the door, and the wash-hand-stand on its side by the window; and, on the Wednesday fortnight, the tallboy on its face by the bed, and the dressing-table on its back by the door, and the night-stool on its side by the window, and the wash-hand-stand on its head by the fire; and, on the Thursday fortnight, the tallboy on its back by the door, and the dressing-table on its side by the window, and the night-stool on its head by the fire, and the wash-hand-stand on its face by the bed; and, on the Friday fortnight, the tallboy on its side by the window, and the dressing-table on its head by the fire, and the night-stool on its face by the bed, and the wash-hand-stand on its back by the door, for example, not at all rare, to consider only, over a period of nineteen days only, the tallboy, the dressing-table, the night-stool and the wash-hand-stand, and their feet, and heads, and faces, and backs and unspecified sides, and the fire, and the bed, and the door, and the window, not at all rare.

For the chairs also, to mention only the chairs also, were never still.

For the corners also, to mention only the corners also, were seldom vacant.

Alone the bed maintained the illusion of fixity, the bed so tasteful, the bed so solid, that it was round, and clamped to the ground.

Mr. Knott's head, Mr. Knott's feet, in nightly displacements of almost one minute, completed in twelve months their circuit of this solitary couch, His coccyx also, and adjacent gear, performed their little annual revolution, as appeared from an examination of the sheets (changed regularly on Saint Patrick's Day), and even of the mattress.

Of the strange doings above stairs, that had so preoccupied Watt during his time below stairs, no explanation was to be had. But they did not preoccupy Watt any longer.

From time to time Mr. Knott disappeared from his room, leaving Watt alone. Mr. Knott was there one moment, and the next gone. But on these occasions Watt, unlike Erskine, did not feel impelled to institute a search, above stairs and below, assassinating with his tread the quiet house, and pestering his colleague in the kitchen, no, but he remained quietly where he was, not wholly asleep, not wholly awake, until Mr. Knott came back.

Watt suffered neither from the presence of Mr. Knott, nor from his absence. When he was with him, he was content to be with him, and when he was away from him, he was content to be away from him. Never with relief, never with regret, did he leave him at night, or in the morning come to him again.

This ataraxy covered the entire house-room, the pleasure-garden, the vegetable garden and of course Arthur.

So that when the time came for Watt to depart, he walked to the gate with the utmost serenity.

But he was no sooner in the public road than he burst

into tears. He stood there, he remembered, with bowed head, and a bag in each hand, and his tears fell, a slow minute rain, to the ground, which had recently been repaired. He would not have believed such a thing possible, if he had not been there himself. The humidity thus lent to the road surface must, be reckoned, have survived his departure by as long as two minutes at least, if not three. Fortunately the weather was fine.

Watt's room contained no information. It was a small, dingy, and, though Watt was a man of some bodily cleanliness, fetid compartment. Its one window commanded a very fine view of a race-course. The painting, or coloured reproduction, yielded nothing further. On the contrary, as time passed, its significance diminished.

From Mr. Knott's voice nothing was to be learnt. Between Mr. Knott and Watt no conversation passed. From time to time, for no apparent reason, Mr. Knott opened his mouth in song. From bass to tenor, all male registers were employed by him, with equal success. He did not sing well, in Watt's opinion, but Watt had heard worse singers. The music of these songs was of an extreme monotony. For the voice, save for an occasional raucous sally, both up and down, to the extent of a tenth, or even an eleventh, did not leave the pitch at which, having elected to begin, it seemed obliged to remain, and finally to end. The words of these songs were either without meaning, or derived from an idiom with which Watt, a very fair linguist, had no acquaintance. The open a sound was predominant, and the explosives k and g. Mr. Knott talked often to himself too, with great variety and vehemence of intonation and gesticulation, but this so softly that it came, a wild dim chatter, meaningless to Watt's ailing ears. This was a noise of which Watt grew exceedingly fond. Not that he was sorry when it ceased, not that he was glad when it came again, no. But while it sounded he was gladdened, as by the rain on the bamboos, or even rushes, as by the land against the waves, doomed to cease, doomed to come again. Knott was also addicted to solitary dactylic ejaculations of extraordinary vigour, accompanied by spasms of the members. The chief of these were: Exelmans! Cavendish! Habbakuk! Ecchymose!

With regard to the so important matter of Mr. Knott's physical appearance, Watt had unfortunately little or nothing to say. For one day Mr. Knott would be tall, fat, pale and dark, and the next thin, small, flushed and fair, and the next sturdy, middle-sized, yellow and ginger, and the next small, fat, pale and fair, and the next middle-sized, flushed, thin and ginger, and the next tall, yellow, dark and sturdy, and the next fat, middle-sized, ginger and pale, and the next tall, thin, dark and flushed, and the next small, fair, sturdy and yellow, and the next tall, ginger, pale and fat, and the next thin, flushed, small and dark, and the next fair, sturdy, middle-sized and yellow, and the next dark, small, fat and pale, and the next fair, middle-sized, flushed and thin, and the next sturdy, ginger, tall and yellow, and the next pale, fat, middle-sized and fair, and the next flushed, tall, thin and ginger, and the next yellow, small, dark and sturdy, and the next fat, flushed, ginger and tall, and the next dark, thin, yellow, and small, and the next fair, pale, sturdy and middle-sized, and the next dark, flushed, small and fat, and the next thin, fair, yellow and middle-sized, and the next pale, sturdy, ginger and tall, and the next flushed, fair, fat and middle-sized, and the next yellow, ginger, tall and thin, and the next sturdy, small, pale and dark, and the next tall, fat, yellow, and fair, and the next small, pale, thin and ginger, and the next middle-sized, flushed, dark and sturdy, and the next fat, small, ginger and yellow, and the next middle-sized, thin, dark and pale, and the next tall, fair, sturdy and flushed, and the next middle-sized, dark, yellow and fat, and the next thin, pale, tall and fair, and the next ginger, sturdy, small and flushed, and the next dark, tall, fat and yellow, and the next fair, small, pale and thin, and the next sturdy, ginger, middle-sized and flushed, and the next yellow, fat, small and fair, and the next pale, middle-sized, thin and ginger, and the next flushed, tall, dark and sturdy, and the next fat, yellow, ginger and middle-sized, and the next dark, thin, pale and tall, and the next fair, flushed, sturdy and small, and the next ginger, yellow, tall and fat, and the next thin, dark, pale and small, and the next flushed, sturdy, fair and middle-sized, and the next yellow, dark, fat and small, and the next pale, fair, middle-sized and thin, and the next sturdy, tall, flushed and ginger, and the next middle-sized, fat, yellow and fair, and the next tall, pale, thin and ginger, and the next small, flushed, dark and sturdy, and the next fat, tall, fair and pale, and the next small, thin, ginger and flushed, and the next middle-sized, dark, sturdy and yellow, and the next small, ginger, pale and fat, and the next thin, flushed, middle-sized and dark, and the next fair, sturdy, tall and yellow, and the next dark, middle-sized, fat and pale, and the next fair, tall, flushed and thin, and the next sturdy, ginger, small and yellow, and the next flushed, fat, tall and fair, and the next yellow, small, thin and ginger, and the next pale, middle-sized, dark and sturdy, and the next fat, flushed, ginger and small, and the next dark, thin, yellow and middle-sized, and the next fair, pale, sturdy and tall, and the next dark, flushed, middle-sized and fat, and the next thin, fair, yellow and tall, and the next pale, sturdy, ginger and small, and the next flushed, dark, fat and tall, and the next yellow, fair, small and thin, and the next sturdy, middle-sized, pale and ginger, and the next small, fat, flushed and fair, and the next middle-sized, yellow, thin and ginger, and the next tall, pale, dark and sturdy, and the next fat, middle-sized, ginger and flushed, and the next tall, thin, dark and yellow, and the next small, fair, sturdy and pale, or so it seemed to Watt, to mention only the figure, stature, skin and hair.

For daily changed, as well as these, in carriage, expression, shape and size, the feet, the legs, the hands, the arms, the mouth, the nose, the eyes, the ears, to mention only the feet, the legs, the hands, the arms, the mouth, the nose, the eyes, the ears, and their carriage, expression, shape and size.

For the port, the voice, the smell, the hairdress, were seldom the same, from one day to the next, to mention only the port, the voice, the smell, the hairdress.

For the way of hawking, the way of spitting, were subject to daily fluctuation, to consider only the way of hawking, and of spitting.

For the belch was never the same, two days running, to go no further than the belch.

Watt had no hand in these transformations, and did not know at what hour of the twenty-four they were carried out. He suspected, however, that they were carried out between the hours of midnight, when Watt ended his day by helping Mr. Knott into his nightdress,[1] and then into

[1] For the guidance of the attentive reader, at a loss to understand how these repeated investments, and divestments, of the nightdress, did not finally reveal to Watt Mr. Knott's veritable aspect, it is perhaps not superfluous here to note, that Mr. Knott's attitude to his nightdress was not that generally in vogue. For Mr. Knott did not do as most men, and many women, do, who, before putting on their nightclothes, at night, take off their dayclothes, and again, when morning comes, once again, before they dream of putting on their dayclothes are careful to pull off their soiled nightclothes, no, but he went to bed with his nightclothes over his dayclothes, and he rose with his dayclothes under his nightclothes.

bed, and eight in the morning, when Watt began his day by helping Mr. Knott out of his bed, and then out of his nightdress. For if Mr. Knott had modified his appearance during Watt's hours of attendance, then it was unlikely that he could have done so without attracting Watt's attention, if not at the time, at least in the hours following. So Watt suspected that it was in the depths of the night, when the risk of disturbance was small, that Mr. Knott organized his exterior for the day to come. And what went far to strengthen this suspicion in the heart of Watt was this, that when sometimes, in the small hours of the morning, unable or unwilling to sleep he rose and went to the window, to look at the stars, which he had once known familiarly by name, when dying in London, and breathe the night air, and listen to the night sounds, of which he was still extremely curious, he sometimes saw, between him and the ground, lightening the darkness, greyening the leaves and, in wet weather, tinseling the rain, a fascia of white light.

None of Mr. Knott's gestures could be called characteristic, unless perhaps that which consisted in the simultaneous obturation of the facial cavities, the thumbs in the mouth, the forefingers in the ears, the little fingers in the nostrils, the third fingers in the eyes and the second fingers, free in a crisis to promote intellection, laid along the temples. And this was less a gesture than an attitude, sustained by Mr. Knott for long periods of time, without visible discomfort.

Other traits, other little ways, little ways of passing the little days, Watt remarked in Mr. Knott, and could have told if he had wished, if he had not been tired, so very tired, by all he had told already, tired of adding, tired of subtracting to and from the same old things the same old things.

But he could not bear that we should part, never to

meet again (in this world), and I in ignorance of how Mr. Knott put on his boots, or his shoes, or his slippers, or his boot and shoe, or his boot and slipper, or his shoe and slipper, when he did so, when he did not merely put on a boot, or a shoe, or a slipper. So, taking his hands from my shoulders, and laying them on my wrists, he told how Mr. Knott, when he felt the time come, taking on a cunning air would begin to sidle sidle up to the boots, up to the shoes, up to the boot and shoe, up to the boot and slipper, up to the shoe and slipper, sidle sidle little by little with an artless air little by little nearer and nearer to where they lay, in the rack, till he was near enough, pouncing, to secure them. And then, while he put on the one, the black boot, the brown shoe, the black slipper, the brown boot, the black shoe, the brown slipper, on the one foot, he held the other tight, lest it should escape, or put it in his pocket, or put his foot upon it, or put it in a drawer, or put it in his mouth, till he might put it on, on the other foot.

Continuing then, when he had told me this, then he loosed my hands from his shoulders, and backwards through the hole went back, to his garden, and left me alone, alone with only my poor eyes to follow him, this last of many times to follow him, over the deep threshing shadows backwards stumbling, towards his habitation. And often he struck against the trunks of trees, and in the tangles of underwood caught his foot, and fell to the ground, on his back, on his face, on his side, or into a great clump of brambles, or of briars, or of thistles, or of nettles. But ever he picked himself up and unmurmuring went on, towards his habitation, until I saw him no more, but only the aspens. And from the hidden pavilions, his and mine, where by this time dinner was preparing, the issuing smokes by the wind were blown, now far apart, but now together, mingled to vanish.

IV

As Watt told the beginning of his story, not first, but second, so not fourth, but third, now he told its end. Two, one, four, three, that was the order in which Watt told his story. Heroic quatrains are not otherwise elaborated.

As Watt came, so he went, in the night, that covers all things with its cloak, especially when the weather is cloudy.

It was summer, he thought, because the air was not quite cold. As for his coming, so now for his going, it seemed a kindly summer's night. And it came at the end of a day that was like the other days, for Watt. For of Mr. Knott he could not speak.

In the room, passably lit by the moon, and large numbers of stars, Mr. Knott continued, apparently very much as usual, to lie, kneel, sit, stand and walk, to utter his cries, mutter and be silent. And by the open window Watt sat, as his custom was in suitable weather, heard dully the first night sounds, saw dully the first night lights, human and celestial.

At ten the steps came, clearer, clearer, fainter, fainter, on the stairs, on the landing, on the stairs again, and through the open door the light, from darkness slowly brightening, to darkness slowly darkening, the steps of Arthur, the light of poor Arthur, little by little mounting to his rest, at his habitual hour.

At eleven the room darkened, the moon having climbed behind a tree. But the tree being small, and the moon's ascension rapid, this transit was brief, and this obscuration.

As by the steps the light, growing, dying, Watt knew that

it was ten, so he knew, when the room darkened, that it was eleven, or thereabouts.

But when he thought it was midnight, or thereabouts, and he had put Mr. Knott into his nightdress, and then into his bed, then he went down to the kitchen, as he did every night, to drink his last glass of milk, to smoke his last quarter of cigar.

But in the kitchen a strange man was sitting, in the gloaming of the expiring range, on a chair.

Watt asked this man who he was, and how he had got in. He felt it was his duty to do this.

My name is Micks, said the stranger. One moment I was out, and the next I was in.

So the moment was come. Watt lifted the cork lid from his glass, and drank. The milk was turning. He lit his cigar, and puffed. It was an inferior cigar.

I come from ——, said Mr. Micks, and he described the place whence he came. I was born at ——, he said, and the site and circumstances of his ejection were unfolded. My dear parents, he said, and Mr. and Mrs. Micks, heroic figures, unique in the annals of cloistered fornication, filled the kitchen. He said further, At the age of fifteen, My beloved wife, My beloved dog, Till at last. Happily Mr. Micks was childless.

Watt listened for a time, for the voice was far from un-melodious. The fricatives in particular were pleasing. But as from the proscript an encountered nightsong, so it faded, the voice of Micks, the pleasant voice of poor Micks, and was lost, in the soundless tumult of the inner lamentation.

When Watt had finished his milk, and smoked his cigar, until it burned his lips, he left the kitchen. But in a short time he reappeared, to Micks, with in each hand a small bag, that is to say, two small bags in all.

Watt preferred, when travelling, two small bags to one

large bag. Indeed he preferred, when moving from place to place, two small bags, one in each hand, to one small bag, now in one hand and now in the other. No bag, big or small, in either hand, that of course is what he would have liked best of all, when on his travels. But what then would have become of his effects, his toilet necessities and change of body linen?

One of these bags was the grousebag, already perhaps mentioned. In spite of the straps, and buckles, with which it was generously provided, Watt held it by the neck, as though it were a sandbag.

The other of these bags was another and similar grousebag. It also Watt held by the neck, as though it were a club.

These bags were three-quarters empty.

Watt wore a greatcoat, still green here and there. This coat, when last weighed by Watt, weighed between fifteen and sixteen pounds, avoirdupois, or a little more than a stone. Of this Watt was certain, having weighed himself on a machine, first with the coat on, and then with it off, lying on the ground, at his feet. But that was a long time ago, and the coat might have put on weight, since then. Or it might have lost weight. This coat was of such length, that Watt's trousers, which he wore very baggy, in order to conceal the shapes of his legs, were hidden by it from view. This coat was of a very respectable age, as such coats go, having been bought at secondhand, for a small sum, from a meritorious widow, by Watt's father, when Watt's father was a young man, and motoring in its infancy, that is to say some seventy years before. This coat had not, since then, at any time been washed, except imperfectly by the rain, and the snow, and the sleet, and of course occasional fleeting immersion in canal water, nor dry-cleaned, nor turned, nor brushed, and it was no doubt

216

to these precautions that its preservation, as a unit, was due. The material of this coat, though liberally scored and contunded, especially in the rear, was so thick, and so strong, that it remained exempt from perforation, in the strict meaning of the word, nor was its thread elsewhere exposed, than at the seat, and elbows. This coat continued to button, up the front, with nine buttons, various now in shape, and colour, but without exception of such exceptional size as to remain, once buttoned, buttoned. Aloft in the flower-hole brooded the remains of a factitious murrey chrysanthemum. Patches of velvet clung to the collar. The skirts were not divided.

Watt wore, on his head, a block hat, of a pepper colour. This excellent hat had belonged to his grandfather, who had picked it up, on a racecourse, from off the ground, where it lay, and carried it home. Then mustard, now it was pepper, in colour.

It was to be observed that the colours, on the one hand of this coat, on the other of this hat, drew closer and closer, the one to the other, with every passing lustre. Yet how different had been their beginnings! The one green! The other yellow! So it is with time, that lightens what is dark, that darkens what is light.

It was to be expected that, once met, they would not stay, no, but continue, each as it must, to age, until the hat was green, the coat yellow, and then through the last circles paling, deepening, swooning cease, the hat to be a hat, the coat to be a coat. For so it is with time.

Watt wore, on his feet, a boot, brown in colour, and a shoe, happily of a brownish colour also. This boot Watt had bought, for eightpence, from a one-legged man who, having lost his leg, and a fortiori his foot, in an accident, was happy to realize, on his discharge from hospital, for such a sum, his unique remaining marketable asset. He little suspected that he owed this good fortune to Watt's having found, some days before, on the seashore, the shoe, stiff with brine, but otherwise shipshape.

This shoe and this boot were so close in colour, the one to the other, and so veiled, as to their uppers, in the first place by the trousers, and in the second by the greatcoat, that they might almost have been taken, not for a shoe on the one hand, and on the other for a boot, but for a true pair of boots, or of shoes, had not the boot been blunt, and the shoe sharp, at the toe.

In this boot, a twelve, and in this shoe, a ten, Watt, whose size was eleven, suffered, if not agony, at least pain, with his feet, of which each would willingly have changed places with the other, if only for a moment.

By wearing, on the foot that was too small, not one sock of his pair of socks, but both, and on the foot that was too large, not the other, but none, Watt strove in vain to correct this asymmetry. But logic was on his side, and he remained faithful, when involved in a journey of any length, to this distribution of his socks, in preference to the other three.

Of Watt's coat and waistcoat, of his shirt, his vest and his drawers, much might be written, of great interest and significance. The drawers, in particular, were remarkable, from more than one point of view. But they were hidden, coat and waistcoat, shirt and underclothes, all hidden, from the eye.

Watt wore no tie, nor any collar. Had he had a collar, he would no doubt have found a tie, to go with it. And had he had a tie, he might perhaps have procured a collar, to carry it. But having neither tie, nor collar, he had neither collar, nor tie.

Thus dressed, and holding in either hand a bag, Watt stood in the kitchen, and the expression on his face became gradually of such vacancy that Micks, raising in amaze an astonished hand to a thunderstruck mouth, recoiled to the wall, and there stood, in a crouching posture, his back pressed against the wall, and the back of the one hand pressed against his parted lips, and the back of the other pressed against the palm of the one. Or it may have been something else that caused Micks to recoil in this way, and to crouch against the wall, with his hands to his face, in this way, something other than the face of Watt. For it is hard to believe that the face of Watt, dreadful and all as it was at the time, was dreadful and all enough to cause a powerful lymphatic man like Micks to recoil to the wall with his hands to his face, as if to ward off a blow, or press back a cry, in the way he did, and to turn pale, for he turned pale, very properly. For Watt's face, dreadful and all as it undoubtedly was, especially when it wore this particular expression, was scarcely as dreadful and all as all that. Nor was Micks a little girl, or an innocent little choirboy, no, but a big placid man, who had seen something of the world, both at home, and abroad. What may it then have been, if not Watt's face, that so repelled Micks, and drained his cheeks, of their natural high colour? The greatcoat? The hat? The shoe and boot? Yes, the shoe and boot perhaps, taken together, so brown, so peeping, so sharp and blunt, heel to heel in obscene attention splayed, and so brown, such a brown. Or was it not perhaps something that was not Watt, nor of Watt, but behind Watt, or beside Watt, or before Watt, or beneath Watt, or above Watt, or about Watt, a shade uncast, a light unshed, or the grey air aswirl with vain entelechies?

But if Watt's mouth was open, and his jaw sunk, and his eyes glassy, and his head sunk, and his knees bent, and his back bent, his mind was busy, busy wondering which was best, to shut the door, from which he felt the draught, on the nape, of his neck, and set down his bags, and sit down, or to shut the door, and set down his bags, without sitting down, or to shut the door, and sit down, without setting down his bags, or to set down his bags, and sit down, without shutting the door, or to shut the door, from which he felt the blast, on the nape, of his neck, without setting down his bags, or sitting down, or to set down his bags, without bothering to shut the door, or sit down, or to sit down, without troubling to set down his bags, or shut the door, or to leave things as they were, the bags pulling at his hands, the floor pushing at his feet, and the air puffing, through the door, on the nape, of his neck. And the conclusion of Watt's reflexions was this, that if one of these things was worth doing, all were worth doing, but that none was worth doing, no, not one, but that all were unadvisable, without exception. For he would not have time to rest, and grow warm. For the sitting down was a standing up again, and the load laid down another load to raise, and the door shut another door to open, so hard upon the last, so soon before the next, as to prove, very likely, in the long run, more fatiguing, than refreshing. And he said also, by way of a rider, that even if he had the whole night before him, in which to rest, and grow warm, on a chair, in the kitchen, even then it would be a poor resting, and a mean warming, beside the rest and warmth that he remembered, the rest and warmth that he awaited, a very poor resting indeed, and a paltry warming, and so in any case very likely a source, in the long run, less of gratification, than of annoyance. But his fatigue was so great, at the end of this long day, and his bedtime so long past, and the desire for rest so strong in consequence, and the desire for warmth, that he stooped, very likely with the intention of setting down his bags, on the floor, and of shutting the door, and of sitting down at the table, and of putting his arms on the table, and of burying yes of burying his head in his arms, and who knows perhaps even of falling, after a moment or two, into an uneasy sleep, lacerated by dreams, by dives from dreadful heights into rocky waters, before a numerous public. So he stooped, but he did not stoop far, for hardly had the stoop begun, when it ended, and hardly had he initiated his programme of repose, of uneasy repose, when he checked it, and remained fixed, in an aggravation of his semi-upright station, a station so lamentable that he remarked it, and would have smiled, if he had not been too weak to smile, or laughed outright, if he had been strong enough to laugh outright. Inwardly he was diverted, to be sure, and for an instant his mind turned off from care, but less than if he had had the force to smile, or outright to laugh.

In the avenue, somewhere between the house and the road, Watt recalled, with regret, that he had not taken leave of Micks, as he should have done. The few simple words at parting, that mean so much, to him who stays, to him who goes, he had not had the common courtesy to speak them, before leaving the house. An inclination to retrace his steps, and repair this churlishness, caused him to halt. But he did not halt long, but continued on his way, towards the gate, and the road. And he did well, for Micks had left the kitchen before Watt. But Watt, not knowing this, that Micks had left the kitchen before him, for he only realized it much later, when it was too late, felt regret, as he passed on his way, towards the gate, and the road, that he had not taken leave of Micks, however briefly.

The night was of unusual splendour. The moon, if not full, was not far from full, in a day or two it would be full, and then dwindle, until its appearance, in the heavens, would be that compared, by some writers, to a sickle, or a crescent. The remaining heavenly bodies also, though situated for the most part at a great distance, poured down on Watt, and on the hortulan beauties through which he moved, with regret, in his heart, for his neglect of Micks, to Watt's disgust a light so strong, so pure, so steady and so white, that his progress, though painful, and uncertain, was less painful, less uncertain, than he had apprehended, when setting out.

Watt was always lucky with his weather.

He walked on the grass edging, because he did not like the feel of gravel under his feet, and the flowers, and the long grasses, and the boughs, both of shrubs and of trees, brushed against him in a way that he did not find unpleasant. The lapping, against the crown, of his hat, of some pendulous umbel, perhaps a horn's, gave him peculiar satisfaction, and he had not gone far, from the place, when he turned, and returned, to the place, and stood, beneath the bough, attentive to the drag, to and fro, to and fro, of the tassels, on the crown, of his hat.

He remarked that there was no wind, not a breath. And yet in the kitchen he had felt the cold air, on the nape, of his neck.

He was overtaken, in the road, by the passing weakness already mentioned. But it passed, and he pursued his way, towards the railway-station.

He walked in the middle of the road, because of the freestone, with which the path was strewn.

He met no human being, on his way. A strayed ass, or goat, lying in the ditch, in the shadow, raised its head, as he passed. Watt did not see the ass, or goat, but the ass, or goat, saw Watt. And it followed him with its eyes while he passed, little by little, down the road, out of sight. Perhaps it thought that in the bags there was something good to eat. When it could see the bags no more, then it laid back its head, among the nettles.

When Watt reached the railway-station, it was shut. It had indeed been shut for some time, before Watt reached it, and it was so still, when he did. For the time was now perhaps between one and two o'clock, in the morning, and the last train to call at this railway-station, at night, and the first to call, in the morning, called, the one between eleven and twelve o'clock, at night, and the other between five and six o'clock, in the morning. So this particular railway-station closed, at latest, at twelve o'clock, at night, and never opened before five o'clock, in the morning. And as the time was now probably between one and two o'clock, in the morning, the railway-station was shut.

Watt climbed the stone steps and stood before the wicket, looking through its bars. He admired the permanent way, stretching away on either hand, in the moonlight, and the starlight, as far as the eye could reach, as far as Watt's eye could have reached, if it had been inside the station. He contemplated with wonder also the ample recession of the plain, its flow so free and simple to the mountains, the crumpled umbers of its verge. His eyes then rising with the rising land fell ultimately on the mirrored sky, its coalsacks, its setting constellations, and on the eyes, ripple-blurred, staring from amidst the waters. Finally suddenly he focused the wicket.

Watt climbed the wicket and found himself on the platform, with his bags. For he had the foresight, before climbing the wicket, to hoist his bags over the wicket and let them fall, to the ground, on the other side.

Watt's first care, now that he was safe and sound, with his bags, within the station, was to turn, and to gaze, through the wicket, the way back he had come, so recently.

Of the many touching prospects thus offered to his inspection, none touched him more than the highway, now whiter somehow than by day, and of a fairer onrush, between its hedges, and its ditches. This highway, after an unbroken course of considerable length, dipped suddenly, and was lost to view, in a deplorable confusion of vertical vegetation.

The chimneys of Mr. Knott's house were not visible, in spite of the excellent visibility. On fine days they could be discerned, from the station. But on fine nights apparently not. For Watt's eyes, when he put himself out, were no worse than another's, even at this time, and the night was exceptionally fine, even for this part of the country, reputed for the fineness of its nights.

Watt had always great luck with his weather.

Watt was beginning to tire of running his eyes up and down this highway, when a figure, human apparently, advancing along its crown, arrested, and revived, his attention. Watt's first thought was that this creature had risen up out of the ground, or fallen from the sky. And his second, some fifteen or twenty minutes later, that it had perhaps gained its present position by way of first a hedge, and then a ditch. Watt was unable to say whether this figure was that of a man, or that of a woman, or that of a priest, or that of a nun. That it was not that of a boy, nor that of a girl, was shown, in Watt's opinion, by its dimensions. But to decide whether it was that of a man, or that of a woman, or that of a priest, or that of a nun, was more than Watt could do, strain as he might his eyes. If it was that of a woman, or that of a nun, it was that of a woman, or that of a nun, of unusual size, even for this part of the country, remarkable for the unusual size of its women, and its nuns. But Watt knew too well, too too well, of what dimensions certain women, and certain nuns, were capable, to conclude, from those of this night-wanderer, that this night-wanderer was not a woman, nor a nun, but a man, or a

224

priest. As for the clothes, their testimony was of no more assistance, at that distance, and in that light, than if they had consisted of a sheet, or a sack, or a quilt, or a rug. For from head to foot extended, as far as Watt could see, and his eyes were as good as the next man's, even at this stage, when he gave himself the trouble to focus them, the uninterrupted surfaces of a single garment, while on the head there sat, asexual, the likeness of a depressed inverted chamber-pot, yellow with age, to put it politely. If the figure was indeed that of a woman, or that of a nun, of unusual size, it was that of a woman, or that of a nun, of unusual size of uncommon inelegance. But the giant woman was often dowdy, in Watt's experience, and the giant nun not less so. The arms did not end at the hands, but continued, in a manner that Watt could not determine, to near the ground. The feet, following each other in rapid and impetuous succession, were flung, the right foot to the right, the left foot to the left, as much outwards as forwards, with the result that, for every stride of say three feet in compass, the ground gained did not exceed one. This gave to the gait a kind of shackled smartness, most painful to witness. Watt felt them suddenly glow in the dark place, and go out, the words, *The only cure is diet.*

Watt waited, with impatience, for this man, if it was a man, or for this woman, if it was a woman, or for this priest, if it was a priest, or for this nun, if it was a nun, to draw near, and set his mind at rest. He did not desire conversation, he did not desire company, he did not desire consolation, he felt no wish for an erection, no, all he desired was to have his uncertainty removed, in this connexion.

He did not know why he cared, what it was, coming along the road. He did not know whether shit was a good thing, or a bad thing. It seemed to him that, quite apart from any question of personal feeling of grief or satisfaction, it was greatly to be deplored, that he cared what it was, coming along the road, profoundly to be deplored.

He realized that he could not be content with the figure's drawing merely near, no, but that the figure must draw very near, very near indeed. For if the figure drew merely near, and not very near indeed, how should he know, if it was a man, that it was not a woman, or a priest, or a nun, dressed up as a man? Or, if it was a woman, that it was not a man, or a priest, or a nun, dressed up as a woman? Or, if it was a priest, that it was not a man, or a woman, or a nun, dressed up as a priest? Or, if it was a nun, that it was not a man, or a woman, or a priest, dressed up as a nun? So Watt waited, with impatience, for the figure to draw very near indeed.

Then, as Watt still waited for the figure to draw very near indeed, he realized that it was not necessary, not at all necessary, that the figure should draw very near indeed, but that a moderate proximation would be more than sufficient. For Watt's concern, deep as it appeared, was not after all with what the figure was, in reality, but with what the figure appeared to be, in reality. For since when were Watt's concerns with what things were, in reality? But he was for ever falling into this old error, this error of the old days when, lacerated with curiosity, in the midst of substance shadowy he stumbled. This was very mortifying, to Watt. So Watt waited, with impatience, for the figure to draw near.

He waited and waited, his hands curled round the bars, of the wicket, so that his nails pricked his palms, his bags at his feet, staring through the bars, staring at this incomprehensible staffage, suffering greatly from impatience. His agitation became finally so great, that he shook the wicket, with all his might.

What so agitated Watt was this, that in the ten minutes or half an hour that had elapsed, since he first became aware of this figure, striding along, on the crest of the road, towards the station, the figure had gained nothing in height, in breadth or in distinctness. Pressing forward all this time, with no abatement of its foundered precipitation, towards the station, it had made no more headway, than if it had been a millstone.

Watt was puzzling over this, when the figure, without any interruption of its motions, grew fainter and fainter, and finally disappeared.

Watt seemed to regard, for some obscure reason, this particular hallucination as possessing exceptional interest.

Watt picked up his bags and advanced, round the corner of a wall, on to the platform. A light was burning in the signal-box.

The signal-man, an elderly man of the name of Case, was waiting in his box, as he did every night, with the exception of the night from Sunday to Monday (strange), for the upgoing express to go up safely, through the station. Then he would set his signals and go home, to his lonely wife, leaving the station deserted.

To while away the time, and at the same time improve his mind, Mr. Case was reading a book: *Songs by the Way*, by George Russell (A.E.). Mr. Case, his head flung back, held this book out at arm's length. Mr. Case had a very superior taste in books, for a signal-man.

Mr. Case read:

?

Mr. Case's heavy moustache followed the movements of his lip, as it espoused, now pouting, now revulsed, the various sonorities of which these words were composed. His nose too responded, with its bulb and nostrils. The pipe moved up and down, and from the corner of the mouth the spittle fell, unheeded, on the waistcoat, which was of corduroy.

Watt stood in the cabin as he had stood in the kitchen, his bags in his hands, his open eyes at rest, and the door open behind him. Mr. Case had once caught, through the windows, of his box, a glimpse of Watt, on the evening of his arrival. So he was familiar with his appearance. This stood him now in good stead.

Could you tell me what time it was, said Watt.

It was as he feared, earlier than he hoped.

Could I be admitted to a waiting-room, said Watt.

Here was a teaser, to be sure. For Mr. Case might not leave his box, until he left it to go home, to his anxious wife. Nor was it possible, detaching the key from the bunch, to hand it to Watt, saying, Here, sir, is the key of our waiting-room, I shall call for it on my way home. No. For the waiting-room opened off the booking-office, in such a way, that to reach the waiting-room it was necessary to pass through the booking-office. And the key of the door of the waiting-room did not open the door of the booking-office. Nor was it possible, slipping the two keys off the ring, to hand them to Watt, saying, Here, sir, is the key of our waiting-room door, and here that of our booking-office door, I shall call for them on my way out. No. For the booking-office communicated with the station-master's sanctum, in such a way, that to reach the station-master's sanctum it was only necessary to traverse the booking-office. And the key of the door of the booking-office opened the door of the station-master's sanctum, in such sort, that these two doors were represented, on each bunch of station keys, on Mr. Gorman's the station-master's bunch, on Mr. Case's the signal-man's bunch, and on Mr. Nolan's the porter's bunch, not by two keys, but by one key only.

In this way an economy of no fewer than three keys was

realized, and it was Mr. Gorman's the station-master's intention to reduce still further the number of station keys by having fitted, at no distant date, and at the company's expense, to the door of the waiting-room a lock identical with the now identical locks of the doors of the booking-office and of his private sanctum. This design he had communicated, in the course of a recent conference, both to Mr. Case and to Mr. Nolan, and neither Mr. Case nor Mr. Nolan had any objections to offer. But what he had not confided, either to Mr. Case or to Mr. Nolan, was his determination to have fitted, in the near future, little by little, at the company's expense, to the wicket and to the doors of the signal-box, of the porters' restroom, of the luggage-office and of the ladies' and gentlemen's lavatories, locks so contrived that the key which now opened, with such perfect ease, the door of the booking-office, and the door of the station-master's sanctum, and which so soon would open, without the least difficulty, the door of the waiting-room, would open all those other doors also, one after the other, in the fulness of time. So he would leave, at his retirement, if he did not die before, or on his death, if he did not retire first, a station unique, in this respect, if not in any other, among the stations of the line.

The keys of the till, which Mr. Gorman carried, the one on his watch-chain, lest his trouser's pocket should develop a hole, as trouser's pockets are so apt to do, or the key, which was minute, be drawn forth with the small change, and lost, and the other, lest his watch-chain should be lost, or stolen from him, in his trouser's pocket, these little keys Mr. Gorman did not number among the station keys. And indeed the keys of the till were not properly speaking station keys at all. For the station till, unlike the station doors, did not remain in the station, all day, and all night, but left the station with Mr. Gorman, when he went home in the evening, and did not return until the following morning, when Mr. Gorman returned to the station.

Mr. Case considered all this, or such parts as he deemed germane, weighing the for, and weighing the against, without passion. He came finally to the conclusion that he could do nothing, for the moment. When the express-train had come, and gone, and he was free to go home, to his unquiet wife, then he could do something, then he could admit Watt to the waiting-room, and leave him there. But he had no sooner come to the conclusion that he could do this, in order to oblige Watt, when he saw that he could do so only on condition that he locked the door of the booking-office, behind him. For he could not go away, leaving the door of the booking-office open, in the sleeping station. But on this condition, that Watt submitted to be locked into the booking-office, he could oblige Watt, once the express-train had come, and gone. But he had hardly decided that it would be possible for him to oblige Watt, on this condition, when he realized that, even on this condition, it would not be possible for him to oblige Watt, unless Watt consented to being locked, not only into the booking-office, but into the waiting-room also. For it was out of the question that Watt should have free access, all night long, in the sleeping station, to the station-master's sanctum's antechamber. But if he had no objection to being locked, till morning, not only into the booking-office, but into the waiting-room also, then Mr. Case saw really no reason why the waiting-room should not be placed at his disposal, as soon as the express-train had passed safely by, with its passengers, and valuable freight.

Mr. Case now informed Watt of what he had settled, in his mind, with reference to Watt's request, that he should be admitted to the public waiting-room. The reasons that had led Mr. Case to settle this, in his mind, rather than something else, Mr. Case had the delicacy to keep to himself, as being more likely to cause Watt pain, than to cause him pleasure. In the morning, said Mr. Case, as soon as Mr. Gorman, or Mr. Nolan arrives, you will be let out, and free to come and go, as you please. Watt replied that that would indeed be something to look forward to, and a comfort to him during the night, the prospect of being enlarged, in the morning, by Mr. Gorman, or Mr. Nolan, and made free to come and go, as he listed. If in the meantime, said Mr. Case, you care to come in, to the box, and shut the door, and take a chair, I should be happy to have you. Watt replied that it would be better if he waited outside. He would be on the platform, walking up and down, or sitting on a seat.

Watt lay on the seat, on his back, with his bags under his head, and his hat over his face. Thus the moon was in a measure kept off, and the lesser beauties of this glorious night. The problem of vision, as far as Watt was concerned, admitted of only one solution: the eye open in the dark. The results given by the closed eye were, in Watt's opinion, most unsatisfactory.

Watt first considered the matter of the express-train, so soon due to thunder, with irresistible impetus, through the sleeping station. He gave very full and close attention to this matter. Finally suddenly he ceased, as suddenly as he had begun, to think.

He lay on the seat, without thought or sensation, except for a slight feeling of chill in one foot. In his skull the voices whispering their canon were like a patter of mice, a flurry of little grey paws in the dust. This was very likely a sensation also, strictly speaking.

Mr. Case was obliged to explain his insistence. But a few words were sufficient. A few words from Mr. Case, and

231

all came back to Watt. Mr. Case carried a storm-lantern in his hand. From it issued a yellow beam, of extraordinary debility. Mr. Case spoke of the train, with professional pride. It had left on time, it had passed on time, and it would arrive, at its destination, if nothing supervened to delay it, on time.

Here then was the explanation of the recent external commotion.

It was now fully two hours since Watt had passed water. And yet he felt no need, nay, no desire, to pass water. Not the least drop, or globule, of water could I pass, he reflected, good, bad or indifferent, if I were paid not to do so. He who hourly passed an urgent water, a delicious water, in the ordinary way. This last regular link with the screen, for he did not count as such his weekly stool, nor biannual equinoctial nocturnal emission in vacuo, he now envisaged its relaxation, and eventual rupture, with sadness, and gladness, distinctly perceptible in an alternation of great rapidity, for some little time, and dying blurred together away, in due course.

Watt stood on the floor, with his bags in his hands, and the floor was like stone under his feet, and his faithful body did not fall, his relentless body, suddenly on its knees, or on its coccyx, and then forward on its face, or backward on its back, no, but it preserved its balance, in a way not unlike the way that its mother had taught, and the conformism of youth confirmed.

Faintlier, faintlier came the footfalls to his ear, until of all the faint sounds that came, by the abandoned air, to his ear, not one was a footfall, as far as he could judge. This was a music of which he was particularly fond, the parted quiet closing like a groom, behind departing footfalls, or other disturbances. But Mr. Case's way brought him behind the station, and his footfalls came again, four or five, a little wale of stealth, to Watt's ears, which stuck out wide on either side of his head, like a   ?   's. Before long they would come to Mrs. Case, to her ears weary of the stepless murmurs, stronger and stronger, till they reached the grass. Few sounds, if any, gave Mrs. Case more satisfaction than these. She was a strange woman.

Part of the waiting-room was faintly lit, by light from without. The passage from this part to the other was more abrupt, now that Watt had ceased to listen, than he would have believed possible, if he had not seen it, with his own eyes.

The waiting-room was empty of furniture, or other objects, as far as Watt could see. Unless there was something behind him. This did not strike him as strange. Nor did it strike him as usual. For his impression was, such as it was, as he drooped sigmoidal in its midst, that this was a waiting-room of which even the nicest degrees of strange and usual could not be affirmed, with propriety.

Whispering it told, the mouth, a woman's, the thin lips sticking and unsticking, how when empty they could accommodate a larger public than when encumbered with armchairs and divans, and how it was vain to sit, vain to lie, when without the rain beat down, or the sleet, or the snow, with or without wind, or the sun, with greater or lesser perpendicularity. This woman's name had been Price, her person was of an extreme spareness, and some thirty-five years earlier she had shot, with colours flying, the narrows of the menopause. Watt was not displeased to hear her voice again, to watch again the play of the pale bows of mucus. He was not displeased either when it went away.

The waiting-room was now less empty than Watt had at first supposed, to judge by the presence, some two paces to Watt's fore, and as many to his right, of what seemed to be an object of some importance. Watt could not tell what this was, though he went so far as to advance his head, not without torsion of the neck, in its direction. It was not part of the ceiling, nor of a wall, nor, though it seemed in contact with the floor, of the floor, that was all that Watt could affirm, of this object, and even that little he affirmed with reserve. But that little was enough, for Watt the possibility was enough, more than enough, that something other than he, in this box, was not intrinsic to its limits.

A smell exceptionally foul, and yet at the same time in some way familiar, made Watt wonder if there were not hidden, beneath the boards, at his feet, the decaying carcass of some small animal, such as a dog, a cat, a rat, or a mouse. For the floor, though it felt to Watt like stone, was in reality contabulated, all over. This smell was of such virulence that Watt was almost obliged to put down his bags and draw forth his pocket-handkerchief, or, more exactly, his roll of toilet-paper, from his pocket. For Watt, in order to save himself the washing, and no doubt also for the pleasure of killing two birds with one stone, never blew his nose, except when the circumstances permitted of a direct digital emunction, in anything but toilet-paper, each separate slip, when thoroughly imbibed, being crumpled up into a ball, and thrown away, and the hands passed through the hair, to its great embellishment, or rubbed the one against the other, until they shone.

This smell however was not what Watt had at first supposed, but something quite different, for it grew weaker and weaker, as it would not have done, if it had been what Watt had at first supposed, and finally ceased, altogether.

But in a short time it returned, the same smell exactly, dilated and passed off, as before.

In this way it came and went, for some hours.

There was something about this smell that Watt could not help but like. Yet he was not sorry, when it went.

In the waiting-room the darkness gradually deepened. There was no longer a dark part and a less dark part, no, but all now was uniformly dark, and remained so, for some time. This notable change took place by insensible degrees.

When the waiting-room had been quite dark, for some time, then in the waiting-room the darkness slowly lightened, throughout, by infinitesimal stages, and continued to do so, at the same rate, until every part of the waiting-room was faintly visible, to the dilated eye.

Watt saw now that his companion all this time had been a chair. Its back was turned towards him. Little by little, as the light grew, he came to know this chair, so well, that in the end he knew it better than many a chair he had sat on, or stood on, when the object was beyond his reach, or shod his feet on, or toileted his feet on, one after the other, paring and curetting the nails, and scouring the web-holes, with a spoon.

It was a high, narrow, black, wooden chair, with arms, and castors.

One of its feet was screwed to the floor, by means of a clamp. Not one of the remaining feet, but all, carried similar, if not identical irons. Not one, but all! But the screws, which no doubt had once fixed these to the floor, had very kindly been removed. Through the bars, which were vertical, of the back, Watt saw portions of a grate, heaped high with ashes, and cinders, of a beautiful grey colour.

This chair then had been with Watt, all this time, in the waiting-room, all these hours, of scant light, of no light, and it was with him still, in the exhilarating dawn. It would not be impossible, after all, to take it away, and put it somewhere else, or sell it by auction, or give it away.

Otherwise, as far as Watt could see, all was wall, or floor, or ceiling.

There next emerged, without haste, from the wall, a

large coloured print of the horse Joss, standing in profile in a field. Watt identified, first the field, then the horse, and then, thanks to an inscription of great   ?   , the horse Joss. This horse, its four hooves firmly planted on the ground, its head sunk, seemed to consider, without appetite, the grass. Watt pushed forward his head, to see if it was really a horse, and not a mare, or a gelding. But this interesting information was hidden, just hidden, by a haunch, or tail, of more decency than breeding. The light was that of approaching night, or impending storm, or both. The grass was sparse, sere, and overrun with what Watt took to be a species of cockle.

The horse seemed hardly able to stand, let alone run.

This object too had not been always here, would perhaps not be always here.

The flies, of skeleton thinness, excited to new efforts by yet another dawn, left the walls, and the ceiling, and even the floor, and hastened in great numbers to the window. Here, pressed against the impenetrable panes, they would enjoy the light, and warmth, of the long summer's day.

A merry whistling now sounded, afar off, and the nearer it approached, the merrier it grew. For Mr. Nolan's spirits always rose, as he approached the station, in the morning. They rose also, invariably, in the evening, when he left it. Thus Mr. Nolan was assured, twice a day, of a rise in spirits. And when Mr. Nolan's spirits rose, he could no more refrain from whistling, merrily, than a lark from singing, when it rises.

It was Mr. Nolan's habit, when he had flung open all the station doors, with the air of one storming a bastille, to retire to the porters' restroom, and there drink a bottle of stout, the first of the day, over the previous evening's paper. Mr. Nolan was a great reader of the evening paper. He read it five times, at his tea, at his supper, at his breakfast, with his morning stout and at his dinner. In the course of the afternoon, for he had a very gallant nature, he carried it to the ladies' house of office, and left it there, in a conspicuous position. Few pennyworths gave more joy, than Mr. Nolan's evening paper.

Mr. Nolan then, having unlocked and hurled, against their jambs, the wicket and the booking-office door, came to the door of the waiting-room. Had his whistle been less piercing, and his entry less resounding, he might have heard, behind the door, a disquieting sound, that of soliloquy, under dictation, and proceeded with care. But no, he turned the key and dealt, with his boot, the door a dunt that sent it flying inwards, at a great speed.

The innumerable semicircles thus brilliantly begun did not end, as on all previous mornings, in the bang that Mr. Nolan loved, no, but they were all cut short, all without exception, at the same point. And the reason for that was this, that Watt, where he stood, swaying, murmuring, was nearer the waiting-room door than the waiting-room door was wide.

Mr. Nolan found Mr. Gorman on his doorstep, taking leave of his mother.

Now I am at liberty, said Watt, I am free to come and go, as I please.

There were four armpits, where the friezes met, four fair armpits. Watt saw the ceiling with an extreme distinctness. It was of a whiteness that he would not have believed possible, if it had been reported to him. It was a rest, after the wall. It was a rest too, after the floor. It was such a rest, after the wall, and the floor, and the chair, and the horse, and the flies, that Watt's eyes closed, a thing they never did by day in the ordinary way on any account, except very briefly now and then, to prevent themselves from becoming too dry.

Poor fellow, said Mr. Gorman, shall we telephone for a policeman.

Mr. Nolan was all in favour of telephoning for a policeman.

Help him to rise, said Mr. Gorman, perhaps he has a bone broke.

But Mr. Nolan could not bring himself to do this. He stood in the middle of the booking-office, unable to move.

You do not expect me to help him to rise, all alone, said Mr. Gorman.

Mr. Nolan expected nothing.

Together let us levvy him to his feet, said Mr. Gorman. Then, if necessary, you will telephone for a policeman.

Mr. Nolan dearly loved to telephone. It was a treat seldom vouchsafed him. But in the door of the waiting-room he stopped short, and said he could not. He was sorry, he said, but he could not.

Perhaps you are right, said Mr. Gorman.

(Hiatus in MS.)

Yet we cannot leave him there like that, said Mr. Gorman. The five-fifty-five will be upon us—he consulted his watch—in thirty-seven and . . . (Hiatus in MS.) . . . in a lower voice, And the six-four will follow hard behind. The thought of the six-four seemed to trouble him particularly, for some reason. There is not a moment to lose, he exclaimed. He drew himself up, threw back his head, lowered the hand that held the watch to the level of the glans (Mr. Gorman had a very long arm) penis, laid the other to his temple and took the time. Then suddenly flexing his knees, and hunching his back, he cuddled the watch to his ear, in the attitude of a child cringing away from a blow.

It was as he feared, later than he hoped.

Run fetch a bucket of water, he said, perhaps who knows

238

if we souse him thoroughly he will get up of his own free will.

Perhaps the hose—, said Mr. Nolan.

The bucket, I said, said Mr. Gorman, from the tap.

What bucket? said Mr. Nolan.

Bloody well you know what bucket! cried Mr. Gorman, not however an impatient man as a rule. The muck bloody bucket, blast your bloody . . . He paused. The day was Saturday. Your bloody eyes, he said.

Watt distinguished fragments of a part:

.... *von Klippe zu Klippe geworfen*
Endlos in.........................hinab.

Mr. Gorman and Mr. Nolan advanced together, stooping, the bucket, heavy with slime, held between them.

Sister, sister......beware of a sullen silent sot........ *always musing......never thinks.*

Gently does it, said Mr. Gorman.

Is that the gob? said Mr. Nolan.

Gently, gently, said Mr. Gorman. Have you got a firm holt on her?

I have not, said Mr. Nolan.

Don't let go whatever you do, said Mr. Gorman.

Or is it a hole in his trousers? said Mr. Nolan.

Never mind what it is, said Mr. Gorman. Are you right?

Hold back the handle, said Mr. Nolan.

To hell with the bloody handle, said Mr. Gorman. Tilt the bucket when I tell you.

Tilt her with what? said Mr. Nolan. With the hair on me chest?

Mr. Gorman spat violently into the bucket, Mr. Gorman who never spat, in the ordinary way, if not into his pocket handkerchief.

Put down the bucket, said Mr. Gorman.

They put down the bucket. Mr. Gorman took the time, as before.

Lady McCann will be upon us in ten minutes, said Mr. Gorman.

Lady McCann was a lady who daily left the neighbourhood by the first train in the morning, and returned to it by the last at night. Her reasons for doing this were not known. On Sundays she remained in bed, receiving there the mass, and other meals and visitors.

Hell roast her, said Mr. Gorman. Good morning, Mr. Gorman, lovely morning, Mr. Gorman. Lovely morning!

And Arsy Cox, said Mr. Nolan.

And Herring-gut Waller, said Mr. Gorman.

And Cack-faced Miller, said Mr. Nolan.

And Mrs. Penny-a-hoist Pim, said Mr. Gorman.

That old put, said Mr. Nolan.

Do you know what she says to me the other day? said Mr. Gorman.

What was that? said Mr. Nolan.

In my private burreau, said Mr. Gorman. Placing his thumb and forefinger on his cheekbones, he pushed up the long yellow-grey moustache. Shortly after the departure of the eleven-twenty-four, he said. Mr. Gorman, says she, winter may be in my hair, but there is still plenty of spring in my do you follow me.

(MS. illegible.)

The right hand firmly on the rim, said Mr. Gorman, the fingers of the left curled round the——

I follow you, said Mr. Nolan.

They stooped.

God knows why I give myself all this trouble, said Mr. Gorman. Tilt when I say the word.

The bucket slowly rose.

Not all at one go, said Mr. Gorman, there is no point in soiling the floor unnecessarily.

Mr. Nolan now releasing his hold on the bucket, Mr.

240

Gorman, who did not care to wet the outside of his trousers, was obliged to do the same. Together rapidly in safety they gained the door.

I declare to God she sprang out of me hands, like as if she was alive, said Mr. Nolan.

If that doesn't get him up, nothing will, said Mr. Gorman.

Blood now perfused the slime. Mr. Gorman and Mr. Nolan were not alarmed. It was unlikely that a vital organ was touched.

Mr. Case arrived. He had passed an unrefreshing night, in a sense, but his humour was excellent. He carried, in one hand, a can of hot tea, and, in the other, *Songs by the Way*, which the untoward events of the early morning had caused him to forget to leave behind, in his cabin, on the shelf, as his habit was.

He wished good morning to, and shook hands warmly with, first Mr. Gorman, and then Mr. Nolan, who in their turn, and in that order, wished a very good morning to him, and shook him heartily by the hand. And then remembering, Mr. Gorman and Mr. Nolan, that in the heat of the morning's vicissitudes they had forgotten to wish each other good morning, and shake each other by the hand, they did so now, most cordially, without further delay.

Mr. Case's narrative was of great interest to Mr. Gorman, and to Mr. Nolan, there shedding light, as it did, where until now all had been dark. Much however remained to be elucidated.

You are sure it is the same? said Mr. Gorman.

Mr. Case picked his way, to where Watt lay. Bending he scraped, with his book, a little mire from the face.

Oh, you'll spoil your nice book, cried Mr. Gorman.

The clothes seem to me the same, said Mr. Case. He went to the window and turned over, with his boot, the hat. I recognize the hat, he said. He rejoined Mr. Gorman and Mr. Nolan in the doorway. I see the bags, he said, but I cannot say that I recognize the face. It is true, if it is the same, that I have only seen it twice before, and both times the light was poor, oh very poor. And yet I have a great memory for faces, as a rule.

Particular a face like that, said Mr. Nolan.

And for arses, added Mr. Case, as an afterthought. Let me once catch a fair glimpse of an arse, and I'll pick it out for you among a million.

Mr. Nolan murmured something to his superior.

Grossly exaggerated, said Mr. Gorman.

Otherwise my memory is poor, said Mr. Case, oh very poor, as my wife could tell you.

Lady McCann joined the group. Greetings were exchanged, and salutes. Mr. Gorman told her what they knew.

Do I see blood? said Lady McCann.

A mere trickle, my lady, said Mr. Case, from the nose, or perhaps the lug.

Arsy Cox and Herring-gut Waller arrived together. Following the usual compliments, and prescribed motions of the head, and hands, Lady McCann informed them of what had passed.

Something must be done, said Mr. Cox.

At once, said Mr. Waller.

A breathless boy appeared. He said he was sent by Mr. Cole.

Mr. Cole? said Lady McCann.

Of the level-crossing, my lady, said Mr. Case.

Mr. Cole desired to know why Mr. Case's signals were against Mr. Cole's five-fifty-seven, now rapidly approaching, from the south-east.

God bless my soul, said Mr. Case, what can I have been thinking of.

But he had not reached the door, when Mr. Gorman, on a sign from the boy, desired him to stay.

Mr. Cole, said the boy, would also be very happy to learn for what reasons Mr. Case's signals were against Mr. Cole's six-six, now hastening towards him, from the north-west.

Return, my little man, said Lady McCan, to him that sent you. Tell him that — has been the scene of terrible events, but that now all is well. Repeat now after me. The scene . . . of terrible . . . terrible . . . events . . . but that now . . . all is well . . . Very good. Here is a penny.

Cack-faced Miller arrived. Cack-faced Miller never greeted anyone, orally or otherwise, and few people ever greeted Cack-faced Miller. He knelt down beside Watt and inserted his hand under the head. In this touching attitude he remained for some time. He then rose and went away. He stood on the platform, his back to the line, his face to the wicket. The sun had not yet risen, above the sea. It had not yet risen, but it was rising fast. As he watched, it rose, and shone, with its faint morning shining, on his face.

Watt now also rose, to the no small diversion of Messrs. Gorman, Nolan, Cox and Waller. Lady McCann was less amused.

Who the devil are you, said Mr. Gorman, and what the hell do you want?

Watt found his hat and put it on.

Mr. Gorman repeated his question.

Watt found his bags, first one, then the other, and settled them in his hands, in the way that irked him least. The group fell away from the door and he passed out, into the booking-office.

Who is he? said Mr. Cox.

And what does he want? said Mr. Waller.

Speak, said Lady McCann.

Watt halted before the ticket-window, put down his

243

bags, once more, and knocked on the wooden shutter.

Go and see what he wants, said Mr. Gorman.

When Watt saw a face on the other side of the window, he said:

Give me a ticket, if you please.

He wants a ticket, cried Mr. Nolan.

A ticket to where? said Mr. Gorman.

Where to? said Mr. Nolan.

To the end of the line, said Watt.

He wants a ticket to the end of the line, cried Mr. Nolan.

Is it a white man? said Lady McCann.

Which end? said Mr. Gorman.

What end? said Mr. Nolan.

Watt did not reply.

The round end or the square end? said Mr. Nolan.

Watt reflected a little longer. Then he said:

The nearer end.

The nearest end, cried Mr. Nolan.

There is no need to bellow, said Mr. Cox.

The voice is low, but clear, said Mr. Waller.

But what an extraordinary accent, said Lady McCann.

I beg your pardon, said Watt, I mean the farther end.

What you want is a free pass, said Mr. Nolan.

Issue him a third single to — , said Mr. Gorman, and let us have done.

One and three, said Mr. Nolan.

Watt counted out, in the fluted trough, one shilling, two sixpences, three threepences, and four pennies.

What's all this? said Mr. Nolan.

Three and one, said Watt.

One and three, roared Mr. Nolan.

Watt put the difference in his pocket.

The train! exclaimed Lady McCann.

Quick, said Mr. Cox, two there and back.

It was Mr. Cox's and Mr. Waller's practice, though they travelled daily, on this line, to and from the city, to buy their tickets every morning anew. One day it was Mr. Cox who paid, and the next it was Mr. Waller. The reasons for this are not known.

Not many minutes later the six-four entered the station. It did not take up a single passenger, in the absence of Mrs. Pim. But it discharged a bicycle, for a Miss Walker.

Mr. Case, free now again to leave his box, joined Mr. Gorman and Mr. Nolan, before the wicket. The sun was now well above the visible horizon. Mr. Gorman, Mr. Case and Mr. Nolan turned their faces towards it, as men will, in the early morning, without heeding. The road lay still, at this hour, leaden, deserted, between its hedges, and its ditches. From one of these latter a goat emerged, dragging its pale and chain. The goat hesitated, in the middle of the road, then turned away. The clatter came fainter and fainter, down the still air, and came still faintly when the pale had disappeared, beyond the rise. The trembling sea could not but be admired. The leaves quivered, or gave the impression of doing so, and the grasses also, beneath the drops, or beads, of gaily expiring dew. The long summer's day had made an excellent start. If it continued in the same manner, its close would be worth coming to see.

All the same, said Mr. Gorman, life isn't such a bad old bugger. He raised high his hands and spread them out, in a gesture of worship. He then replaced them in the pockets, of his trousers. When all is said and done, he said.

Riley's puckaun again, said Mr. Nolan, I can smell him from here.

And they say there is no God, said Mr. Case.

All three laughed heartily at this extravagance.

Mr. Gorman consulted his watch.

To work, he said.

245

They parted. Mr. Gorman went in one direction, Mr. Case in another and Mr. Nolan in a third.

But they had not gone far when Mr. Case hesitated, went on, hesitated again, stopped, turned and cried:

And our friend?

Mr. Gorman and Mr. Nolan stopped and turned.

Friend? said Mr. Gorman.

Mr. Gorman was between Mr. Case and Mr. Nolan, and so did not need to raise his voice.

Is it the long wet dream with the hat and bags? cried Mr. Nolan.

Mr. Nolan looked at Mr. Case, Mr. Case at Mr. Nolan, Mr. Gorman at Mr. Case, Mr. Gorman at Mr. Nolan, Mr. Nolan at Mr. Gorman. Mr. Case at Mr. Gorman, Mr. Gorman again at Mr. Case, again at Mr. Nolan, and then straight before him, at nothing in particular. And so they stayed a little while, Mr. Case and Mr. Nolan looking at Mr. Gorman, and Mr. Gorman looking straight before him, at nothing in particular, though the sky falling to the hills, and the hills falling to the plain, made as pretty a picture, in the early morning light, as a man could hope to meet with, in a day's march.

ADDENDA[1]

her married life one long drawsheet

— — —

Art Conn O'Connery, called Black Velvet O'Connery, product of the great Chinnery-Slattery tradition.

— — —

the Master of the Leopardstown Halflengths

— — —

who may tell the tale
of the old man?
weigh absence in a scale?
mete want with a span?
the sum assess
of the world's woes?
nothingness
in words enclose?

— — —

judicious Hooker's heat-pimples

— — —

limits to part's equality with whole

— — —

dead calm, then a murmur, a name, a murmured name, in doubt, in fear, in love, in fear, in doubt, wind of winter in the black boughs, cold calm sea whitening whispering to the shore, stealing, hastening, swelling, passing, dying, from naught come, to naught gone

— — —

[1] The following precious and illuminating material should be carefully studied. Only fatigue and disgust prevented its incorporation.

Bid us sigh on from day to day,
And wish and wish the soul away,
Till youth and genial years are flown.
And all the life of life is gone.

— — —

Watt learned to accept etc. Use to explain poverty of Part III.
Watt cannot speak of what happened on first floor, because
for the greater part of the time nothing happened, without
his protesting.

— — —

Note that Arsene's declaration gradually came back to
Watt.

— — —

One night Watt goes on roof.

— — —

Watt snites.

— — —

Meals. Every day Mr. Knott's bowl at a different place.
Watt marks with chalk.

— — —

the maddened prizeman

— — —

the sheet of dark water, the widening fret of ripples, the
deadening banks, the stillness

— — —

never been properly born

— — —

the foetal soul is full grown (Cangiamila's *Sacred Embryology* and Pope Benedict XIV's *De Synodo Diocesana*, Bk. 7,
Chap. 4, Sect. 6)

— — —

sempiternal penumbra

— — —

248

for all the good that frequent departures out of Ireland had done him, he might just as well have stayed there

— — —

a round wooden table, of generous diameter, resting on a single massive conical frustum, filled the middle space

— — —

zitto! zitto! dass nur das Publikum nichts merke!

— — —

on the waste, beneath the sky, distinguished by Watt as being, the one above, the other beneath, Watt. That before him, behind him, on all sides of him, there was something else, neither sky nor waste, was not felt by Watt. And it was always their long dark flowing away together towards the mirage of union that lay before him, which ever way he turned. The sky was of a dark colour, from which it may be inferred that the usual luminaries were absent. They were. The waste also, needless to say, was of a dark colour. Indeed the sky and the waste were of the same dark colour, which is hardly to be wondered at. Watt also was very naturally of the same dark colour. This dark colour was so dark that the colour could not be identified with certainty. Sometimes it seemed a dark absence of colour, a dark mixture of all colours, a dark white. But Watt did not like the words dark white, so he continued to call his darkness a dark colour plain and simple, which strictly speaking it was not, seeing that the colour was so dark as to defy identification as such.

The source of the feeble light diffused over this scene is unknown.

Further peculiarities of this soul-landscape were:

The temperature was warm.

Beneath Watt the waste rose and fell.

All was silent.

Above Watt the sky fell and rose.
Watt was rooted to the spot.

— — —

Watt will not
abate one jot
but of what

of the coming to
of the being at
of the going from
Knott's habitat

of the long way
of the short stay
of the going back home
the way he had come

of the empty heart
of the empty hands
of the dim mind wayfaring
through barren lands

of a flame with dark winds
hedged about
going out
gone out

of the empty heart
of the empty hands
of the dark mind stumbling
through barren lands

that is of what
Watt will not
abate one jot

— — —

die Merde hat mich wieder

— — —

pereant qui ante nos nostra dixerunt

— — —

Second picture in Erskine's room, representing gentleman seated at piano, full length, receding profile right, naked save for stave-paper resting on lap. With his right hand he sustains a chord which Watt has no difficulty in identifying as that of C major in its second inversion, while with other he prolongs pavilion of left ear. His right foot, assisted from above by its fellow, depresses with force the sustaining pedal. On muscles of brawny neck, arm, torso, abdomen, loin, thigh and calf, standing out like cords in stress of effort, Mr. O'Connery had lavished all the resources of Jesuit tactility. Beads of sweat, realized with a finish that would have done credit to Heem, were plentifully distributed over pectoral, subaxillary and hypogastrical surfaces. The right nipple, from which sprang a long red solitary hair, was in a state of manifest tumescence, a charming touch. The bust was bowed over the keyboard and the face, turned slightly towards the spectator, wore expression of man about to be delivered, after many days, of particularly hard stool, that is to say the brow was furrowed, the eyes tight closed, the nostrils dilated, the lips parted and the jaw fallen, as pretty a synthesis as one could wish of anguish, concentration, strain, transport and self-abandon, illustrating extraordinary effect produced on musical nature by faint cacophony of remote harmonics stealing over dying accord. Mr. O'Connery's love of significant detail appeared further in treatment of toenails, of remarkable luxuriance and caked with what seemed to be dirt. Feet also could have done with a wash, legs not what you could call fresh and sweet, buttocks and belly cried out for hipbath at least, chest in disgusting condition, neck positively filthy, and seeds might have been scattered in ears with every prospect of early germination.

That however a damp cloth had been rapidly passed at a recent date over more prominent portions of facies (Latin word, meaning face) seemed not improbable.

(Latin quote.)

Moustache, pale red save where discoloured by tobacco, advancing years, nervous chewing, family worries, nasal slaver and buccal froth, tumbled over ripe red lips, and forth from out ripe red jaw, and forth in same way from out ripe red dewlap, sprouted, palely red, doomed beginnings of bushy pale red beard.

— — —

like a thicket flower unrecorded

— — —

Watt's Davus complex (morbid dread of sphinges)

— — —

One night Arthur came to Watt's room. He was agitated. He thought he had been taken for Mr. Knott. He did not know if he felt honoured or not.

Walking in the garden he said, Now I am walking in the garden, not with any great pleasure it is true, but nevertheless, up and down, I am walking in the garden.

He watched his legs as under him they moved, in and out.

I stand first on one leg, he said, then on the other, so, and in that way I move forward.

Notice how without thinking you avoid the daisies, he said. What sensibility.

Halting, he contemplated the grass, at his feet.

This dewy sward is not yours, he said. He clasped his hands to his breast. He lifted them towards the maker, and giver, of all things, of him, of the daisies, of the grass. Thanks, Boss, he said. He stood easy. He moved on.

This is said to be good for the health, he said.

Not many moments had elapsed since this aphorism when Arthur began to laugh, so heartily that he was obliged to lean for support against a passing shrub, or bush, which joined heartily in the joke.

When he had recovered his calm, he turned to examine the bush, or shrub. All he could say was that it was not a rush.

Now he saw, advancing towards him over the grass, an indistinct mass. A moment later it was an old man, clothed in rags.

Who can this be, I wonder, said Arthur.

A penny for a poor old man, said the old man.

Arthur gave a penny.

God bless your honour, said the old man.

Amen, said Arthur. Good day.

I remember you when you was a boy, said the old man. I was a boy meself.

Then we was boys together, said Arthur.

You was a fine lovely boy, said the old man, and I was another.

Look at us now, said Arthur.

You was always wetting your trousers, said the old man.

I wets them still, said Arthur.

I cleaned the boots, said the old man.

If it hadn't been you, it would have been another, said Arthur.

Yer father was very good to me.

Like father like son, said Arthur. Good day.

I helped to lay out this darling place, said the old man.

In that case, said Arthur, perhaps you can tell me the name of this extraordinary growth.

That's what we calls a hardy laurel, said the old man.

Arthur went back into the house and wrote, in his journal:

Took a turn in the garden. Thanked God for a small mercy. Made merry with the hardy laurel. Bestowed alms on an old man formerly employed by Knott family.

But this was not enough. So he came running to Watt.

This was the first time Watt had heard the words Knott family.

There had been a time when they would have pleased him, and the thought they tendered, that Mr. Knott too was serial, in a vermicular series. But not now. For Watt was an old rose now, and indifferent to the gardener.

— — —

das fruchtbare Bathos der Erfahrung

— — —

faede hunc mundum intravi, anxius vixi, perturbatus egredior, causa causarum miserere mei

— — —

change all the names

— — —

descant heard by Watt on way to station (IV):

Sop. With   all our heart breathe head awhile darkly apart
Alt. With   all our heart with   all   – our heart – – –
Ten. With   all – our   heart   –   – – – –   – – –
Bas. Breathe – –   –   breathe –   –   – – –   – – –

Sop. the   air   exile of ended smile of ending care
Alt. breathe breathe – – of – end   – ing – care –
Ten. breathe breathe – – the – –   – ex –   –   –
Bas. –   –   – phew! the– –   – ex –   –   –

Sop. darkly awhile the exile air
Alt. the – ex – ile – air –
Ten. ile – – – air – – –
Bas. ile – – – air – – –

254

Watt looking as though nearing end of course of injections of sterile pus

— — —

parole non ci appulcro

— — —

Threne heard by Watt in ditch on way from station. The soprano sang:

— — —

no symbols where none intended

— — —

Paris, 1945.